Girls From Da Hood 12

Girls From Da Hood 12

Treasure Hernandez, Katt and Paradise Gomez

www.urbanbooks.net

Urban Books, LLC
300 Farmingdale Road, NY-Route 109
Farmingdale, NY 11735

ISBN 13: 978-1-62286-693-9
ISBN 10: 1-62286-693-2

First Mass Market Printing June 2018
First Trade Paperback Printing August 2017
Printed in the United States of America

10 9 8 7 6 5 4 3 2 1

Distributed by Kensington Publishing Corp.
Submit Orders to:
Customer Service
400 Hahn Road
Westminster, MD 21157-4627
Phone: 1-800-733-3000
Fax: 1-800-659-2436

Short Stacks

by

Treasure Hernandez

Chapter 1

Slap!

"I asked you where the fucking money is!"

Standing in the living room of a luxury hotel suite was a woman no more than five foot five. Her long, naturally curly hair was combed up and neatly tucked into a ninja bun with her baby hairs slicked to the nines. The makeup on her golden-brown face had been applied to perfection. The light pink two-piece pantsuit she wore hugged her full, curvy shape, making her backside look like a plump apple. Honey was what most would call a rare beauty. She had the kind of beauty that deserved to be on the cover of a magazine or the big screen . . . not pistol-whipping a man in the face with a small army of soldiers behind her. But she had long since signed her life over to the streets.

The man she'd just slapped in the face with the butt of her Glock 19, DeAngelo Allan, was what most would call a very dangerous man. He was the kind of man that, when angry, people ran the other way to escape his wrath. However, he was also a man with a debt to an even more powerful man, and Honey was there to collect. Raising her gun again, she brought it down harder on his face than she had the first time.

"*Agh!*" DeAngelo grunted, and his head whipped to the side.

Honey didn't stop there. She continued beating him with her gun until a thick, bloody gash appeared above his left eye, and his cheek looked like he was eating a jawbreaker. He tried to muscle his way free of the two big men holding his arms, but they had a grip of steel on him. When Honey was done, she'd barely broken a sweat, but her irritation level was growing. A few splattered blood droplets had found a new home in her clothing, and her nose flared.

"Shit! This is my favorite suit," Honey said, looking down at the red stains on her pretty pink. "Now, on top of the fifty thousand you owe El-Jihad, you owe me a new Tom Ford. This is a *$5,000* suit!"

On her last word, Honey hit him again. She was growing tired of the games and had already been there longer than she intended to be. After she and her five goons had tailed DeAngelo for five days, they finally decided to make their move the night they saw him pull up to a Marriott in downtown Chicago. Honey watched him tell his own security to get lost as he got out of the backseat with a barely dressed, drunken woman. All it took was five crisp hundred-dollar bills to get the room number and an extra five hundred to cut all cameras on DeAngelo's floor. The look on DeAngelo's face was one mixed between rage and terror when Honey's goons kicked in the door and raided the room. DeAngelo had literally been caught slipping with his pants down, and Honey would grant him no mercy. She had the girl tied up naked in the bathroom tub while she proceeded to beat the truth out of DeAngelo in nothing but his boxers.

A few months back, he came to El-Jihad asking for help in order to keep his empire afloat. He was fronted with $25,000 worth of product with the agreement that he would pay back double that. However, when it was time to pay back what he owed, it was like DeAngelo had fallen off of the face of the earth.

"Fu-fuck that suit," DeAngelo coughed. "And fuck El-Jihad too. I'm not paying him a penny."

"Oh?" Honey raised her eyebrows. "It's fuck us, huh? You gon' say fuck *us* because *you* can't pay what *you* owe? OK."

She shook her head and held her hand out to her most skilled shooter, Dank, who placed a silencer in her hand. She screwed it on without even looking at the weapon as she took a few steps forward and knelt down. When her full mocha lips were inches away from his ear, she parted them and spoke in a voice that only he could hear.

"I'm going to give you one more chance to tell me where the money is, or you will pay with your body instead. The pain you feel right now is *nothing* compared to what I have in store for you."

Breathing heavily, DeAngelo contemplated his options and realized that he only had one. He knew by not paying back his debt that he was gambling with the devil himself. When he made back three times more than what he calculated from the original front, greed had gotten the best of him. The last thing he wanted to do was send that wire to El-Jihad . . . so he didn't. Instead, he tightened up on security and kept his business running. For five months, he had made being a ghost look easy, but he was a fool to think that what he'd done wouldn't catch up to him. Still, there was no part of him that wanted to give El-Jihad any piece of green. If he hadn't put in the legwork, the dope would have just been sitting in some warehouse of El-Jihad's making no money. He lifted his head with a weak neck so that he could look Honey in her eyes.

"Send me to hell, bitch," he snarled and spit a bloody glob of mucus on Honey's white Christian Louboutin pointed-toe red bottoms.

Honey shifted her heel and looked down at the greenish-red wet spot now at the tip of her heel. She sighed and gritted her teeth. She wouldn't let DeAngelo know that although she would kill him, and she really wanted to, she couldn't. Truth be told, that was always the last-case scenario when it came to El-Jihad and his money. Honey's job was, and had always been, to collect money, whether it was collecting owed dues or moving work in the streets. Either way, El-Jihad was all about revenue, and Honey refused to come home empty-handed. She had already fumbled on two dealings, and a third one was something she couldn't afford. The kind of grasp El Jihad had on her life made Honey ruthless. She would do anything to stay on her boss's good side.

"You knew how hot the water would be if you bailed out on the deal," Honey said, standing back straight. "And now you owe me a new pair of Christians." Aiming her gun at his left ear, Honey let one round off and blasted it from his head. "Send you to hell? I need you to beg a little harder."

DeAngelo yelled from the seething pain coming from the left side of his face, but it hadn't even fully set in before he felt a bullet hit his shoulder.

"*Aaghhh!*"

"Aaghhh is right," Honey told him. "Tie this nigga to that computer chair and hold his fingers out. I brought fifteen clips with me. Blowing off ten fingers ain't gon' be shit."

"Yo, aim right like that, shorty," Dank teased, watching the other goons tie army knots around DeAngelo's wrists with the hotel sheet.

"Brother, name a time I missed my target." Honey looked side-eyed at her tall, chocolate friend.

"I'm just saying," Dank grinned. "You got our people holding this greasy motherfucka's hands. That's a pretty close mark if you ask me."

Honey glanced at the three goons holding DeAngelo's fingers up with their own. She knew they trusted her, but the looks on their faces read that they prayed her aim was on point that day.

"Well, I'm not asking you, Dank. And I don't know why you're smiling and shit. If we don't get this paper, it will be *your* ass too, not just mine." Honey turned her attention back to DeAngelo and was unmoved by his tattered appearance.

"You supposed to be the king of the Chi, but you look like a little bitch to me."

Pfft!

With the aim of an expert marksman, she shot off DeAngelo's ring finger and smiled at his agonizing scream. The blood on his face was now mixed with tears, and Honey pointed the nose of her weapon at the severed finger on the ground.

"Since you'll never marry, I don't see a point in you having that," she said, aiming for the thumb on his right hand next.

The exact moment that she applied pressure to the trigger to let another one off, the sound of somebody banging on the door stopped her. The room they were in had no neighboring suites, but maybe somebody walking past had heard the torment going on behind the closed door. They were all still for a second . . . until the knock came again, and Honey realized that it wasn't the door to the suite. It was the bathroom door down the hall.

"Please! Please, let me go-ooo," the sobs of the woman DeAngelo had brought with him cried. "Please don't kill me! I have a daughter. She needs me! Ple-easse!"

"Breezy, shut that bitch up!" Dank called down the hallway to his friend who was supposed to be keeping watch.

"Man, Dank, I done tried!" Breezy called back. "This bitch done chewed through the duct tape, *twice!*"

"Bring her up here then!" Dank said. "Get that tape too."

In less than thirty seconds, Breezy, a young knucklehead from Memphis, Tennessee, brought the kicking and screaming redbone from the back. Her short, auburn haircut was disheveled, and mascara was running down her sharp cheekbones. If her face wasn't twisted up in a grimace, she would have been very pretty, but the way she had her mouth open resembled a saber-toothed tiger.

"Yo, hog-tie that bitch!" Honey barked from where she stood. "You should have done that when the ho was in the bathroom!"

"Ahhh! No! I just met him tonight. I don't have shit to do with his bullshit! Please! Please! Please!" As Dank and Breezy put duct tape on her wrists and her ankles she saw the state that DeAngelo was in. The sight of all of the blood let her know that she wasn't getting out of there alive. Her screams turned to hopeless whines, and she clenched her eyes shut. "Oh my God! You're going to kill me. I don't want to die."

The emotion in her voice would have made any woman feel empathy, but Honey wasn't any woman. She leered down at the woman and cocked her head.

"What's your name?" she asked.

"Tari," the woman answered after a few seconds.

"Well, yes, Tari. You're about to die over some dick. Didn't your mother teach you not to fuck with greasy-ass niggas?" Honey focused back to the broken "boss" before her. "Put tape over her mouth. I don't need her screaming and fucking up my mojo. And you? Since you don't want to tell me where I can find El-Jihad's $50,000—"

"Fifty thousand dollars?" Tari's shaky voice interrupted Honey.

Breezy kept trying to put the sticky piece of tape over her mouth, but she kept jerking her head back and forth. Tari glared at the man she'd left the club with, and suddenly, the fear she felt was replaced with anger. DeAngelo was no longer the man with clout that she thought he was. She had met him in the VIP section popping bottles like a rich man, and he was either too trusting or too drunk because when he ran out of cash, he sent her to the club's ATM machine to grab another stack. After the transaction had processed, it asked her if she wanted to check the balance. Tari, being the nosy woman that she was, printed a receipt and saw exactly how much money DeAngelo was working with.

"Fifty thousand dollars?" Tari's scream was directed to DeAngelo. "You selfish bastard! You're going to let me die because you owe fifty thousand fucking dollars?"

She'd heard of men being stubborn, but not *this* stubborn. She didn't care about any underlying issue between the woman with the gun and DeAngelo. All she knew was that she'd seen more zeros in his account than she'd ever seen in her life living in the hood. All she could think about was the fact that she'd told her mother that she'd be home before nine o'clock the next day, and she needed to keep that promise. She didn't really have a child, but she made the mistake of hoping they would show her leniency if they thought she did. As she wormed around trying to keep the tape from around her mouth, she knew she had to do something before they decided to knock her out—or worse. DeAngelo might have been willing to die over his money, but Tari wasn't. Trying to place herself in the position to mess with a baller had landed her in a hotel room with murderers.

"Wait!" she yelled steadying her voice. Breezy had finally caught one of the corners of her mouth with the tape. "I know where the money— *mmmm! Mmmm!*"

Breezy finally had clamped her big mouth shut. She was working his nerves, and the last thing he needed was Honey ragging on him later. To his surprise, Honey came over and ripped the tape back off.

"What the fuck, Honey?" he asked incredulously, throwing his hands up. "First, you want me to gag the bitch, which was hard as shit. This bitch is part snake or something. *Then,* you take the tape off so she can start screamin' again!"

"Shut up, stupid, and open your ears!" Honey snapped, and then looked at Tari. "What did you just say?"

"I said, I know where the money is!"

DeAngelo heard the revelation and shot daggers into Tari's face with his eyes.

"You better not say shit! Do you hear me!"

Honey ignored the dead man talking and grabbed Tari's arm so that she could sit up and put her back on one of the walls in the room. Honey got down to her level and used the gun to move Tari's bang piece to the side.

"You have very pretty eyes," Honey said when her face was directly in front of Tari's. "Not quite hazel but . . . almost. They say the eyes are where you can detect any lie. You wouldn't lie to me, would you, Tari?"

"No. I don't know you enough to lie to you."

"Then why did you say that you have a child?" Honey laughed when Tari's eyes widened in shock. "I went through your phone to make sure nobody knew where you were when we first busted in here. Now, I'm not a mother, but if I was, I'd have pictures of my baby all throughout my phone. In yours, all I see is you, Tari, the *party girl.* So tell me why I should believe that you know where my *fuckin'* money is if you already lied to me."

"I—"

"Uh-uh." Honey placed her finger on Tari's mouth. "Think about your answer *very* wisely. I usually give three strikes, but you only get two before you're out."

Honey slowly removed her finger from Tari's mouth, and Tari felt like she was looking into the face of death herself. Out of all of the men in the room standing over her, the woman who was inches away from her face seemed the deadliest. The men all followed her every command as if afraid of what she might do. Tari swallowed the lump in her throat. Her mother had always taught her that the only way to stand a chance against a powerful person was to be equal to it. Right then, with duct tape on her wrists and ankles, she wasn't quite equal. But she did have something on her side. Leverage.

"OK." Tari nodded her head. "You're right. I don't have a child. I thought—no—I *hoped* that you would feel sorry for me and let me go. I lied then to save my life."

"What would make me believe that you won't do that again?"

"Because . . ." Tari looked across the room at DeAngelo. The men around him had gagged his mouth and were using him as a punching bag. "I don't want to be tortured. And that's what you will do to me if I don't tell you what I know." Her eyes jumped from each man in the room and recognized that they all wore the same hardened expression as the boys she'd seen working her own block. She turned back to the woman in pink and wrinkled her brow. "What is your name?"

"Honey."

"Honey, if I tell you where you can find your money . . . will I live?"

No witnesses.

The thought flashed through Honey's head. She usually had a strict policy involving those who witnessed the horrible crimes committed by her and her crew. Nobody was ever left with any breath to tell the tale. Still, though, there was something about the girl in front of her and the audacity she had to barter for her life.

"What do you do for a living, Tari? Other than look for a come up with these niggas?"

"I work full time at a dentist's office," Tari told her not understanding why she cared. "I'm the secretary."

"Did you go to college?"

"I wasn't able to. My mother got sick my senior year in high school. Breast cancer. She was too weak to work the way that she used to, so as soon as I graduated, I got a job."

"Why?"

"Why?" Tari forgot that the woman was holding a gun and looked at her like she was off. "What do you mean why? Isn't it obvious? I had to help her with bills and hospital expenses."

"Is that something that you wanted to do?"

"No," Tari answered honestly. "But there is so much that I do want to do, and it won't be worth doing if my mama ain't here to see it. She's at home now. I promised that I'd be there in the morning. I have to make sure she takes her medicine. She's been having one of her sick bouts again."

"What were you doing here tonight if your mother is at home sick?" Honey's question must have struck a nerve because Tari averted her gaze instantly. When she didn't answer right away, Honey placed her gun on Tari's chin and forced their eyes to meet again. "You didn't hear the question or something?"

"Mama's cancer has been really aggressive. The shit the doctors are giving her isn't working, and the radiation is causing too much stress on her body. At the rate they're going, they're killing her more than the cancer is. I've been doing research, and there is this man in Africa, he's an herbalist. He uses nothing but natural compounds, and he has documented where he has cured multiple cases of cancer completely. It's expensive, though. Very, very expensive and—"

"You thought that if you went to the club and bagged a baller, then you could get the money for her treatment?" Honey removed the gun from Tari's chin and shook her head.

"Yea. Stupid, right?"

"Stupid as hell." Honey's response was harsh, but her tone was softer than it had been before. "This nigga wasn't going to do nothing but fuck you and call an Uber to take your ass back to the hood. You thought you could woo him with some pussy? This greedy pig?"

"Look," Tari whispered and closed her eyes tight, "I've seen a lot of shit where I live at, so a piece of me knows I ain't getting out of here alive. Mama and I live in a house in Riverdale, on Union Avenue. You can't miss it. We painted it light pink last year because Mama always wanted a pink house. Please make sure she gets the $20,000 for the treatment." She opened her eyes and pointed down the hallway to the bedroom in the suite. "His wallet is back there. He has a card connected to a bank account with $300,000."

"She lyin'!" Breezy piped up. "How this bitch know that shit? She just tryin'a buy time before we pop her ass."

"I know because his drunk ass sent me to the ATM at the club." Tari shot him a dirty look.

"Yeah, whatever. Even if he do got a card with the money on it, we don't have the bank account info to make a transfer. And while you two were having a powwow, these other niggas done beat our real mark to a coma."

He pointed to the men standing around DeAngelo's limp body with sheepish expressions on their faces. DeAngelo's chin was touching his chest. He didn't move. Blood trickled down the center of his nose, dripping off the tip of it, and he looked dead.

"We don't need him."

"How? You gon' rob the bank?"

"No, stupid." Tari rolled her eyes. "I see why you were put on babysitting duty now."

"You real lippy for a bitch that's just about to be eating dirt."

"Breezy, shut the fuck up and let her talk!" Honey yelled, motioning for Tari to continue.

"You don't need his bank information if you make a transaction. I'm not just a secretary. When my mother got sick and began losing her hair, I started making wigs for her. When I got really good at it, I actually started an online store called Beauty's Calling where I make quality wigs for women. I can create you an invoice for all of the money in his account, and you can pay it. When it's in my account, you can just transfer it all in your account. All you need is a phone and his card."

The room was silent for a minute before Honey nodded her head at Breezy.

"Go get his wallet and her clutch," she instructed and pulled out Tari's cell phone.

She didn't have to ask for the Web site information because it pulled up as soon as she clicked on the Internet app. Scrolling through the information on it, she saw that Tari had been telling the truth. Still, she didn't trust that Tari wouldn't try to run if she was cut free. When Breezy brought the card and the receipt to her, Honey created an invoice for the balance in the account and sent it to Tari's e-mail. She then used the card to make the payment. When the page on the screen told her the transaction was successful, the phone made a pinging noise. The notification bar of the phone read something that gave Honey a huge wave of relief.

Tari Knowles. A deposit of $346,869 has been made to your account. If you have any questions, please contact us at the telephone number listed below.

Opening the e-mail, Honey clicked on the link to take her to Tari's online banking. Tari didn't hesitate to give her the log-in information, and Honey transferred the money to her own account. There was a two-day wait for the transfer to be completed, but she wasn't expected back home in LA for three.

"That was easy," Honey said and stood to her feet. She turned to the goons and said, "I don't want the body found. And get somebody up here to clean this room up."

With that, she made her way to the door but stopped when she was in front of Tari again. She reached into her own clutch and threw an object down on the ground right beside the bound girl.

"You have five minutes to gather all your things and wash that smeared makeup off of your face,"

Honey said smoothly. "My car leaves in five minutes. Be in it by then or join DeAngelo."

She exited the room with Breezy and Dank behind her, leaving Tari scrambling to cut herself free with the switchblade.

Chapter 2

Days Gone By . . . April 2011

"Lisa!"

Seventeen-year-old Honey Broadway stood in the doorway of her foster mother's room. It was seven in the morning on Friday, and her ride to school would be there within the next fifteen minutes. The check Lisa got for keeping Honey had come in the previous week, and she knew Honey needed the remainder of what she owed for her cap and gown. Lisa lay unmoving in her queen-sized bed, intertwined in the covers. Honey turned her nose up as she looked around the room. Trash and clothes were strewn everywhere on the ground and on the mahogany-colored dressers. There was always a lingering sex smell inside, and the musk danced disgustingly at the tip of Honey's nose. Reluctantly, she stepped foot inside because it was apparent that her voice would not be enough to wake Lisa up from her slumber.

"Lisa," Honey said in a softer voice and shook the sleeping woman by the shoulder. "Lisa!"

"Hmmm," Lisa groaned and tried to tuck herself deeper under her burgundy comforter. When the cover was snatched away and the cold air hit her face, she sprang up. "What the hell do you want? What! What is it?"

Lisa blinked her puffy eyes and tried to focus on the pretty young lady before her. She saw that Honey was fully dressed in a tight pair of skinny jeans, a red zip up hoodie with a camisole underneath, and a pair of fresh white Air Force Ones. The gold chain that Honey never took off dangled slightly because of the way she was bent over Lisa. She stood up when Lisa, furrowing her brow and scratching her disheveled hair, sat up.

"Where are you going this early in the morning? It's Saturday!"

Her voice was shaky, and Honey studied her bright yellow face. There were bags under her eyes, and not the ones that came from being tired. There was a point in time where Honey was sure Lisa was the finest girl on the block, but now, she just looked burnt out and frail.

"It's Friday, Lisa," Honey said looking at her like she was crazy. "And you said you would give me the rest of the money for my graduation stuff."

"Money?" Lisa stared blankly at Honey and licked her dull, black lips.

"Yeah," Honey told her and stepped away from the bed. She began rummaging through all of Lisa's drawers to find the cash. "I need some of the $400 you got last week."

"Oh!" Lisa answered moving her hair from her face. "*That* money."

Getting up on wobbly legs, wearing nothing but a blue Texas Cowboys T-shirt and a pair of red panties, she began helping Honey look through her things to find where she put the money. She knew that she had cashed it as soon as she got it, but she didn't know where she'd put it afterward.

Honey began to grow frustrated. If Lisa had not been so busy smoking all night, then she could have remembered where the money was. Honey was on her knees looking under the bed when she heard the distant sound of a horn being blasted outside.

"Shit," she said getting up from the floor. "My ride is here. Lisa, today is the last day to make my payment! If I don't get my cap and gown, then I can't walk with my class!"

"I'm sorry," Lisa said and sat back down on her bed. She put her hand to her forehead and looked at Honey, genuinely distraught. "I don't know what I did with the money. When I find it I'll bring it up to the school, OK?"

"What do you me—"

"Money? What money?"

Honey's statement was cut short by the sound of a deep baritone voice.

She turned toward the doorway and saw Lamont, Lisa's on-again, off-again boyfriend, standing there. Lamont was a little taller than six foot and was blacker than a panther. The hair on top of his head was scraggly, as was his beard. He was wearing nothing but a pair of blue boxers and a white Hanes T-shirt showing his beer belly, letting Honey know that he must have stayed the night.

"The money from the state," Honey answered because Lisa was too spaced out to.

"Aw, *that* money," he said and gave a sly smile. "She cashed that yesterday to pay my car note. Then we got something to sip and smoke on."

"What?" Honey asked and felt her chest tighten. She faced Lisa again, and that time, she had fire in her light brown eyes. "Is he telling the truth?"

"Oh, yea. That's what I did with it." Lisa shrugged her shoulders and let her head roll to the side. "I need Lamont to take me to work."

"Stupid bitch!"

The frustration in Honey's chest built quickly, and it took everything in her not to slap the high out of Lisa. A year ago, the only reason she accepted living with an addict was because she was able to come and go as she pleased. Now, she regretted not running away a long time ago.

"Hey, you watch your mouth when you're talking to me!" Lisa jumped up and tried her hardest to stand still. "You've been living in my house rent free, you little bitch! That's *my* money! Be lucky I didn't sell your pretty ass to the niggas poking around on the streets. They would'a loved your pretty pussy!"

"Fuck you! Fucking junky." Honey turned her back on Lisa and started for the door. Lamont was still standing there, leering down at her. His eyes traveled every curve on the young girl's body, and Honey sneered at him. "Get out of my way. My ride is here."

"You know if you need the money . . ." He licked his dry lips at her and grabbed at his crotch. "I just got some last night. You just gotta do a little something, something for me too."

"I ain't never gon' be hurting that bad for a dollar," Honey said, wanting to throw up at the fact that he would even *think* that was an option.

She pushed past him without another word to either one of them and went back to her room to grab her backpack. While there, she also threw a couple of outfits in the bag because she had no plans on coming home that evening. After tossing the bag over her shoulder, Honey briskly left the small, one-story house, ignoring Lisa's calls behind her.

"Fuck that bitch! You need to get the fuck up so we can go to my house before—"

Honey slammed the door before she could hear the rest of Lamont's statement. She was tired of them both already, and the day had just started.

"Honeyyyyyy!"

Parked outside next to Lisa's beat down green Grand Am was a light blue 2011 Chevy Cruze that had its darkly tinted windows rolled all the way down. Hanging out the passenger's side was Honey's best friend, Lanai, with a big smile on her pretty brown face. Her hair was braided neatly back into two long Cherokee braids, and the pink gloss on her lips made them pop fiercely in the sunlight. In response to her hearty welcome, Honey gave a head nod and grunt when she got in the passenger's seat.

"Uh, when is Lisa gon' get that door fixed? That one white door looks a mess!" Lanai raised her perfectly arched eyebrow when Honey didn't speak. "Why yo' shit stink so bad already?"

"Because it's early as fuck, and you're too damn happy for me."

Lanai pulled away from the curb and drove in the direction of their high school. Honey was quiet, with her head turned to the window most of the ride, and Lanai knew what that meant.

"What did Lisa do this time?"

Her question made Honey's jaw clench, and for a second, Lanai thought she pissed her friend off even more.

"She spent all the money," Honey finally answered.

"Are you serious, Honey? Didn't she know you gotta get your shit for graduation by today?"

"Yup, she figured paying that nigga's car note was more important, though." Honey put her head back on the headrest on her seat. "I ain't gon' be able to walk with y'all. . . . After all of this, I ain't gon' be able to walk!"

Pissed wasn't the word to describe what she was feeling. For the last five months, Honey had been meeting with tutors and doing tons of extra assignments just to make sure she had all of the credits needed to graduate. After her mother was killed, she bounced around a lot. Out of all the homes that she had been to, Lisa's was the best, and that wasn't saying much. If it did anything, it gave her the gumption to want to get out of the system with her feet on the ground, running. Now, all of the effort she'd made had been thrown back fiercely in her face with a nice "fuck you."

"How much do you owe?"

"I only needed a hundred." Honey shook her head and clenched her fists. "That dopehead couldn't even give me one hundred stinking dollars, Ny!"

Lanai didn't say anything else for a while, she just turned the last few corners to get to on their school. When they got to the student parking lot of Jefferson High School ten minutes before the bell, running inside with the big group of students was the last thing on Lanai's mind. She sighed and had an inward battle with herself on what she was about to offer her friend. Once that door was open, there was no way of shutting it and nowhere to run after having passed through it. Facing Honey, she saw that her head was still toward the window and the stony expression on her face hadn't changed in the slightest.

"Yo," she said, but Honey didn't budge. "Look, what Lisa did is fucked up, and there ain't no way of getting around that. I could give you the hundred for the rest of your graduation gear. That little hundred dollars ain't shit to me."

That got Honey's attention. She turned to face Lanai, expecting to see her hand outstretched with the money, but all she saw was a determined face.

"I *could* give you the money but—"

"But what? You don't *want* to?"

"Nah, that ain't it. I'ma give it to you, but what's gon' happen when you need some more money? You turn eighteen in two weeks, girl. You already know Lisa ain't gon' let you live there once that check stops coming."

"I'ma have to get a job." Honey shrugged it off. "They had a hiring sign on that new burger joint around the corner from the house. I'll probably try to fuck with that."

Lanai laughed like Honey had just told the funniest joke of the century. A burger joint was the last place that she could see Honey working . . . herself, too, for that matter.

"Girl, bye," Lanai said, still giggling. "You ain't finna be putting fries in nobody's grease, stop it! Plus, everybody knows ain't no real bread in that. But I feel you. You *are* going to have to get a job. If you want, I can put you on with something, and you'd be getting hella cash too."

"How do you know?"

"What do you mean? Have you seen my clothes? My car?" She pointed at the light blue Ralph

Lauren sweat suit she had on and the all-white Jordan 12s on her feet. "How do you think I was getting all this shit?"

To be honest, Honey always thought Lanai was spoiled. The two became close at the beginning of the school year, and Honey always wondered why somebody as cool as Ny wanted to be friends with somebody like her. Back then, Honey's clothes were shabby, and the shoes on her feet usually came from a Payless or a Walmart. Kids in the high school always made fun of her, so she was always fighting. After Lanai took Honey under her wing, she gave her clothes and shoes so nobody would ever tease her again. Honey thought it was because she felt sorry for her, but nonetheless, she was thankful for the friendship.

"Do you ever wonder why out of all these bitches in this school, you're the only one I really fuck with?"

"Yeah," Honey answered looking at her hands. "I always wondered that."

"It's because you remind me of myself."

"How I remind you of yourself? You ain't never been in foster care or had to jump house to house."

"Nah, I haven't, but I might as well have been." Lanai's eyes got glossy, and she avoided Honey's eyes. By then, the sounds of the kids yelling and running into the school had come and gone. It was just them outside in the parking lot. "My mom ain't shit, Honey. In some ways, her and Lisa are identical."

"W-wait." Honey put her hands up. "I thought she was some big-time lawyer or some shit."

"Nah," Lanai shook her head. "Maybe some years ago, but not anymore. Not since she met this man named James. He was supposedly this big-time contractor. At first, they used to just smoke weed and drink, normal shit. Then he got her into popping pills, and that was enough for her for a while. She was still able to go to work like a normal person, but then . . ." Her voice trailed off.

"But then what, Ny?" Honey stared at her friend's face, and she didn't just see the sadness there, she felt it too.

"It was the beginning of second quarter," Lanai's voice was barely louder than a whisper. "I walked in on her and James doing lines in the living room, and when she heard me come in, she looked up, and I could tell she didn't even know who I was. She was so high, and I ignored the way James looked at me. I just went to my room and shut the door. I should have locked it. I don't know why I didn't. I tried to go to sleep and ignore their loud-ass music. We had that English test the next day, so I was trying to be well rested. I-I went to sleep in a T-shirt like I always did, and in the middle of the night, I felt something wet between my legs. When I turned on my light, I just screamed. I screamed so loud. It was James. He was . . . He was licking my pussy!"

"Oh my God, Ny!" Honey exclaimed and reached out for her friend's hand. She was almost afraid to ask what happened next. "Did he . . . did he . . . you know?"

"No," Lanai shook her head. "I wasn't trying to go out like those girls in the movies. I snatched my lamp from the wall and cracked it on his head. He passed out. But to this day, I can still feel and see him on me like that." She shuddered slightly. "I packed up all the shit I could and left."

"Wait. What do you mean you left?" Honey asked. "I'm at your apartment almost every day."

"Yeah, you're at *my* apartment."

"You always tell me your mom is at work when I come over after school."

"I lied," Lanai answered bluntly. "I ain't seen that bitch since the day her nigga tried to fuck me. And she ain't tried to look for me, either. Probably too doped up on that powder."

"I'm sorry, Ny," Honey said. She thought about the nice two-bedroom apartment that Lanai lived in and about how decked out it was. "That's really your spot? You pay the bills and all that?"

"Yup," Lanai said. "Living on the streets was never an option, so I had to get some bread and fast. You know Nard from algebra?"

Honey nodded. How could she not? Bernard Brown was a fine chunk of chocolate with a baby face, and many times, Honey had fantasized about doing a few ungodly things to him. She also knew what kind of things he was into and what most of the girls who hung around him and his friends did to stay around them.

"Well, let's just say he does a little more than just help me with my math homework."

"You selling pussy, Ny? 'Cause I'm not down with that."

"No!" Lanai said, feeling the smile coming to her face again. "Stupid. This pussy is priceless! Open my glove compartment."

Honey looked at the handle to the glove compartment in front of her and was hesitant to open it. When Lanai prompted her again, she reluctantly reached out her hand and pulled the handle.

Click!

Honey's eyes widened and went back and forth between the contents of the compartment and Lanai's face.

"Yo, what the fuck, Ny? Is this a nine?"

"Grab it and find out."

Honey wasted no time wrapping her skinny fingers around the butt of the handgun. She looked around to make sure nobody was watching them inside the car before she held it up. It fit perfectly in her hand.

"This is dope, Ny," she said admiring the chrome on the weapon.

"You're right. That's a nine-millimeter pistol," Lanai answered. "Good for handling any nigga that gets out of hand."

"What do you mean 'any nigga that gets out of hand'? Why do you need a gun, Ny?"

"I told you, Honey," Lanai shrugged her shoulders. "I had to get some money fast. Bernard put me on."

"Put you onto what?"

"The streets. I move now."

"Like move . . . drugs?"

"Yeah," Lanai said and laughed at the look on Honey's face. "Look, Honey, before you completely turn your nose up, hear me out. It's not as bad as it sounds, for real. There is money out there, so much fucking money that I never even knew existed. And the way me and my team move, we clock in thousands every week."

"Thousands?"

"*Thousands*. I bought this car for six stacks cash, Honey. I just brought one of the older niggas in the movement with me and made him pretend to be my dad and shit. One of the girls on the team put her name on my lease since I wasn't old enough to get a place of my own. It's like a family. I just wanna get my diploma so I can move the way I want to. I'm too smart to be a high school dropout behind the streets. So what's up? My people got this little job they gotta do today, and I was going to sit it out, but fuck it. We can go get this money now and be a little late for school, or you can go up in there and tell the principal that you can't walk with us."

Honey's mind was trying to process a hundred thoughts a minute. There was no "if" to it. She knew what Lanai was saying was the truth. She wanted to tell her no and go inside the school, but at the end of the school day, what would she have? Nothing. She'd turn eighteen at the beginning of June, and the check Lisa blew was the last one she'd ever receive from the state. With her back to the wall, Honey realized she only had one choice.

"A'ight, Ny, but have me back here by fifth period. We're making enchiladas today in Culinary."

"Behind that cash, get murked. I'm talking big shit, nigga, join my hit list, nigga!"

36 Treasure Hernandez

The sound of Lil Wayne's mixtape *No Ceilings* was cranked so loud that Honey could hear it outside of the shabby two-story house Lanai had her standing outside of. They were about twenty minutes from the school in a different neighborhood off of Slauson, and Lanai had to bang on the door a second time before anyone came to open it. On the other side of the slightly ajar door stood a man that looked to be in his early twenties. He almost smiled when he saw Lanai, but when his eyes brushed Honey, his expression hardened.

"Yo, who this?"

His scowl showed Honey that she wasn't welcome, but Lanai grabbed her arm to keep her still beside her.

"She with me," Lanai said and pushed the door all the way open. "Now open the fuckin' door, nigga. Y'all already pissed me off by making me wait longer than I should have." She looked at Honey and nodded her head. "Come on."

The dude, Mo, watched Honey like a hawk as she walked past him. The hood in Honey made her look him up and down with her lip turned up for the disrespect.

"Yoooo!" Lanai called out happily to the room of people with her arms in the air.

Honey was blown away by the setup of the small house, if you could call it that. The main level had no walls up, it was just a big room. There were four big windows, and on every wall there was a sixty-inch TV. The TV next to the door had several miniscreens on it with the surveillance cameras around the house. The one on the left wall was playing reruns of *Law & Order SVU*, the one on the far wall had every game system a person could think of connected, and the TV on the right was showing highlights of sports games. The soft orange carpet, tan plush chairs, and colorful bean bags made the room look like a teen recreational center, except that it wasn't. As Honey looked around at the five people in the room, she took notice that they all were strapped with either a handgun or an automatic.

That's an AK, she thought to herself, eyeing the gun in the hand of the last boy Lanai dapped up in greeting.

The welcome of Lanai was short lived when they saw the girl she'd brought with her. Instinctively, they all put their hands on their weapons and grilled Honey with their eyes.

"Honey, this is Dank, Snow, Willie, Ron Ron, and you met Mo at the door." Lanai went around the room and pointed everyone out to her.

"What's good, everybody?" Honey lifted her chin but only got animalistic grunts in return.

"What is this, Ny?" the chocolate-skinned boy, Dank, asked.

"Chill, Dank. She's my best friend."

Dank walked up on Honey, snatching his arm away from Lanai when she grabbed it. Any other time, Honey might have given Dank the googly eyes. He had a fierce jawline and chestnut-colored eyes. His hair was cut into a tapered fade with sideburns lined up leading perfectly into his little goatee. He loomed over Honey, perhaps trying to intimidate her by his muscular build, but she stood her ground. He looked her up and down, and then turned back to Lanai.

"Yea?" Dank finally said with his square forehead bunched up. He put the AK-47 on his shoulder and scowled. "Well, what the fuck is she doing in my spot?"

"Why are any of us in the spot? We're all tryin'a eat." Lanai took a few steps and stood between Dank and Honey. "Now back up off of her before we have a problem, my guy. And put that fuckin' gun down unless you gon' use it. Let's talk business. All y'all relax." She looked over her shoulder at her best friend and pointed at one of the plush chairs. "Honey, you can sit in the chair by Dank. He ain't gon' do shit to you."

Honey had never seen that side of Lanai. The authoritativeness in her voice calmed down the entire room, and although everyone else shot Honey skeptical looks, they didn't say another word until Lanai spoke again. Honey sat in the chair that she was instructed to next to Dank, and the man named Mo sat on the other side of her. Lanai waited until everyone was seated before she turned off all of the TVs and poised herself in front of them all.

"Listen," Lanai scanned the room with a hard expression on her face, "my homegirl is tryin'a get down with the get down," she said. "And because she's my peoples, I'm tryin'a give her a shot."

"Why should we trust her? Homegirl don't even got a piece!"

The voice came from the person sitting on a bean bag in front of Honey. Honey's eyebrows raised because she could have sworn everybody in the room beside her and Lanai were men, but she was wrong.

"Because she came from the gutter just like the rest of us. And, Snow, you act like it's gon' be hard to strap her up. Stop it."

"I just met the bitch," Snow rebutted. "Shit, barely that. The ho acting like she scared to speak for herself. I don't trust no bitch that don't talk."

"You the one out here fooling people." Honey couldn't help it. She snapped, glaring at Snow. "Bitch really sitting up here looking like and pretending to be a nigga, but talking about trust."

"What, slut?" Snow stood to her feet and flexed her five-foot-seven frame at Honey, who stood up too.

"Bitch, I'd work yo' little ass," Honey said, tucking her chain.

Snow was still puffing her chest out when Honey took the first swing at her face. The punch had so much power behind it, Snow would have been sure to be knocked flat on her back. Too bad it didn't connect. All Honey felt was air on her fist and an arm around her waist as she was yanked back.

"Chill, ma," Dank said making her sit back down. "You too, Snow, before I let shorty loose on yo' ass."

"Yo, shorty got them dukes!" Ron Ron said, laughing and dapping Willie up.

The two were cousins but resembled each other so much people thought they were brothers. They both had almond-colored skin and auburn-colored hair with light freckles sprinkled over their faces. The only differences were that Ron Ron's hair was in a brush cut while Willie's was braided into cornrows. And Ron

Ron was skinny while Willie was built like he hit the weights faithfully.

"On God, she was finna hit Snow with that blamer!" Willie's cosign made Snow's brown skin turn hot.

"Shut yo' ass up! You always instigating some shit," she said and ran her hand over the short curls on top of her head.

"Don't be mad 'cause yo' dyke ass almost got knocked the fuck out!"

Honey couldn't help it. She started laughing so hard that the she almost fell out of the chair. Lanai's high-pitched laugh joined hers, and soon, the whole room was cracking up.

"Look," Honey said holding her hand up when the room got quiet again, "I'm just tryin'a get some money. Ny said y'all had some work today, so I'm trying to see if I can slide in with y'all."

Dank looked at Honey and could tell by the expression on her face that she was serious. He didn't know what she was going through, but it was obvious that she was thirsty for a dollar, just like the rest of them. Although Snow had a point on why they shouldn't trust her if they just met her, he was having a hard time determining why not trust her. He trusted Lanai—with his life on several occasions—so if she was saying Honey was good peoples, he would give her the benefit of the doubt. There was only one missing piece to the puzzle.

"She plugged in with El-Jihad?" he asked Lanai, and the look on her face answered his question. He shook his head and sighed deeply. "Ny . . ."

"El-Jihad?" Honey's attention spiked at the mention of LA's kingpin.

Everyone knew El-Jihad. He was what people called the devil of the underworld. Honey figured that Lanai was down with big cats in the game, but never in her right mind would she have guessed El-Jihad.

"I figured we'd put her on first," Lanai smiled sheepishly at Dank and ignored Honey. "And hopefully, he'd see what a great asset she is to our team and let her stay."

It was an unspoken fact that she and Dank were the heads of their team. They respected each other and never made a decision without checking with each other first. It was also a fact that their team was the most efficient one moving El-Jihad's work for him. Not only that, they made the most precise hits when he requested them to be made. She knew that if she had Dank backing her up on it, then it was less likely that El-Jihad would be angry about bringing a new face in his mix.

"What y'all think?" he asked the rest of the crew.

"Nigga, that bitch almost let one off on me," Snow spoke up, and Honey thought for sure that she was going to tell him hell no. "Give her a gun and see what she do with it."

Honey grinned at her, and Snow shot back an approving look.

"A'ight, then," Dank said when he got no disapproving answers. "Let's take her to the lab."

Chapter 3

"The Lab" turned out to be the upper level of the house.

That level of the house was open too. It was one big room, except it had a few more bells and whistles, and a smaller bedroom off of it. Whereas the house didn't have a kitchen on the main level, there was one up there in the far corner. Honey didn't ask questions, she just looked around and saw that she was wrong to assume that the seven of them were the only ones in the house. Up there were four women with face masks on, seated at a round table a little way away from the staircase. They were all voluptuous in the white camis and boy shorts they wore and didn't budge when they heard the newcomers. They were too focused on the white powder they were cutting and bagging. Next to the work, they each had a pistol within arm's reach.

"This is the trap?" Honey asked, even though she didn't need an answer.

"Yup," Willie said walking around her. "The main one. We keep this shit up here so when the hoes be cooking, the smell ain't that potent."

"Yeah, that's why we was so skeptical on Ny bringing a fresh face here," Snow said, patting Honey on the back. "But now I see that you're too green to be a snake."

"Be nice, Snow." Lanai rolled her eyes and pushed Honey to follow the guys into the one bedroom down there. Walking up to the circular table, she examined the work the women were bagging up. "Good job, ladies. If y'all get this order done before night hits, I'll throw in an extra five hundred apiece."

She turned her back on them before she could see how quickly their fingers began to move, and followed her team into the bedroom they'd turned into an arsenal. On every wall were weapons of all kinds, even explosives. In the middle of the room was a glass compartment with knives and switchblades of all sizes, as well as bulletproof vests. She was going to tell them to start her with a Ruger first, but they had other plans.

"You gon' need something light to start with," Ron Ron was saying and handed Honey a Glock 19. "This bitch right here is powerful, but she won't knock you off your feet."

Lanai studied Honey to make sure that her friend wasn't overwhelmed at what she'd seen so far. To her satisfaction, it seemed as if Honey was just soaking it all in. It reminded her so much of when Bernard introduced her to his big cousin, Dank. The first time she saw the trap, she couldn't say that she was scared . . . more like ready for whatever was to come her way. After running away from her mother, Lanai didn't have anything but the streets and Honey. She hated having to hide that part of her life from her best friend, but now she was happy that she could mix the two. She watched the guys and Snow showing her how to aim the gun and shoot it without her shoulder snapping back, and laughed at the show Ron Ron and Willie were giving. They were all so enthralled in getting Honey ready for the small job they had to go on that they didn't hear the footsteps coming up the stairs.

"Ahem."

The sound of a throat being cleared made all of them stop doing what they were doing. They all turned around, most already knowing who was behind them. El-Jihad stood in between two men aiming Uzis with banana clips attached. He was a good-looking, pecan-colored man in his upper thirties. He wore his hair cut low and had a clean-shaven face, except for the thin mustache above his top lip. His face held no wrinkles, giving him more youth than what he really had, and he stood no taller than five foot nine. He wasn't skinny, nor was he muscular, but it wasn't his size anyway that made him menacing. It was his aura.

"What's popping, God," Willie spoke up trying to cut the tension in the air.

El-Jihad ignored him and instead, placed his cold, dark eyes on the only person in the room that he didn't recognize. He ignored her beauty and the fact that she seemed as sweet as honey. All that he was concerned about was why she was in his spot with his people.

"That's what I'm tryin'a figure out." El-Jihad's deep voice was venomous. "Give me a reason why I shouldn't let my Rottweilers start barking in this bitch. Nobody is on their post. That's money gone if somebody was to run up in my place of business. Who is this?"

"El-Jihad," Lanai said. "I can explain. This is—"

"My name is Honey," Honey interrupted.

She stepped forward to face him, trying not to look at the two burly men holding the guns. By the way the others were acting, it was apparent that the he was the head honcho. The way his eyes bore into her caused the hairs on the back of her neck to stand up.

"Good. You speak for yourself. Now that I know who you are, tell me why you're here."

"I needed some money, and my friend said she could put me on to some."

El-Jihad's laugh came as a shock, and it almost caused her to jump. It was a sinister laugh, and Honey didn't think he even found anything funny. He stopped laughing abruptly and frowned. He snatched the Uzi from the hands of the man on his right and advanced on Honey. From the corner of his eye he saw Dank holding Lanai back, and he made a mental note to handle her later. Placing the nose of the gun to Honey's temple, he placed his lips close to her ear and applied pleasure to the trigger.

"I don't like unfamiliar faces, Honey," El-Jihad breathed in her ear. "They make me *uncomfortable*. I'm the only one who can put anybody on to some money, and today? Well, let's just say I'm feeling generous. I'm going to give you three seconds instead of one to tell me why I should open my doors to you."

Honey caught her breath and felt her body go rigid. She felt the cold gun on the side of her head and tried to think of a good answer. When Lanai said she could get her the money, she would have never guessed that an hour later she would have to barter for her own life.

"One," El-Jihad's counting started too fast. She wasn't done thinking.

What the fuck can you offer this man, Honey? Think. Think.

"Two."

Oh my God, I'm about to die.

"Thre—"

"I'm hungry," Honey blurted out just in time. Her heart was pounding so loud that she could hear it. When she realized that she was still alive, but the gun was still connected to her head, she figured there was no better time to be completely honest. "I-I don't have anything else to dedicate my time to. I'm tired of living like a mole and having to borrow my homegirl's clothes. I want my own shit. I don't want to have to go home to my foster mother so her boyfriend can fuck me and get away with it."

She paused, hoping that was good enough.

"And?" El-Jihad jerked his neck slightly like he was annoyed. "You said you was hungry, but all I'm hearing is a sob story."

She inhaled and decided to go all the way in. What she was about to say she never told anyone, not even Lanai. It was like a fantasy of hers, something that she never felt would happen.

"I be seeing niggas hitting the block from the window in my bedroom," she confessed, closing her eyes, thinking about the young hustlers in her neighborhood. "I know how dangerous it is and shit. At any moment, somebody could come rob them or lock them up or whatever, but it don't matter. Every time I see them, from my window or up close, they look happy. Because they have *money*. I'm smarter than most people my age, but I ain't no scholar. I don't want to be a doctor or a lawyer, none of that. But I want money, and a lot of it. I've been cooped up so long around fucked-up people that I've had time to think about what I want."

"And what is that?"

"I want to live *good*," she replied and nodded back toward Lanai and the others. "Around loyal people. I don't really know all of them like that, but from what I see, I fit in with them."

El-Jihad let her words soak in, and he found himself chuckling. Removing the gun from her head, he stepped back to study her. He didn't trust her quite yet, but he'd heard the sincerity in her voice. She was green, but street, and he liked that.

"OK," he said and handed the gun back to its owner. "This is what I'm going to do. I'm going to give you a job. *One* job to prove to me that you're about what you're talking. If you succeed, I'll let you get down with the best team in my operation. But—" His eyes lowered, and Honey held her breath. "If you fail, I'ma let my goons tie a brick to each ankle and throw you in the ocean alive. You feel that?"

"Y-yeah," Honey nodded her head.

"And you," El-Jihad addressed Lanai with a look so venomous that it was a surprise that he didn't strike. "Give her a phone. I'll be calling later with details on the job. Let this be the last time you bring a fresh face into my facility."

He didn't wait to hear a response because he turned and walked away, taking his goons and cold aura with him. Nobody spoke until they heard the footsteps leave and the front door to the house slam shut. After that, it was like everyone in the room sighed with relief.

"I thought for sure he was gon' kill all of us," Ron Ron said, leaning up against one of the weapons walls.

"Hell, yea! You see how he was looking at her?" Snow said, referring to Honey.

"We're his best team," Lanai spoke up, trying to shake the goose bumps on the backs of her arms. "OK, back to business. When do we leave for this hit?"

"Nah," Dank said, shaking his head. "Y'all get back to school. This is just an easy pickup any-ways. You need to, for real, talk to your homegirl about what she just signed up for, straight up."

"Did you just hear what she said?" Lanai argued. "She knows what this shit is about."

"Yeah, whatever," Dank shook his head. "We gon' see."

"I'm still standing right here, you know," Honey butted in on their quarrel.

"I see you." Dank's voice sounded angry, but his eyes told a different tale. There was a file cabinet in the room that had a couple of burner phones in it. He grabbed a flip phone out of it and handed it to Honey after sending a text message. "Here. It's active, and he got your number now. If I were you, I'd do my best to not miss that call. You on your own now, ma. Willie, give her that gun y'all was showing her, with a couple of clips." He eyed Honey's tight jeans and shook his head again. "You gon' need some baggier pants too. Try some cargos or something. Easier to conceal something like that."

Honey tried to ignore the fire in her chest and the fact that everyone in the room was looking at her as if she'd just signed her death warrant. She wanted to ask them what they thought he was going to have her do, but then decided that she didn't want to know. She didn't want to get scared because, in all honesty, it was too late for that.

"Come on, Honey," Lanai told her after Willie gave her the strap. "Let's go back to school."

"Wait." Honey had started behind her but stopped. "The reason we came here was because I needed some money, like right now."

"How much you need, ma?" Dank asked.

"One hundred dollars for my graduation fees."

"Here." He reached in the pocket of his Levi jeans and pulled out a roll of cash. He not only peeled off a one hundred-dollar bill, but five more after that. "Now be easy, and don't miss that phone call."

Honey nodded and followed after Lanai, leaving the others in the basement to their own thoughts.

"Damn, G," Ron Ron said when he heard the front door slam. "She sold her soul to the devil for one Ben?"

Dank had been thinking the same thing. He had been watching Honey since she came in, and it was obvious that she was naïve to a lot of things; however, she wasn't afraid, either. It made him wonder what kind of demons she was hiding because she signed her life over way too easy.

"Some people use this lifestyle as a quick come up, and then get out," he said locking the file cabinet up again. "And others? Others just succumb to the life the hood spits at them."

"This nigga tryin'a sound like Ghandi or some shit," Ron Ron laughed.

"Ole Nelson Mandela-ass, nigga!" Willie threw in, joining his cousin's laughter.

"Yeah, yeah," Dank laughed a little bit too. "Fuck both of you niggas. Come on, let's get to this drop."

The sound of running water filled the air, and Honey relished in the feel of the hotness filling the tub she was relaxing in. Her head was thrown back, and she wished she could stay there in that moment forever. The school day was over, and although she paid for her cap and gown, she was beginning to wonder if it was worth what she paid. The volume to the flip phone had been turned up as loud as it could possibly get since she got it, and was sitting on the toilet seat next to the tub. She and Lanai had gone straight to Lanai's house, and neither girl had barely said a thing to the other.

Knock! Knock!

Honey jumped slightly in the water when she heard the knob on the bathroom door turn. When Lanai entered, Honey realized just how on edge she was.

"My bad," Lanai apologized. She set the towel and pair of pajamas she had in her hands down on the counter by the sink. "I didn't mean to scare you."

"It's cool, thank you."

"You a'ight?" Lanai asked, picking up the phone so that she could pop a squat on the closed toilet seat.

"I don't know how to answer that," Honey said, washing her body. "What did you have to do, Lanai?"

"What?" Lanai asked, playing dumb.

"You know what I mean," Honey said, rolling her eyes. "Bitch, what did you have to do to get put on?"

"Honey—"

"Don't 'Honey' me, Ny." Honey finished her bath and stepped out to dry her body.

"I'm not tryin'a scare you."

"It's too late to think like that." Honey popped the tags on the underwear and bra so she could put them on. "Tell me."

Lanai left the bathroom without telling her a thing. Honey followed her to the master bedroom as soon as she was dressed in the baby blue cotton shorts and white T-shirt she'd been brought.

"Tell me," Honey repeated, climbing on the queen-sized bed and nestling herself in Lanai's beige comforter.

"What I had to do doesn't matter," Lanai said from where she sat on the edge of the bed. "What matters is that you listen to what I'm about to tell you. My plan was to break you in with a small job and sneak you in through the back door. You know, ease you into this shit."

"Now what?"

"I feel you've been tossed in a pool of sharks before you were ready to swim. Listen, El-Jihad ain't no joke, and he don't like when people he doesn't know is in his mix."

"If you knew you wasn't supposed to bring me, why did you? Now you got me in his sights. I've seen what niggas like him do to people. Enough bodies have been tossed out on my block."

"I know, Honey, and I'm sorry. I ain't expect him to pop up like that, and you can curse me out if you want to, but what is that going to do? Now, I can tell you on how to survive a night with El-Jihad so you can get some money, or you can die broke and with nothing." When Honey was quiet, she continued. "Step one, don't put your trust in people, put your trust in situations. If some shit don't feel right, it ain't right. Step two, always know what you're doing, and if you don't know, look like you know. And step three, if you pull your fire out—"

Bzzzz! Bzzzz!

"you better shoot," Lanai finished with wide eyes as the flip phone vibrated loudly in Honey's hand.

Honey answered the phone before it could ring again, and put the receiver to her ear.

"Hello?"

"Wilson's Place. One hour. A car will be outside for you in fifteen minutes."

Click!

The phone hadn't even been pressed against her face for thirty seconds before she was disconnecting it. Honey jumped up from the bed and went to Lanai's walk-in closet.

"What did he say?" Lanai asked.

"He said someone is coming to get me in fifteen minutes," she said flicking the light on. "Do you have some cargo pants?"

She turned to face Lanai but saw that she was gone. Before she could call her name, Lanai was coming back in the room. Not only did she have the gun with the clips that Dank gave Honey, but she also had a bulletproof vest.

"Huh?" Lanai said handing Honey the vest. "Put this over your T-shirt. Move right quick." She moved by Honey to get in the closet and snatched a few items. "These should fit you. Sit at my vanity when you're done so I can braid you up."

Within five minutes, Honey was dressed and ready to go. Lanai spent the last ten minutes making sure Honey knew how to reload and tuck her gun correctly.

"I wish I had enough time to show you how to aim," she said, walking Honey to the front door. She hugged Honey and pulled back. "Just be as real as you can."

Honey nodded, even though she didn't understand what Lanai meant by that. There was no time to ask either. She turned away from Lanai's apartment door and walked away before her nerves caught up to her head. The door shut behind her as soon as she hit the corner on the end of the well-lit hallway. She could see the headlights of a car parked right outside of the apartment building entrance and figured that was her ride. She made sure the hoodie covered the gun tucked in her cargo pants before she stepped foot outside of the building and approached the darkly tinted Mercedes-Benz. The door unlocked the moment she put her hand on the handle, and she got in the backseat. The leather seats were light in color and comfortable to sit on. The partition window between her and the driver rolled down when she shut the door, and a voice asked, "Honey Broadway?"

"Y-yeah," Honey answered trying to hide the shock from coming to her face. She didn't know how he could possibly know her name. "That's me."

He didn't say anything else to her. The partition window just rolled back up and left Honey to stare at her reflection in the window. She felt the car pull off, and it suddenly hit her that she really didn't know what she'd gotten herself into. She didn't even see the driver's face. He could be taking her anywhere. Honey closed her eyes tightly and told herself to get it together. It didn't matter where he was taking her. . . . She was already in the car. All she could do was prepare for what would happen when she opened the door to the car once again.

Leaning back in the seat, she put her hood on. She looked around the luxury car and wondered how much it cost to buy. Being bounced from foster home to foster home, Honey always daydreamed about what it would be like to have nice things and be rich. She ran her fingers on the hard top of the armrest in the middle of the backseat and came across a button. Letting curiosity get the best of her, she pressed it, causing the armrest to click and the hard top to open upward like double doors. Inside was a .38 revolver and a small strap. She felt the car coming to a stop, so she hurried to strap the gun on her right leg. She had just pulled her pants leg down when the passenger's side back door opened. A tall man wearing a suit got out of her way when she stepped out of the car. She was confused because she thought "Wilson's Place" was some sort of restaurant, but there she was, standing in the parking lot of a closed auto body shop. There were a few client cars parked around her, but from what she could see, there was nobody in the building. No lights were on, and she couldn't hear anything. Not only that, but it looked to be the only building for some miles. Honey turned around to ask the driver if he'd brought her to the correct place, but he was already driving off.

"Aye!" Honey yelled, but he didn't stop driving. "Shit!"

Turning back to the building, she checked the time on the phone she had in her pocket and saw that she only had five minutes to get to wherever El-Jihad wanted her to be. She gave the location a once-over one more time before her eyes brushed against the sign on the building's front window.

"*Wilson's Place,*" she read to herself and slowly approached the front door.

She pulled the metal handle, and the door opened easily, giving her access to the place. The light being provided from the windows made it easy to see that she'd stepped into the lobby of the business. There was a high desk in front of her with two seats and two computers. Behind the desk was the entrance to the big garage on the left of the building. To the right of her were six chairs around an oval wooden table facing where a TV was propped up over a coffee machine. Farther to the right was an open door that said *"Employees Only,"* and Honey saw that it was the entrance to a hallway. At the end of the hallway she could make out a light and, naturally, she gravitated to it. She walked into what looked like the break room for the business's employees, and El-Jihad was there, waiting for her.

"Right on time," he said and smiled, pleased at her ability to be punctual. He sat at the head of the long, rectangular table with his hands crossed. "Sit."

Honey tried to ignore the fact that the air around her felt as cold as it did the first time she was around El-Jihad, and did as she was told. She sat at the other end of the table so she could face him and look him in his eyes. His were so dark in the weak lighting that she could have sworn she was looking into the face of a demon.

"What are we doing here?" she asked taking notice of the six men El-Jihad had lined up against the walls in the room. Three on the left and three on the right, all standing tall and dapper in their suits.

"Impatient, aren't we, Honey Broadway? It takes patience to become rich. Has anybody told you that?"

"No," she responded. "But then again, I ain't never been around no rich people. How do you know my name?"

"I make it my business to know everyone I do business with." He reached in his suit pocket and pulled out a cigar, a lighter, and his cell phone. Placing the phone in front of him on the table, he lit the cigar and took a long drag. "When I first met you, the blankness in your eyes intrigued me. You were . . . *unreadable* for a lack of a better term and only a few things make a person that way. It didn't take long for me to figure out, it pays to have friends in high places." He leaned back with the cigar resting between his fingers and cocked his head slightly. "I know that you turn eighteen soon and that you come from absolutely nothing. You were born to a

woman who never told you who your father was.
She was so hooked on pain pills that she was
probably passed out high when they came to
take you away. You were eight years old in the
system, placed with families, some more cruel
than others. You had to fight, sometimes you
won, but sometimes you lost. Like that time your
foster siblings jumped and stabbed you. After
you got out of the hospital, instead of pressing
charges, you were placed in a different home.
And that brings us to the relevance of this entire
spiel of mine. You see, I was going to have you
run the streets of some of my youngins to see
how much heart you had, but that was before I
found out how useful you could be to me."

"Useful how?" Honey was confused.

"Lisa Montgomery." El-Jihad shook his head
at the name. "They let anybody foster kids these
days, even the ones hooked on dope. She still got
that old '99 Grand Am with the one white door,
I see." He chuckled to himself, but Honey knew
there was nothing funny. "Are you familiar with
Lamont Ferguson?"

"Yes," Honey answered, not understanding
what her foster mother and her boyfriend had to
do with anything. "I didn't know his last name

was Ferguson, but we have to be talking about the same one."

"Sometime last night, one of my young runners got a call from someone asking for $400 worth of product. An hour later, one of my spots got robbed of $5,000 or $10,000 and another ten in product and guns. Now, imagine my surprise when I played back the security cameras and saw the niggas that robbed me hop into the *same* green Grand Am with the white door."

El-Jihad's words sent electricity through Honey's whole body. Not only had Lisa lied to her about what she did with the $400—she still had it. Honey wouldn't even be seated at the table with El-Jihad if Lisa would have just given her $100.

"I already had some niggas sweep through her house and—"

"They weren't there," Honey interrupted absentmindedly. Her anger had made her lips purse and her brow wrinkle. "This morning, I heard them talking about going to Lamont's house. Nobody knows about it, but Lisa drove me by there before. Why are you telling me all of this? What do you want?"

"Isn't it obvious, my dear Honey? I want their souls. Tonight. I was going to give you five hours to get the job done, but now you have exactly three hours to fulfill the job. I want them dead and the stolen items in the house Lanai so graciously took you to—or else I will kill both of you. Succeed, and you will live."

Honey said the only thing that she could think of without getting a bullet to her head right then and there.

"OK."

Chapter 4

"Come on, bitch! Give me some pussy before we hit the road!"

Honey sat outside of Lamont's one-story brick house. The neighborhood that the home was in was shabby, and many of the houses on his block were condemned. His looked like it wasn't too far from being declared that as well. The bottom looked like it was sinking into the ground, and on the left side of the house, mold was building up. El-Jihad had given her a car to use so she could get to where she was going. It was a silver Audi A8, and she'd never ridden in anything that drove so smooth like this before. Honey thought that maybe she should have parked a little farther away when she arrived at her destination, but it was too late now.

"Safety off," she told herself holding the gun tightly in her hand.

She got out of the car with her hood over her head and checked her surroundings. She didn't see anything but a few stray cats roaming the streets. Other than that, the night was quiet. The only thing she could hear was Lamont begging for some pussy plain as day. She advanced on the white front door and pressed her ear against it.

"Man, nigga, if you don't drag that ho in the back and get some pussy . . . you ain't gotta ask a whore for shit!"

The second male voice speaking to Lamont threw Honey completely off. She didn't recognize it from anywhere and decided to go with a different approach. She removed her hood and tucked her gun before knocking three times on the door. She heard footsteps coming closer to her, and then they stopped. She figured that whoever it was, they were looking through the peephole to see who was knocking on the door that late at night.

"Who is it, Monty?"

"Just this bitch's foster kid," Lamont said over his shoulder as he opened the door. "What the fuck you want, bitch?"

"I was . . ." Honey put on her most innocent face and tried to peer inside the house. So far, she could make out three other people, including Lisa, in the small living room. There was a coffee table on top of an old ragged rug that had a stack of cash and an open kilo of cocaine on it. "I was looking for Lisa. I went home, and she wasn't there. Is she here?"

Honey didn't wait for him to tell her what she already knew before she stepped in the house. She cleared her throat at Lisa to get her attention right before she snorted a line of the white powder. Lisa looked up and squinted her eyes at Honey until she figured out who she was.

"What you want, girl?"

"You said you didn't have the money I needed earlier," Honey said pointing at all the money on the table. "What's that, then?"

Lisa looked at the money Honey was pointing to and started laughing. She leaned into the skinny man sitting next to her. "Butch, this little bitch is still mad at a hundred dollars."

"That's your foster daughter, sis?" Butch asked her and looked Honey up and down with a small smile. "She looks mighty fine. How old is she?"

"She's seventeen. She turns eighteen in a little bit, though." Lisa stopped laughing to look seriously at Honey. "You know what that means, bitch? No. More. Money. So I ain't got no more use for ya!"

"I might have some use for her." Butch licked his lips at her.

Honey was trying to understand how a bunch of crackheads robbed the most notorious kingpin around, but she knew to never underestimate her enemy.

Slap!

"Damn, your ass is fat!" Lamont had come up behind her and palmed one of her ass cheeks. "I've been wanting to dive in that since I first saw it. I wanted some of Lisa's pussy tonight, but I think I'ma take yours instead. Y'all can do her with me. Lisa, make sure you don't sniff all the coke. We gotta sell some of it!" Lamont said, and then put his mouth to the back of Honey's ear. He reached his hand to the front of her and tried to palm her pussy too. "I'm about to make you fuck me and suck me the way I like."

When he licked her neck, Honey lost it. She pulled the gun from her waist and whipped around to face Lamont before he could react.

"I'm not here for you to fuck me. I already told you that would *never* happen," she said and was pleased at his shock at the gun pointed in his face. "I'm here because you robbed a very powerful man, and you gotta pay the price."

"You ain' no gangsta!" Lamont puffed his chest out and hit it with his own fist. "You ain't shit but a stray that nobody wanted!"

"Exactly. I don't have shit to lose."

Bang! Bang!

She pulled the trigger twice and held on to the gun the way Willie had showed her so she would have control of the weapon. Lamont fell to the ground with half of his face missing, and the wall behind him was sprayed crimson. Lisa's scream sounded far away, although she was right there, and Honey felt an adrenaline kick that she never knew existed. When Lisa came charging at her like a wild beast, Honey fired again, catching her foster mother in her throat. Lisa gripped her neck and gurgled on her blood as she dropped to her knees.

Butch and the other shaggy man in the room jumped into action. They each pulled out a pistol, and Honey dove for cover as soon as she heard them start shooting. Her body was behind a love seat, and she could hear the bullets ripping holes through it. Suddenly, she had an idea. It was risky, but she had to try it. She forced her body to collapse all the way on the floor so she was lying on her stomach. She stretched her legs out so that her feet showed at one end of the love seat and she lay lifelessly on the ground.

"Aye, man! We got her!" she heard Butch yell over the gunfire. "Grab the money and the coke and let's get out of here!"

The moment their guns stopped shooting was the moment that Honey used to her advantage. She jumped up while they were bending down and stuffing the cocaine and cash into duffle bags and pulled her trigger nonstop. Their bodies hit the floor and their blood mixed in with the other two dead bodies'. She didn't have time to sit and stare at her handiwork. She grabbed up the duffle bags and ran through every room of the house to make sure she wasn't forgetting anything. When she realized that she had everything she'd come for, she stepped over the bodies and ran for the door. Although the neighborhood was one that law enforcement would take their time getting to *if* someone called them, she didn't want to be anywhere near it when the pigs came sniffing around.

Honey's heart was still pumping as she turned the car on and sped away from the crime scene. She thought that she would feel differently about what she'd just done. On her way to the hit, she had asked herself if she could really take a soul. Now she knew how easy it was. She felt no remorse. If anything, she felt reborn. She felt . . . powerful.

When she got to the trap house, Dank and El-Jihad were already there waiting for her. Dank was surprised to see her since she was an hour early, and he was even more surprised to see that she had everything El-Jihad had asked for. There were a few dried blood spots on her hoodie, but instead of saying anything, he just looked her in the eyes and nodded his approval.

"Nicely done," El-Jihad said after he counted the money. Then he did something that surprised Honey. He handed her the duffle bag containing the money. "I don't give none of my soldiers shit that they don't work for. This is your payment for the job. You need a new place to stay, right? And a way to buy a car? Dank will teach you how to flip work, and you can re-up from there."

"Thank you," Honey said, taking the bag back from him. "I won't let you down."

"That's what I always hope," El-Jihad hissed. "But sometimes, hope isn't enough. I'm going to tell you what I tell all of my employees: two strikes and you're out. But I like your spunk, so for you? I'll add on one more. If you fuck up three times . . . Well, I don't think I need to explain. I'll show you. Bring him in here!"

He called behind him, although his eyes were still on Honey. She shifted her gaze from him to a man that Snow and Ron Ron were bringing from the upper level. He had a pillowcase over his head, and his hands were bound behind his back. They half-walked and half-dragged him down the stairs. He looked like he was trying to yank away from them, but his body had been beaten so badly it was a wonder that he even had any strength left. They brought him in front of El-Jihad and Honey and forced him to kneel.

"This is Malone." El-Jihad yanked the pillowcase from the man's head and removed his gag. El-Jihad's voice reminded Honey of an infomercial, and it made his words more menacing. "Malone is the one who let his entire trap house get robbed by four crackheads. Malone has hit his second strike . . . and now, Malone must die."

Malone's hair was matted with blood, and his face was so cruelly beaten that Honey couldn't even make out his features. Both of his eyes were swollen, and his lips were puffed up and bloody. His mouth couldn't shut all the way because his jaw had been cracked, and his eyes went to the only familiar face in the room. He began crying and begging for Honey to save him.

"The way he dies is up to you." El-Jihad stepped closer to Honey so that he could speak directly in her ear.

"What if I don't want him to die?" Honey subconsciously knelt so that she was eye to eye with Malone. "He hasn't done anything to me." She recognized him from Lisa's neighborhood.

"One thing I don't need from anybody who is on call for me is a conscience."

There was nothing Honey could do to save Malone, no matter how much he begged her, and suddenly, she wondered why she even wanted to. She didn't know how. All she saw before her was a sorry man in need. However, she knew nothing about his inner demons. She'd sold her soul not even an hour before, and it wasn't to save a two-bit hustler; it was to save herself.

"You've beat him up bad enough," Honey said and saw a flicker of hope creeped into Malone's eyes. She stood up tall next to El-Jihad again and turned her nose up at Malone. "He was trying to run when they brought him down the stairs, now I wanna know how fast he can go. Put him in a room with some hungry pit bulls and see what he does."

The smile that formed on El-Jihad's face was a slow and thoughtful one. He chuckled to himself and wondered why he, the king of torture, had never thought of doing that.

"I like how you think," he said, and motioned for Snow and Ron Ron to take him back to wherever they had him. "I like it a lot."

Chapter 5

Present Day . . .

Honey sat quietly in the backseat of the car beside a tattered Tari. Neither woman spoke, but both were trying to catch the vibe of the other. The last time Tari had used her voice was when they first stopped outside a raggedy-looking motel, and she was confused.

"This is where y'all were staying?"

"Low profile," Honey answered. "DeAngelo has been so good at playing ghost because he knew exactly who El-Jihad would send to collect. The last thing I needed was for him to be tipped off that I was in town. Now, pray that my shit don't have no roaches in it when I bring it back to the car."

At the time Tari had almost laughed. Now, there they were again riding in silence, and she didn't know what to do. Tari sat up and turned around to look out the back window, and sure enough, a black Audi A8 was following close behind. She'd given the driver the address to her house and wondered how she was going to explain three house guests to her mother.

"Do you have a mirror?" Tari's voice seemed to startle Honey.

"For?"

"So I can see exactly how much like shit I look before I walk in my house."

"You don't need a mirror for what I can tell you. You look like old man shit, the green kind."

The laugh almost got stuck in Tari's throat, and when it came out, it sounded like she was choking.

"The green kind?" Tari exclaimed and touched her face with her fingers. The makeup smeared right off, and she groaned. "My mom is going to flip shits. I don't want her to call the police."

"Here." Honey reached into the makeup bag by her feet. It was the only thing that she removed from the duffle bag she'd placed in the trunk. "There should be some makeup wipes inside. I think there's a comb and some bobby pins too. I don't think I have anything for them edges— whoo!" Honey looked at Tari's hair and shook her head. "You better say you sweated them bitches out."

"I guess that won't be too much of a lie," Tari smiled to herself.

Sure enough, in the MAC makeup bag, she found some MAC makeup wipes, a small comb, and three bobby pins. Tari combed through her short hair and pinned it back as neatly as she could. She then cleaned her face, removing the fake eyelashes that she was wearing, and threw all of her trash out the window of the moving car.

"That's it?" Honey asked, nodding at the pink house Tari had described earlier.

"Yeah," Tari said. "Pull into the driveway. We don't have a car, and Mama should be asleep."

The house wasn't much, and Tari was almost embarrassed to bring them there. Little did she know, Honey was admiring her home. Her eyes brushed the little lit-up flower garden in the front yard and noticed how neatly the grass was trimmed around it. The house looked like it was older than the owners, but Tari and her mother had kept it up.

"Pretty," Honey said.

"Yeah, right," Tari replied, looking around in the backseat to make sure she had everything she came with. "You probably live in some big-ass mansion or some shit."

Although she didn't live in a mansion, Honey couldn't lie and say that her three-story sub-urban home wasn't the bee's knees. When she didn't say anything, Tari shook her head and scoffed before getting out of the car.

"You probably don't know shit about living in the hood. You look like you've been spoon-fed all your life."

"Ha!" Honey laughed at the fact that Tari had tried her. "You'd be surprised at what I've been through. Money used to be a foreign language to me. Just because I speak it fluently now doesn't mean I've always known how to."

Honey grabbed her duffle bag from the very back of the truck and told the driver to go to the other motel where the others were. The plan was to all go home that night, but since the transaction wouldn't clear for a few days, Honey, Dank, and Breezy would hang back. Dank pulled in the driveway as the truck was backing out, and surprisingly, he got out of the car by himself.

"Where's Breezy?"

"He said his baby mama is tripping on him, and he needed to get home to handle family business." Dank shrugged his shoulders. "He figured we got this since all we doing is waiting on the transaction to process. And shit, I'm not about to come between no man and his family."

"Whatever," Honey shook her head. "He still gon' touch down and go fuck on all of his little hoes before he makes it home."

"Come on," Tari waved for them to follow her to the sidewalk that led to the front door.

"My neighbors are nosy. If they see us, they're probably going to think we're about to have a threesome."

"You into that shit, ma?" Dank asked jokingly but caught a quick jab to the arm from Honey.

"Stupid ass," Honey mugged him and wanted to hit him again because he was laughing so hard.

"Chill, ma," Dank said when Tari unlocked the front door.

The moment they were all through the threshold, the smell of clean linen hit their nostrils. To their right was a living room that had a baby blue couch and love seat. On the glass coffee table were two burning candles that gave enough light to see where they were going. Directly in front of them was a long hallway that would take them to the back of the house, and to their right was the dining room and kitchen.

"What have I told her about going to sleep with the candles burning," Tari murmured to herself and rushed to blow them out. They'd been burning for so long that the wax was all the way to the bottom of the glass holders. "She gon' fuck around and burn the whole house down."

Since the house was completely dark now that the candles were out, Tari reached out and grabbed Honey by the wrist to show her where they'd be staying. She showed them where the bathroom was and took them to the guest room. After she flicked on the light in there, she pointed down the hallway.

"That's Mama's room. Mine is right next to it," she said. "I'ma tell her that y'all are my friends from work and your lights are off, so you need to stay with me for a few days."

"We pulled up in an Audi," Dank shook his head. "Look, I don't want her to call the police. Just say we're your friends from high school and we're in town for a few days. Tell her you didn't want us to stay in a hotel if you had an extra room."

"OK," Tari said, liking his lie much better. "Y'all can relax and go to sleep. I'll put some fresh towels in the bathroom if y'all want to shower."

Dank thanked her and let her go to her own room. He waited a few seconds before shutting the door and examining the room. It was smaller than what he was used to, but it was clean and well decorated. He decided to take Tari up on her offer and hit the shower first. He too had brought in a bag with his belongings, and from it, he pulled out a pair of Ralph Lauren pajamas. He left the room for about thirty minutes and returned to Honey sitting on the bed the exact way that he left her. She seemed lost in thoughts.

"This reminds me of my grandma's house," he said and sat down on the tall, full-sized bed.

"I don't have a grandmother's house to compare it to." Honey had salt dripping from her tone as she took off her heels.

"My bad, Honey." Dank instantly noticed the change in her demeanor and knew why.

"Don't apologize. It's not your fault that my family threw me away like a rag doll," she told him, wiggling her toes, happy that they were finally free. "This 'sultry killer' shit is painful. I'm about to go back to cargos and Jordans!"

"You always change the subject."

"Huh?" Honey tried to play dumb when Dank scooted next to her.

"You always change the subject when your past gets brought up. Why?"

"Because there is nothing happy to remember, Dank." Honey shrugged her shoulders, trying to play it off like it was no big deal. "There was nothing special about the shit I remember about life before the system."

"Maybe nothing special, what about painful?"

"I'm not really trying to talk about this right now, Dank. I'm just trying to chill out until that deposit hits, and then I'm out of this bitch."

"Nah," Dank grabbed Honey's arm softly when she tried to pull away from him. "I'm not letting you get away that easily. You know, I always wondered why you would sell your life to El-Jihad for $100. That shit used to boggle the fuck out of my mind, but the closer I get to you, the more I understand. Your life had to have been pretty fucked up to sell your soul for one hund—"

"Nigga, I *said* I didn't want to talk about this," Honey snapped and leaned away from him. "But since you wanna know so bad, here it is. My mom was so fucked up when I was a kid. I be tryin'a forget that shit, but I can't. I never hated her . . . never. Not even when she used to put out her blunts out on my legs. Not when she forgot to feed me dinner, and not even when she left me home alone for days. In fact, that was heaven compared to the homes they shipped me to. I was ten years old and scared to go to sleep because I didn't want to wake up to anyone playing with my pussy. I was twelve when my foster parents at the time made their three foster kids sit in a circle and cut each other. All so they could get more money for us— to still not do shit for us. I was sixteen when I was almost murdered for *not* letting my foster brothers run a train on me.

"So, no, I didn't sell my soul to El-Jihad for $100. At first, I thought I sold it the night I caught my first bodies, but, no. I didn't even have a soul then. My soul left the moment those white motherfuckas came and got me when I was eight. The system took my soul, and no justice was ever made to give it back. So that's why it was so easy to say yes to El-Jihad and his three strikes."

Dank was quiet when Honey got done talking. She had told him way more than he thought, and none of it was anything he would have guessed. Reaching for her hand, he wrapped it in his.

"I'm sorry, ma," he said and kissed her fingers. "That's horrible. I shouldn't have pressed like that."

"You wanted to know."

"Well, now I know, and that shit don't even matter no more, especially when we get back home." He wrapped his arms tenderly around her waist and pulled her to him. "We only have one strike left each. There ain't no better time to bow out than now. It's what Lanai would have wanted."

Honey nodded her head, thinking about all the money she and Dank had saved up over the years. El-Jihad always said that if they could bring him $1 million, then anyone under him would be a free man. He knew that was almost impossible, mainly because most of his employees were comfortable and always spending. However, after five years, she and Dank both were $25,000 away from that million mark in their savings, and when they went home, they would cash in. In another account, they had almost the same amount that they planned to live off of for a while, and that thought alone should have made Honey very happy. But her eyes instantly watered at the mention of her best friend's name, and she stood to her feet.

"I'm about to take a quick shower."

She didn't want him to see her cry, so when she grabbed the things she needed from her bag, including a small flask, she left the room. She remembered where the bathroom was and shut the door behind her. The bathroom was the same color pink as the outside of the house. It smelled great in there, like Sweet Pea, and fabric with from on the soft white rug nestled in between Honey's toes as she sat on the toilet. The bathroom was small, so to turn the shower on, all she had to do was reach with her left hand and turn the knob. As the steam filled the room, she tossed the flask back and emptied out the Hennessey she had there.

"Mmm," she moaned when the burning sensation hit her chest.

She felt the effects of the alcohol almost immediately, since she didn't really have anything in her stomach except a sandwich she'd eaten right before the job. Getting up from the toilet, she began undressing, noticing that the slightest touches to her skin felt amazing . . . like the steam against her nipples and the running water thumping against her bare pussy when she stepped in the tub.

"Mmmm," she moaned again, that time in bliss.

It had been awhile since she'd been taken down, and she didn't know how much she needed it until that moment. She and her "boo," as she liked to call him, had both been too busy working to really get busy, but, oh, how she missed the feel of his rock-hard dick beating down her walls. She needed him. . . . So it was a good thing that he was in the other room. She finished her shower and left the bathroom naked, with all her clothes in her hand. Her buzz was walking for her, and she didn't care who in the house opened the door and saw her in her birthday suit. Water was still trickling down her smooth skin when she opened the door to the guest room, since she hadn't bothered to dry off.

The lights were still on, but Dank was lying back on the bed with his eyes shut. He opened them when he heard the door close and froze when he saw that Honey was naked. Her chocolate nipples were looking him square in the eyes, and her completely shaven pussy was begging him to put his mouth on her. The bulge in his pants grew, and he shook his head. Honey had always been the only girl to ever get him hard without touching him. He had been a hustler his whole life, and the last thing he ever wanted was to be thrown off his game by a female. Honey changed that, though. He knew when Lanai brought her around the first time that Honey would be a problem. Her gangster attitude alone had made him want her, and when he penetrated her body for the first time, he realized she was a rare gem . . . one that he would never let get away, no matter how many times they told each other they weren't in a relationship.

"Honey, what are you doing, ma?"

"I want you to lick my pussy, Daddy." Honey called him by the name that let him know she was submitting to him for the moment. She dropped the clothes in her hands and advanced on the bed. "Like you did last time, please. Daddy?"

Honey crawled sexily over his body until her fat pussy lips were positioned over mouth.

"Honey . . ."

"I won't sit until you tell me to, Daddy," she breathed. "But I want to so bad. *Please,* Daddy. Suck on my pussy."

Her voice alone was driving him crazy. He couldn't take it anymore. He gripped her wide hips and pulled her down on his face. His tongue went to work as soon as her love button touched it. He wasn't going to suck on it the way he did the last time they were intimate. He set a goal to do it better. He slurped up every drop of juice that tried to slide down his face, and he beat her clit with his tongue until she reached her first orgasm. He held her tightly so that she couldn't run from him and wrapped his lips around her clit so that he could suck it like she had begged him to do.

"Uhhhh!" she squealed. "Daddy! Uhhh!"

Honey's eyes rolled in the back of her head, and her thighs quivered. He had sucked her clit so good that it brought on two orgasms, back to back. Her body was telling her to go to sleep, but the Hennessey was telling her to lie on her back and spread her legs.

"Fuck me, nigga," she commanded and tried to pull him on top of her, but he didn't budge.

"Is my name nigga or Daddy?" Dank whispered and rubbed her wetness with his hand. He stuck his long middle finger in her tight opening and used his thumb to rub her still-throbbing clit. "Huh? And since you want to forget who's in charge, I'ma make you beg for this dick."

Honey moved her hips, not understanding how one finger and a thumb could feel so good. His finger was stoking her so good she couldn't wait any longer to feel what she really wanted to.

"I'm sorry, Daddy," she whined reaching for his face. Bringing it hers, she began planting soft kisses on his lips. Slowly, she slid her tongue in his mouth and intertwined it with his, kissing him deeply. Everything about him felt so good right then, and if he wanted her to beg, she had no problem doing so. She broke the kiss when she felt her third orgasm, and she wrinkled her forehead up at him. "Ple-ease—ahhh! Ahhh! Oh my God, Daddy, please fuck me! I want to feel that again."

"I'm Daddy?" Dank said, removing his pajama pants and positioning himself between her legs.

"Yes!"

"Say it again."

"You're my *Daddyyyyy!*" Honey's back arched when Dank plunged deep inside of her. "Oooo! You're so big, Daddy!"

Dank didn't say anything back because he was too busy relishing in the feel of her good pussy. He stroked her long and hard because he didn't want to hear words. He wanted to make her scream. He wanted to punish her pussy for being away from him for too long, so he put her legs behind her head and drilled into her until she squirted her juices on his stomach. But he also wanted to make love to her for having the best pussy he'd ever had, so he made her wrap her legs around his waist.

"You're so beautiful, ma," he whispered in her ear, thrusting into her repeatedly. "You hear me? Huh? Don't you ever give my pussy away. This Daddy's pussy! You hear me, bitch?"

"Yes! Yes! Yes! Yes!" Honey screamed, not caring who heard her. Her legs were shaking violently, and she bit into Dank's shoulder because her last orgasm was the most vicious. She didn't think she could take anymore, but she planned to leave her legs open until he was done getting all that he wanted. "I love you, Dank."

Her last whisper in his ear was all that he needed to hear. He released his nut into her with an animalistic grunt and gripped her tightly until he was done. Breathing like he'd just run a track meet, he rolled over to the side of her and pulled her close.

"I love you too," he said in a tired voice, kissing her forehead.

"I know," Honey replied with a giggle. "You're so *nasty*!"

"And you'll be able to get all the dick you want when we buy our way out."

"I can't wait!"

Chapter 6

"That's ugly!"

Honey laughed and made a face at the item Tari was holding up. It was an olive-green dress with the back cut out into an X. Hearing Honey's disapproval made Tari turn her nose up and roll her eyes. The day that the money would finally transfer over had come, and before Honey left the city, she wanted to do some shopping. If there was one thing she loved about Chicago, it was its downtown shopping area. She always went back home with tons of goodies, usually more than what she needed. The women had stopped into a boutique that had an array of sexy night life dresses and shoes. Honey had seen Tari's closet and told herself that before she left, she would boss the girl's life up. Tari thought that they were just out shopping for Honey, but Honey had a trick up her sleeve. She wasn't sure if it was because she was feeling a void, but she'd taken a quick liking to the girl. She'd even let Tari pick out a cute yellow summer dress with matching sandals to wear from her suitcase that day. She herself had opted for a comfortable pair of jean shorts, a black tube top that had ruffles at the bosom, and a pair of black Toms. Her appearance never gave off that she was as deadly as a black mamba, and that's the way she liked to keep it.

"You just don't have a sense of fashion," Tari responded and went back to admiring the dress. "This shit is sexy."

"Yeah, maybe if you're going to an eighteen-and-up party. Ooh! Come look at this one. You *have* to try this one on, bitch."

Reluctantly, Tari put the olive dress back on the rack and joined Honey by another that had a red, sleeveless body suits on it. She had to admit, Honey had an eye for beautiful things. The one Honey had picked up had diamond sequins subtly along the bra line and was made of a stretchy cotton that would hug every curve you asked it to. The front was cut low enough to tease, but not so low that it wasn't classy.

"This would go perfectly with this Marc Jacobs blazer I have at home. I can send it to you. I bought it and never wore it."

Tari took the jumpsuit from her and admired it for a few more seconds before reaching for the price tag.

"Twelve hundred dollars!" she exclaimed and tried to put it back, but Honey stopped her. "I can't afford that, Honey. A hundred-dollar dress would be too damn much for my budget."

"Do you like it?"

"I mean, yes, it's gorgeous, it's just too much—"

"Then get it. I'm footing the bill for everything today. Go find some shoes to match too. We can go up there to the Michael Kors store and grab some bags too when we leave here. Let's go get some more stuff to try on."

Honey snatched the jumpsuit from her and a few more in different sizes before walking away from that rack and heading for the shoes. Tari was speechless. She couldn't fathom the fact that the woman who had almost killed her two nights before was being so nice to her now. Yes, Tari had opened the doors to her home to Honey and Dank, but it wasn't like she had much of a choice either. She didn't move from that spot until Honey smiled at her from across the room and waved her over.

"What size shoe do you wear?" she asked, holding up a pair of nude, open-toe heels.

"An eight and a half. Oooh," Tari said, getting googly-eyed taking the shoe from her. "This ankle strap sets these shoes off! These shoes are fire! They're—$800! Honey, no, I can't let you spend all this money on me. You don't even know me like that. And, come on, it's not like we're even friends like that."

"Girl, if you don't shut yo' ass up," Honey giggled at the look of horror on Tari's face. "You look just like you did when Breezy brought your ass from the bathroom."

"That's not funny. Y'all were trying to kill me that night."

"But we didn't," Honey said in a singsong voice. She nudged Tari playfully with her shoulder. "Look, it's just been awhile since I was able to go out shopping without a group of niggas around me. I haven't done this since . . ." Honey got quiet, and a look of sadness rippled across her face.

"Since what?" Tari pressed.

"Since my best friend was murdered a few years ago," Honey finished. She took the shoe from Tari and flagged down one of the sales associates. "Size nine, please," she told the short Hispanic woman, purposely getting a half size bigger than Tari's actual shoe size.

They sat patiently on the bench in front of the shoe wall and waited for the nice woman to bring back the shoes. Honey pulled out her phone and started checking her text messages while Tari was still thinking about what she had just said.

"How was she murdered? Your best friend."

Honey stopped scrolling through her inbox and clenched her jaw. A part of her wanted to snap on Tari for being nosy, but she understood that it was her fault. She was the one who had put the knowledge out there, so she couldn't blame Tari for prying.

"We were set up, and she took a bullet that was aimed for my chest." No matter how many times Honey had answered that question, it never got any easier. She blinked a few times to try to push the painful memory back to the furthest depths of her mind, because the last thing she needed to do was break down in front of a girl she barely knew. "I haven't really got over it. I guess I never had the time. Because the same day I buried her, I had another job to do."

"Damn, she must have really loved you. What was her name?"

"Lanai. We all called her Ny, though. You wouldn't think I was so tough if you met her," Honey smiled to herself. "Now, *that* was one thorough-ass bitch."

"She would have killed me?"

Honey thought about it for a second and then shook her head.

"No, not if you would have started talking like you did. You would have reminded her of me . . . just like you remind me of her. She's the one who put me on when I didn't have shit and nowhere to go. Now I have everything and can go wherever I want. I learned that money is everything, but at the same time, it ain't shit, because I can't take it with me when I'm gone. And right now, I have a lot of it, so I don't mind spending it on you. Look at it as your payment."

"I thought my mother's treatment was my payment," Tari said, alarmed, hoping that Honey wasn't backing out.

"DeAngelo is paying for that." Honey gave her a wicked smile. "This little shopping spree is from me. Truth be told, you saved my ass." Tari didn't look anything like Lanai, but the vibe she gave off made Honey comfortable with her. She was saying more than she should, but not regretting it either. "The man I work for—"

"El-Jihad," Tari said, remembering the name.

"Yeah," Honey nodded. "He's king where I'm from in LA. Think of the devil but 100 times worse. The shit we did to DeAngelo is light work compared to the things I've seen him do to his enemies."

"Damn," Tari said, thinking about DeAngelo's bloody, bludgeoned body. She couldn't imagine what other horrors could be done to a person—or she didn't want to. "So I overheard you talking to your boyfriend last night."

"Dank?" Honey scoffed. "He is *not* my boyfriend."

"I couldn't tell," Tari giggled and dropped it before Honey tried to hit her. "Anyway, I heard you say something about a third strike. What does that mean?"

"You're nosy as hell."

"Our walls are just thin." Tari gave a fake smile, and Honey rolled her eyes. Tari watched her face, and it was obvious that she was having an inward battle with herself on whether she should spill the beans. "I already saw more than what I would like to know last night. Some words ain't gon' hurt."

She was right, and Honey knew it. She sighed and sucked her teeth trying to formulate the right words to say. The Hispanic woman chose that moment to bring back the shoes that she was sent off to find and set them in front of Tari's feet. Honey used the time that Tari was trying on the shoes to make the choice to tell her some, but not all, of what the three strikes meant.

"When El-Jihad opened the doors to his operation to me years ago, he told me I had a three fuck-up limit. I already fucked up twice, once a few months after that. I let my heart overpower my head like the silly young girl I was. Our team was El-Jihad's most thorough, and we handled distribution to the runners. Whenever they got more product, they paid what they owed, and at the same time, re-upped their work. One night I was laid up, and I had one of my other team members take my place in handling a drop." Honey shook her head thinking about how dumb she'd been back then. "I thought everything had gone smoothly . . . until Lanai called me and told me that she pulled up to the drop house and found all the little niggas in there dead. The money and the work was gone. Snow turned on us."

"Snow?"

"Yeah, the dyke bitch. In the beginning, there was seven of us. Me, Lanai, Dank, Ron Ron, Mo, Willie, and Snow. Snow was always the *iffy* one out of all of us. She never liked me, but I didn't think it would get between the money. But as it turned out, she had been plotting on El-Jihad way before I came in the picture. I just gave her the perfect opportunity. She and her people literally painted the wall in those youngins' blood. It was a massacre."

"What happened to her?" Tari asked, standing up, admiring her foot in the shoe.

"El-Jihad found her," Honey said and slightly winced, thinking about what he did to her. "He put two hooks in her back and hung her naked in a butcher's freezer until she told him where to find what she stole."

"T-then he let her go?" Tari asked sitting back down.

"Nah." Honey turned her nose up like something stank. "He hacked her body apart . . . limb by limb."

"Ooo-kay." Tari's eyes were wide, and she tried to erase the visual from her mind. "That was strike one. What about strike two?"

"Strike two . . ." Honey's expression became cold. "We were in North Carolina handling some business. A new customer that Lanai had been plugged to named Charles Bentley. He was legit and moved well in his state. She trusted that it would be a good business venture between our two states. He said that he wanted to buy fifteen from our camp, and Lanai told him she would throw in twice as much if he let our people set up shop there. He agreed . . . or so we thought. We got to the warehouse and began conducting the business meeting, but suddenly, I started hearing gunshots, I knew right then we'd been set up. He never planned to buy shit from us, or accept our business in Charlotte."

"Is that when she . . ."

"Yeah, they disarmed us, and then he aimed his gun, a 9-mm Luger, if I can remember right, and shot directly at my chest. The bullet never found me, though. Lanai jumped right in front of it."

"I love you, Honey. Blood didn't make you my sister. Life did."

Honey looked away from Tari as she remembered Lanai's dying words to her. She shook her head, trying to will the guilt pains to remove themselves from her chest. When the sadness subsided, she continued the story.

"How did you get out?"

"We had a few niggas stay back, just in case. They saved the day just in time, but I made sure I was the one to kill Charles. I emptied an entire clip into his face, and then another in his heart."

"I'm sorry about your friend, Honey," Tari said sincerely.

"Me too," Honey said standing up. "But enough of this sad shit. Go try these jumpsuits on so we can go. Do the medium first. Your ass is almost as big as mine. I don't think it will fit in a small."

Tari gladly took the clothing and went to the dressing room. It took her about five minutes to come out and hand the lady the size small and large. Honey smiled smugly because she knew she was spot-on about Tari's size. The two women walked side by side to the register, and Honey couldn't help but to smile inwardly at the giddy expression on Tari's face.

"You don't have any friends?" Honey asked after they were back on the sidewalk.

"I don't have time for friends," Tari answered. "Plus, the bitches here are the kind who will fuck your man behind your back and listen to you tell them how good he is to you."

"The type that will steal your money and help you look for it," Honey added, laughing.

"Bitch! The kind that will pop the tags off your shit and front on Instagram like it's theirs!"

The two went back and forth just like that all the way to where the car was parked on the street. They were laughing together like they'd known each other for years. Once there, Honey checked her phone and saw that they had a few more hours to kill.

"Your bank said the money will be available at five o'clock," she said taking Tari's bag from her and tossing it in the backseat. She opened the driver's side door, but instead of getting in, she leaned on the black paint and talked to Tari over the hood. "It's only three. Did you *want* to go look at bags?"

"Hell, ye—Honey, look out!" Tari had started her statement with a smile, but it quickly turned to a look of shock. She pointed her finger to warn Honey of something behind her.

Honey tried to turn around to see what Tari was so afraid of, but before she could, she felt a big body pressing forcefully on her back. She tried to scream, but a white cloth covered her mouth and prevented that. She inhaled deeply—and instantly felt herself losing consciousness. The last thing she remembered hearing were Tari's screams. . . . Then everything went black.

Chapter 7

Drip. Drip. Drip.

"Mmmm!"

The sound of dripping water stirred Honey from the deep sleep that she was in. She tried to open her eyes and focus them, but the pain in her head caused her to keep clenching her eyes shut. She felt something cold on her cheek, and wherever she was, it was lit up brightly.

"Honey!"

Honey heard the frantic whisper but didn't know where it was coming from. It sounded close. She tried again to open her eyes and keep them open. Figuring that rubbing them might clear her vision, she tried to bring her hands to her eyes, only to find out that she was bound to something.

"Honey! It's me, Tari!"

She heard the voice again, and that time, she sat up.

"Tari?" she said to herself and looked around. She was in a bathroom, a nasty one at that. Everything in it was filthy, including the stained tile floors. The dripping sound was coming from the tub's faucet as it dripped into a filled tub. Honey's wrists and ankles were tied together under the toilet bowl, and her head had been resting on the cold seat. Her head throbbed again, and all of the memories came flooding back in. She remembered the robbery and going shopping with Tari. The last thing in her mind was of somebody's hand over her mouth, and then nothing. "Chloroform. Shit! Where are we?"

"I-I don't know!" Tari said. "I woke up when they were dragging us out of the car, but I was too scared to open my eyes. I-I didn't want them to know I was awake. All I saw was the vehicle we were in. They just left for a second. I heard a door open and close. Honey, they took all our stuff."

"OK," Honey said. "Are you in the hallway?"

"Yes," Tari said. "Right outside the bathroom. My legs and arms are tied together. I can't even roll if I wanted to."

"Tari," Honey tried to even her voice out because Tari sounded terrified. "I need you to relax. We're going to be OK."

"Do you really believe that?" When Honey was quiet, Tari let out a soft sob. "They want the money we took from DeAngelo. They said they would let me leave if I give them my bank information. But I know they're lying. My God, now I know how DeAngelo felt knowing that no matter what, he was going to die."

"We aren't going to die!" Honey replied. "You said you saw the car we were in. What was it?"

"It wasn't a car, it was a truck. A black truck. It had a rental tag in the window."

"A black truck?" Honey said.

Her mind was moving so fast and so many dots were connecting, but she didn't want to believe it. But nobody else could know about the bank transaction. Nobody. A little ways away she heard a door shut, and Tari became frantic.

"Oh my God, they're back," she sobbed. "They're going to torture me! Please, Honey, don't let them kill me!"

"I won't, I promise," Honey said although she had no clue how she was going to keep that promise.

She listened as the footsteps got closer, and was angry that she couldn't even turn her head enough to look at the doorway.

"No!" she heard Tari scream. It sounded like she'd been hoisted off of the ground and was trying to fight. "Nooooo!! Honeyyy! Noooo!"

"Good job, my niggas," a voice Honey knew all too well was saying. "Y'all can take her to the back room and do whatever y'all want with her while I finish up in here."

Honey fought against her restraints, but they didn't budge.

"Tari!" she screamed over and over until eventually, she couldn't hear Tari's cries anymore. "No!"

"Tsk tsk tsk!" the deep voice said. "You've probably thought about how you would die a million times, but I bet it was never like this, huh?"

"What do you want, Breezy?" Honey's voice was malicious.

"At first, it was about money," Breezy sat on the toilet seat so that the crotch of his grey sweatpants was in Honey's face. "Now, it's about respect. You talk to me crazy, Honey. Like I won't turn up on ya ass. Now look at you."

"You got your money," Honey said. "Now let me go."

"So you can tell El-Jihad about my little stunt? Nope." Breezy shook his head and chuckled. He waved a finger in front of Honey's face before punching her in the eye with a closed fist. "Stupid bitch. Fuck you mean let you go? You ain't shit but El-Jihad's pet, but after this, *I'm* going to be the one moving up in the rankings."

Honey tried to rest her forehead down on the toilet seat, but Breezy yanked her head back up by her hair. She could feel the pain around her eye that already started to swell, and was forced to look up into his gleeful face.

"At first, I was just going to get the money and start fresh, but now, I'm thinking, why not make myself look like a hero? Listen to this. You and Dank got the money from DeAngelo and planned to skip town with it, but I was here to stop the two of you and bring the boss back his money. Yeah . . . and guess what? Either way—you die!"

"Stupid young-ass nigga." It was Honey's turn to laugh and shake her head. "El-Jihad knows I would never turn on him. Especially not for three hundred bands."

Breezy got close to Honey's face, and she wondered why she ever thought he was handsome. Right then, he looked like an evil little troll, and his demeanor matched.

"Well, he's going to believe it today."

He still had her hair gripped in his hand when he proceeded to beat her face with his free fist. He then stood up and began kicking and stomping her body. He knocked her wits out of her and didn't stop until she was coughing up blood. Breezy reached in the pocket of his grey hoodie and pulled out a knife. Using it, he cut the ties on Honey's wrists and ankles, causing her to fall weakly to the side.

Honey used that moment to try to catch her breath. Her adrenaline was pumping, so right then, she didn't feel the pain from the ass whooping he'd just unleashed on her. But she hoped there wasn't another one following behind it. When he cut her loose, she pretended to be weaker than what she really was, hoping to catch him off guard. But he never gave her the opportunity. Breezy hoisted her body up and dropped her instantly. Honey braced for the pain from the tile floor, but instead . . . There was a big splash. Breezy had thrown her in the tub, and the blood from her body was turning the clear water pink. She gripped the side of the tub to escape the frigid water, but Breezy palmed her face and threw her head back.

"I want to feel the life leave your body," Breezy told her with a crazed look in his eyes. "You think I'm beneath you? I'm going to put *you* beneath *me,* bitch! Do you know it takes the average person thirty seconds to drown?"

Honey tried to back away from him, but the water slowed her down, plus the tub was tiny. His hands wrapped around her neck tightly and submerged her in the water. Honey fought him and could get her head back out of the water a few times, but in the end, Breezy succeeded in keeping her under. She felt his thumbs press against her throat, and she knew there would only be one way out—she had to play dead like she did so long ago. She forced herself to close her eyes and began counting.

. . . *Twenty-eight, twenty-nine, thirty!*

Honey put up another fake fight and made her body jerk the way she'd seen in the movies. She was getting light-headed, and she felt that the end was really near. Breezy kept her under water for ten seconds longer than the thirty seconds before he finally let her go and stood to his feet. Naturally, her body rose up, making her face resurface, and her arms floated awkwardly, and her legs were uncomfortably bent in the small tub.

"Stupid bitch," he said again and spit in the water, looking down at her lifeless body in the bloody tub.

He left the bathroom, huffing his chest heavily, and went down the hallway to where Tari was being held. If Breezy would have stared a little closer at Honey's chest, he would have been able to tell that she was taking tiny breaths. She waited until she was sure he was gone before she sat up in the tub slowly, leaning over the side of it to inhale deeply. She wished she could rest there forever, but Tari needed her. She struggled out of the tub since her drenched clothes weighed her down, and found her footing.

Squeak! Squeak!

The water in her Toms made her shoes squeak, so she kicked them off. Glancing around the bathroom, Honey looked for a weapon, and she found a sharp mirror shard under the sink. When she exited the bathroom, she figured out quickly that she was on the lower level of a two-story home. There was no furniture in the house, and it stunk like garbage throughout it, probably because that's all there was. Trash everywhere, in bags or just strewn on the floor. Honey could make out mold on every wall she limped by, and she tried not to touch anything. She was on a search to find the clutch she'd come with. She'd almost made it to the living room when she heard a man mumbling to himself. She ducked down as low as she could go. Peeking around the corner, she saw a man, one of the men who'd traveled to Chicago with them from Los Angeles. His name was Pete or something. She never took the time to learn it. He was a black suit, a goon . . . a nigga who was supposed to do what his boss told him to. He let another money-ass nigga talk him into going against the hand that fed him, so he would pay the price too. He didn't even hear Honey come up behind him until it was too late, and his throat was slit ear to ear. She pinched his nose with her fingers and covered his mouth with her palm until he stopped gurgling and his eyes went blank.

"Gun," she said to herself and grabbed the .48 he had on him.

Not only did she find his gun, she found the car keys and a cell phone too. She opened the phone to call Dank, but a shrill scream cancelled that plan. Dropping the phone, she limped to where the scream had come from. The door to the room Breezy had Tari in was slightly ajar, and when Honey put her face in the slit, she made out Tari on a bed. She was wearing nothing but her bra and her panties, and her arms were bound to the bedposts.

"What's your routing and account number?" Breezy was asking her.

Honey couldn't see him, but from the sound of his voice, she could tell that he must have been at the foot of the bed. Honey's head accidently moved the door slightly, but the only one who seemed to notice was Tari. Honey hurried to put her finger to her lips and shake her head when Tari saw her.

"How many?" Honey mouthed.

"What the fuck are the numbers!" Breezy yelled. "Bitch, you better tell me before I start cutting you up, piece by piece!"

"Um . . ." Tari said breaking her eyes away from Honey. "Three!"

OK, three niggas, Honey thought to herself. All she needed to know was where they were at.

"Where?" she mouthed to Tari when their eyes met again.

"Three?" Breezy's voice sounded beyond impatient. "Three! Bitch, stop fuckin' playing with me! Do you see these guns? I will fucking kill you!"

"I'm sorry!" Tari cried. "The way you're standing in front of me is throwing me off! And the way these niggas are standing on the sides of the bed, almost at the end but not really, are throwing me off too!"

"What? Bitch, are you on crack!"

His question hadn't been out of his mouth for a second before Honey entered the room, gun blazing. She pulled the trigger to the gun twice—hitting the two goons on the sides of the bed with precise head shots. Her senses told her to drop to the floor, and once she did, a bullet hole appeared on door where her head was just at. Honey fired her weapon two more times and caught Breezy in both of his kneecaps.

"Ahhh!" He screamed in agony as he fell back. He dropped his gun when he hit the ground and glared at Honey from across the room. "I killed you!"

"No, stupid," Honey grabbed the doorknob and got back up. "You didn't. Because it takes sixty seconds for a human to drown." She walked closer to him and kicked the gun he was reaching for far out of his grasp. She gazed down at him with a confused look riddled on her face. "You had everything, my nigga. You were young and richer than a lot of people your age. Why be greedy like this? I don't get it. But I don't want to either."

Bang! Bang!

Honey didn't look at Breezy after her bullets demolished his face. She just hurried to get to where Tari was.

"Oh my God, Honey," Tari exclaimed when Honey was bent over her untying her wrists. "Your face!"

"I've been worse, trust me," Honey said trying to sound tough. "Did they hurt you?"

"They touched me, but that guy, Breezy, came in here before they could do what they really wanted to. Ouch!" Tari sat up and rubbed her tender wrists before grabbing for her clothes on the bed beside her.

"Let's get the fuck out of here," Honey said when Tari was dressed.

Tari tried to walk out of the room without looking at the dead bodies, but when she passed Breezy, she kicked him.

"Motherfucka," she said before exiting the room.

She helped Honey limp to the car and ran back in the house to get the cell phone Honey had dropped. Tari didn't recognize the neighborhood that they were in, but the truck had a full tank of gas, and it would be nothing to figure out. She sat there for a second trying to make sense of what just happened. Honey hadn't saved her life once, but twice. She didn't run when she had the opportunity to leave. She'd come back for her.

"Honey, thank—"

Honey threw her arms around Tari before the "thank you" was completely out of her mouth. After the initial shock wore off, Tari wrapped her arms tightly around Honey too. Neither shed a tear, and both were quiet. However, there was much said in silence. When they broke apart, Tari pulled away from the boarded-up white house, and Honey leaned back in the seat, watching Chicago's scenery all the way back to Tari's house.

***

"I'm calling the police! Those girls should have been back by now!"

They heard a frantic voice screaming when they approached the house. Tari's mother was in the front yard yelling at Dank when they pulled into the driveway.

"No! Nooooo! You don't want to do that!" Dank was shaking his head with his palms up, trying to calm the older woman down. "See! There they are!"

"That ain't the car they pulled off in!" Tari's mother tried to walk up to the car, but Tari jumped out first.

"Mama!" Tari said, slamming the truck door shut, not wanting her to see Honey's condition. "I'm OK. We just did a little extra shopping, that's all. Why are you even outside? You should be in bed resting!"

She ushered her mother inside the house, and Dank went to the truck, wondering why Honey didn't get out too.

"Aye, ma, that old lady is a trip! She—" he stopped midsentence when he saw how badly beaten up she was. "What happened to you? Did Tari do this to you?"

"That girl couldn't go toe to toe with me if she tried," Honey told him and grunted in pain when she tried to adjust herself. Breezy had done a number on her ribs, and she hoped nothing was broken. "It was Breezy. He kidnapped us." She went into detail about the last few hours of her life and how Breezy had turned on them all. "I left his ass stinking in an abandoned house," she finished.

Out of all the emotions rushing through Dank, the only one he would allow to surface was relief. He grabbed Honey's hands and kissed each one of her fingers before pressing them to his forehead.

"If something would have happened to you, ma, I woulda aired this whole city out."

"I'm OK, though," she told him with her cheek resting on her seat's headrest. She looked at the house that Tari and her mother had disappeared into and sighed. "I can't go back in there. I've already caused them so much trouble already. Can you go get our bags?"

"No problem. El-Jihad confirmed that the deposit showed up in the account you sent it to, so we're free to go home now. But I'm about to take you to the hospital before we leave. If that nigga wasn't already dead, I'd kill him."

"Wait! Dank?" Honey called his name before he was completely out of the car. "I left $50,000 in her account. Tell her I said thank you."

"For what?"

"Reminding me that it's OK to be normal. And we left that Audi rental downtown. I want to buy it and have it towed here, to Tari's house. It's hers."

Dank looked at Honey and gave her curious look. It looked like he wanted to ask another question but instead, he just smirked.

"You know, I ain't seen you look out for another woman like this since Lanai."

"I know," Honey said and turned away from him to look out the window. She stared up at the sky, and the sun was shining down on her. "Ny been talking to me, and I think it's time that I listened. Tell Tari I'll call her when I get home."

Dank shut the door, and Honey waited patiently for him to return. So much had happened in a few days' time, but so many lessons were embedded in Honey's mind because of it. Since Lanai died, Honey had never been the same, but being able to do for Tari what she hadn't been able to for Lanai brought a small glimmer of light back into Honey's life. A piece of her was even sad to say good-bye so soon, but she knew that she would be saying hello to freedom when she got back home to LA. And that meant she could visit whenever she wanted to, if Tari wanted her to anyway.

"Hey!"

The voice caught Honey off guard, and she turned back to the driver's side to see Tari getting back in the truck. She tossed a bag of clothes and a few pairs of shoes in the backseat before putting her seat belt on.

"I didn't even hear you open that."

"Probably because you got beat the fuck up," Tari grinned, but then straightened her face. "Too soon?"

"Yes, bitch," Honey giggled and gripped her stomach. "It hurts! What are you doing anyway?"

"Dank said y'all were about to leave, and he was about to take you to the hospital. *But* the next flight out of here isn't until the morning, so I talked him into staying here with Mama so *I* could take you to the hospital."

Tari ended her statement with a big fake smile before she started the car and began driving.

"Oh," Honey said and turned her face away from Tari.

"You over there smiling? Awe, Honey! You like me!"

"You a'ight, I guess," Honey replied, rolling her eyes.

"I guess I'll take that. I brought you some clothes and panties since the stuff you have on looks gross. I threw in a brush and comb too, because whoo!" Tari made the same sound Honey had the first night they met and looked at the bird's nest on Honey's head. "My mama would have talked all the shit if she would have seen you. I hope nothing is broken."

The two women talked the whole time to the hospital, and the horrors that had happened to them that day seemed to be farther in the past than they were. Tari helped Honey out of the car when they reached the emergency entrance of the hospital, and when they wheeled Honey to the room, Tari tried to hang back.

"Can you make sure my sister comes in the room with me?" Honey told her nurse, Sally, who was helping her in bed. Honey looked at Tari, who was standing in the doorway of the hospital room, with needy eyes. "I don't want to be alone."

"OK," Tari said, setting the bags in her hands down and taking a seat by the hospital bed.

The last scene the nurse saw before she shut the door was the women holding hands in a consoling manner. She dragged the cart back to where the other nurses were huddled behind the desk.

"She was beat up pretty bad," a woman with brunette hair said to Sally.

"Yeah, she looked pretty dinged up. I can't imagine who would do that to such a beautiful woman like that," Sally responded shaking her head. "But her sister is in there with her now. You can tell they're close. I'm about to go get her vitals. Pam! Don't forget lunch is on you today!"

With that, Sally grabbed everything she needed for her chart and wheeled her cart back down the hall toward the room to give the gift that God gave her . . . healing.

The End

Street Life
Johnny's in Love

by

Katt

Chapter 1

"If you want me to suck your dick, you need to put an extra hundred on the table," Strawberry Shortcake instructed her young white patron.

That Saturday they were in a small motel room that was in major need of an upgrade. The wallpaper looked to have not been updated since the eighties, and the mattress had hard lumps in it. She had no complaints, though. It was the location that her pimp, Sir, had chosen, so she had no choice but to show up. All she knew about the man sitting in front of her was that he was young, kind of cute, and paid well. She didn't ask for his name. Sir made her call all their customers "Johnny."

"An extra hundred?" the young man exclaimed. "I just paid two hundred! I thought that you sucking my dick was included."

"Do I look like a two-bit ho to you, Johnny?" Strawberry asked, motioning to her stacked body.

Johnny followed her hands and got mesmerized for a second. Strawberry had hips for days, and he could see her ass from the front of her. Her D-cup tits sat up perkily, and her pink areolas looked delicious against her olive-colored skin. Her body was perfect, and from where he sat on the bed, he could see no flaws. Even her manicured toes looked scrumptious.

"OK, OK!" He gave in and pulled an extra hundred from the pocket of his brown suit. "But we need to get this show on the road. My lunch is only an hour long."

Smiling big, Strawberry snatched the bill from his hand and set it on the rickety nightstand beside the queen-sized bed. Johnny stripped completely naked and waited patiently to feel Strawberry's warm mouth on him. She put her long, brunette hair in a ponytail on top of her head while slowly moving her hips and staring into Johnny's baby-blue eyes.

"Has anybody ever told you that looking in your eyes is like being lost at sea?" She based him up and lowered herself on her knees. "They say my mouth and my pussy is like being lost at sea too."

She didn't care what his next words were. It was time for her to do her job and make Sir happy. She wrapped her big, full lips on the tip of Johnny's six-inch erection and slid her mouth down to the base. Bobbing her head up and down, she made sounds like she was choking from his size, even though she wasn't.

"Ahhh! Yes, you dirty slut!" Johnny moaned, reaching down to pinch Strawberry's nipple. "You nasty-ass girl!"

He threw his head back when he felt her throat make a swallowing motion on his tip and gripped the back of her head. Tired of her being in control, Johnny stood to his feet, holding both sides of Strawberry's head to keep it still while he ruthlessly fucked her face.

"Nasty bitch!" he said, slamming in and out of her mouth. "Ohhh! That mouth feels so good, you nasty bitch!"

When Strawberry came up for air, he grabbed her arm and pulled her on the bed, telling her that he was ready for her Latina pussy. He bent her over and played with it while he put his condom on. Sliding two fingers in and out of her wetness, he felt himself becoming even harder. His focus wasn't on pleasing her. It was on using her as an object of his own pleasure. Without warning, he shoved the same two fingers that had been inside her pussy in her butt hole.

"Ahhh!" Strawberry shouted in shock.

"Shut up and arch your back," Johnny demanded.

Strawberry did as she was told and let him do to her what he came for. What Johnny didn't have in length, he made up for in thickness. When he rammed his manhood in Strawberry's love canal, he awakened every sense her pussy walls had. Pleasure shot through her body like electricity while he penetrated her two ways, and she arched her back until her nipples rubbed against the bed comforter.

"Is she being good to you, Daddy?" she asked and looked back at him.

He didn't need to answer. Strawberry could tell that he was thoroughly enjoying himself just by the way his face was completely twisted up. She knew that look all too well. It was the "trying to hold a nut" expression. That was her cue to end their session early. Strawberry began throwing her ass back so viciously, the poor man looked like he didn't know what to do. He wasn't trying to get her to come, but she refused to leave without getting something. She felt the pressure building up in her clit, and she bit her own wrist when she felt it explode.

"Ahhh!" they both called out in unison as they climaxed.

Strawberry felt his dick jerking inside of her until he pulled out, holding on to the condom for dear life. The last thing he wanted, Strawberry was sure, was to have a baby with a prostitute. Johnny fell on the bed with his shrunken manhood still out and in the come-filled condom. Strawberry knew what was about to happen next even before she heard him snoring. Johnny had booked her for an hour, and since he only lasted about thirty minutes, that meant she had time to take a quick shower. Gathering her things, she headed for the bathroom to get herself together. She didn't turn her nose up at the small and slightly dirty facility. She'd been to worse places. There were times when she couldn't even clean her swollen pussy after a job, so she was just happy to have access to a bar of soap and running water.

She allowed herself to relish in the feeling of the running water for a few minutes before she cleaned herself and got out. She used one of the towels that was in the bathroom to dry off and wiped the foggy mirror with her hand so she could see herself. Her lipstick was smeared, but other than that, her makeup was still neatly in place. She fixed her lips and put her hair in one neat braid before putting her short red dress and nude four-inch pumps back on. When she opened the bathroom door, she saw that Johnny was still knocked out on the bed. Before she nudged his leg to wake him up, she snatched the $300 from the nightstand, along with her over-the-shoulder nude chain clutch. She put the money in her clutch but grabbed an extra fifty from the pocket of Johnny's slacks on the ground and put that in her bra.

"Sugar," she said sweetly, tapping his leg.

"Hmmmm," he groaned.

"Your time's up, and I need to get going," she told him swishing to the door of the motel room. "Your break is almost over."

She reached in her clutch for her oversized dark shades and put them on before the Memphis sun could blind her when she opened the door.

"Bye," she heard Johnny say behind her, but she'd already slammed the door shut.

She hadn't even taken two steps in the parking lot when a champagne-colored 2016 Cadillac CTS parked in front of her, blocking her way. Smiling big, she reached for the handle and pulled it, but it didn't budge. The passenger's side window rolled down, and she peered inside with a pout on her face.

"Daddy, open the door," she whined to her pimp.

Larry "Sir" Smalls wasn't your typical pimp. He was young, handsome, and didn't rock the normal décor of a pimp. Truthfully, the only thing cliché about him was his car. His hair was cut into a fade, and around his neck, he rocked a thick chain with an "S" hanging from it. He covered six of his bottom teeth with a gold grill and wore many rings on his fingers, though none of them was a wedding band. His skin was brown, and it matched the color of his eyes. Sir blinked at Strawberry and stared at her like he was waiting for something.

"Bitch, where's my money?"

"Daddy, you know I wouldn't come to your car if I didn't have your money," Strawberry gushed and pulled out all the money she'd made that day.

When he saw all the green in her hand, he unlocked the door and rolled the window back up. She handed him the money once she was in the car and watched him count it as she put her seat belt on. She could tell something was wrong since he counted it three times in a row.

"This is only $2,400," Sir said shaking his head. "There's a hundred dollars missin', Strawberry."

"You ain't give me no money this morning," Strawberry replied hurriedly, laying her Hispanic accent on thick. "And since you made me catch taxis to get to all these places, I had to dip into the pot. Don't be mad at me, Daddy."

Sir looked like he wanted to be mad, and Strawberry braced herself for the slap that was sure to come, but it didn't. The angry expression subsided, and Sir put the car back in drive.

"I'll give you some money from now on if I can't drive you where you need to be," he replied. "You hungry? I was finna stop at a burger place and grab some food right quick."

Strawberry nodded and batted her long eyelashes at him. He was so fine, and if she wasn't tainted from another man, she would beg to take him down right then and there. It was no secret that she loved him and would do anything for him. She proved that every day. Many people would say what he made her do was not love, but she begged to differ. She knew Sir loved her, and no matter what, nothing anyone told her would change that. The two had met during Strawberry's sophomore year in college, back when she was just Maria Calico. She'd seen Sir a few times in the club with his boys, and each time, he always looked like a star. He asked her on a movie date one night, and after that, the rest was history. The two were inseparable, and he made her feel like a queen.

Her fairy tale ended after they'd been dating for some months, and Sir's past came to haunt him. He and Strawberry had moved in together, and she was starting to see that the flashy life Sir lived back then was just a show. He didn't have any real money. She was working doubles as a waitress to cover their bills, all the while still attending classes. One night, Sir came running in the house beaten up and bloody, and it scared Strawberry to death. He rambled on about how he owed a man named Honcho $5,000, and he didn't have it. Sir told her that if he didn't pay what he owed that night, then they would come and murder him. He held her hands and told her that there was only one thing that could save him. When she asked him what that was, he explained to her about how everyone knew he had the thickest chick in the city. Everyone wanted a piece of her ass, including Honcho. If she slept with him, then his life would be spared. At the time, Strawberry felt as if her whole life had spiraled out of control within seconds, but the last thing she wanted was for Sir's death to be on her hands.

"Will you still love me if I do this?" she asked him.

"I'll love you more than anything."

Young and naïve, she believed him, and she did it. It was the most demeaning experience of her life, especially since she hadn't given herself to many men before that. But when it was over, everything went back to normal . . . until Sir needed another "favor" . . . and then another. When Strawberry finally got up the courage to tell him no because she didn't want to do it anymore, Sir slapped her so hard that she flew backward.

"You gon' do what the fuck I say, bitch," he hissed in her face. "You my property now. Where else you got to go? Everybody in the city knows you as the ho that fucks for cash. Ain't nobody gon' take you seriously."

His words to her were ones that she would never forget, because he was right. Who would want her? Strawberry never thought that five years later, she would still be whoring for him, but if she did everything Sir told her to, he took care of her. They were a team, he always said. He promised her that when they had enough money saved, he would move her to Hawaii, and they would live their happily ever after.

Sir bought them food with the money Strawberry had just given him and drove them back to their home in East Memphis. It was only five o'clock, and Strawberry hoped that Sir would just let her sleep the rest of the day since she'd literally been working since before the sun came up. She stepped inside the apartment and welcomed the AC blessing her skin. Summers in Memphis were usually hot, but that day, it felt like a sauna. Although she'd already taken a shower, the few seconds she'd spent in the heat walking to the apartment building had caused her back to start sweating.

"I feel gross," she told Sir. "I'm about to go take a shower."

"Nah." Sir wrinkled his eyebrow at her. "I just bought this food. Sit at the table and eat. We have business to discuss."

So much for getting some sleep. She knew what he meant by "business." She sighed and trudged back down the hallway that led to their bedroom and sat at the round table in the dining room. Their two-bedroom apartment was spacious and had a lot more room than the small studio apartment they used to have. It was completely furnished, and Strawberry's favorite spot was the living room. There was a plush leather couch and matching love seat that faced the long balcony. Sitting kitty-corner on the wall next to the balcony window was the entertainment system. Inside it was a fifty-inch TV with three connected game systems and almost 100 DVDs lined up neatly. The two glass end tables on either side of the couch matched the rectangular coffee table, and Strawberry raised her eyebrow because there was incense still burning in its holder.

"I thought you were at work," she asked, taking a bite into her burger. "Why is there incense burning?"

Sir glanced at the living room, and then back at Strawberry. She knew that she was playing with fire by questioning him about his whereabouts, but she didn't care. He said the reason she had to catch a taxi to all her spots that day was because he would be working. The last time she checked, you couldn't be a bank teller at home.

"I was working."

"At home? How can you work for the bank at home, Sir?"

She quickly switched from being a working girl back to being his girlfriend. She could see the agitation building on his face, especially when she called him "Sir" instead of "Daddy."

"Not that it's any of your business, but I quit that job weeks ago."

"Weeks ago?" she exclaimed, not understanding what he was saying. "You quit *weeks* ago? How could that be true when you've been going to work every day?"

"Look, I make more money with you on the streets than I ever could at that bank, shorty. It's time for us to tighten up."

"What do you mean tighten up?" Strawberry's voice rose, and she didn't even know it.

"Everything all right out there, Daddy?"

The voice caught Strawberry off guard, and she looked from where Sir sat across from her, to the hallway of their home, and back at him.

"What was that?" she asked with a confused expression.

"Come on out here, Sugar. You too, Spice!" Sir called down the hall and then focused his attention back to Strawberry. "Like I said, I've been working. I want you to meet a few people."

Two black women came from the back room. Both had on nothing but bras and panties with long weaves hanging down their backs, but that was where the similarities stopped. One of them was tall and light skinned with slanted eyes and puffy pink lips. She was almost as thick as Strawberry, but not quite. Her cute face and voluptuousness was the perfect distraction for her crooked teeth. The other girl was short and had skin the color of toffee. She was flat chested with wide eyes and a wide nose, but her teeth were straight. She wasn't that cute in the face, but her ass was fat and jiggled at any slight movement she made.

"Who the fuck are they?" Strawberry demanded when they took their positions in the large kitchen of the apartment.

"I'm Sugar," the light-skinned one replied.

"And I'm Spice," the other followed.

"I'm not asking you, hoes," Strawberry barked and turned back to Sir. "I'm talking to *him*."

"'Him' couldn't certainly be me," Sir said, calmly placing his Glock 9 mm on the wooden tabletop. "Nah, there ain't no way you're talking to me like that. Like I won't repaint these walls with your blood? Nah, can't be talking to me."

Seeing the gun made Strawberry quickly change her approach, but there was still a hint of salt in her voice.

"I'm just trying to figure out who these girls are in our home, that's all, Daddy."

"These are my new employees," Sir told her like it was nothing. He finished his burger and tossed his trash in the waste bin next to the kitchen counter. "They'll be living here now."

"Living h-here?" Strawberry pointed her fingers to the ground for emphasis. "And what do you mean *new employees?*"

"If you 'sposed to be the bottom bitch, you a little slow," Spice said with a chuckle. "We all finna get this money together, baby."

"Exactly." Sir stood up and went to stand behind the girls. He put a palm on each one of their asses and squeezed. "Mmm. I can't just have you out there working them streets alone, Strawberry. There is only so much you can do in a day. I need more hoes in more places."

Strawberry was appalled, and she now knew why Sir didn't want her to walk to the back room when they'd first got home. She felt tears well up in her eyes so quickly and glared at Sir. Sir had never referred to her as his "ho." He always called her his "business partner." On top of that, she couldn't believe that he was really in front of her fondling Sugar and Spice like that.

"This isn't . . ." Strawberry stood up and shook her head feverishly. "This wasn't the plan. You said that this would only be temporary, not forever! Now, you've quit your job and are trying to bring in more girls."

"Plans change," Sir told her. "And this is the change, and you're going to be OK with it."

"But I'm *not* OK with it," Strawberry told him with tears falling from her eyes. "I don't want them here in the home that I built!"

"Sugar, take Spice back in the room y'all will be staying in," Sir instructed.

His tone was low and deadly. Neither woman opposed. As they walked by Strawberry, she caught their pitiful looks and wanted nothing more than to fire off at them. She glared at them until they were in the room down the hall and the door was shut.

"Are you fucking them?" Strawberry asked.

"I would be a horrible pimp if I didn't test my product."

"Oh my God," Strawberry sobbed. "I hate you! How could you do this to me?"

"Do *what* to you? Fuck another bitch? Strawberry, you let niggas run up in you all day. How could you really expect me to stay faithful to you? I mean, look at you! Plus that pussy lost its grip a long time ago."

"I fuck other people because you ask me to! I don't do it because I want to! I do it because I love you!"

"And I love and appreciate you for that," Sir shrugged her tears off. "But it's time for new blood, Strawberry, so you're either in or out."

"Are you going to fuck them again?"

"Yes." He didn't even think about what she asked. "Whenever I want."

"Then I'm out." Strawberry turned her lip up and tried to storm past him. "I should have left a long time ago! I hate you!"

She opened her mouth to scream at him again, but she didn't get the chance. Sir's hand was wrapped tightly around her throat, and he pushed her until her back was against the front door. He choked her and watched her struggle for a few moments before he spat in her face.

"I *own* you. I could kill you right now and bury your body, do you know that? Who would come looking for you?"

Strawberry couldn't answer. Her hands clawed away at his because he'd completely cut off her ability to intake oxygen. She tried to focus on something to keep her from blacking out, but the only thing that caught her attention was his baritone voice in her ear.

"That's right. Nobody. You are *my* property. I own you until I say you can leave. But you know what? You can go. Get the fuck out and don't come back, bitch."

Sir released her, and she dropped to the floor coughing, holding her neck. Strawberry put her forehead on the floor sobbing through her coughs. She waited for the dizziness to leave her head before standing up and heading to her bedroom to pack her things.

"Nah," Sir grabbed her by the arm and threw her back toward the door. "You ain't taking shit. Everything in this mothafucka is mine. Including those two bitches in the other room. They're in, you're out."

"Noo!" Strawberry tried to dive toward the hallway, but he caught her.

"Strawberry, you're embarrassin' yourself," Sir told her, dragging her to the front door. "You just said you hated me and that you weren't rocking with me anymore. That's cool, but you gotta go. I'm sure it's a whole bunch of niggas out there who would house you, if you ain't fucked 'em already, that is. Get out."

Strawberry yanked away from him and stood to her feet. She was broken, and her pretty braid had come unraveled. She knew she looked like shit, and that's not how she wanted to go into the world. She didn't have anywhere to go. She'd lost all her friends years ago. Plus, all she had on her was the fifty dollars she had hidden in her bra. Sir was growing impatient and knowing him, he would lift her up and throw her out any second. She didn't have a choice. She had to stay.

"Fine," she told him. "I'll get with the program."

"I thought you would change your mind." Sir closed the front door and locked it. "Go in the back and get ready. You look like half a penny. You and the girls have a big party this evening."

Chapter 2

Strawberry sat in front of the vanity mirror in her room and studied her reflection. She was what most called "drop-dead gorgeous," and there was a time that she, too, believed that. Men and women used to admire her when she walked by them and give her nice compliments. Now, the men just asked how much twenty dollars could buy them, while the women looked down their noses at her. East Memphis was big, but not that big. Everybody knew who she was and what she was about . . . except they were wrong. She was still a woman with goals and dreams. She just didn't know how to get to them anymore. She dropped out of college in the middle of her junior year, so she never got her degree. All she ever wanted to be when she was younger was an elementary school teacher, but that got cut short the moment she laid up with Sir.

Most days, Strawberry was happy. She lived comfortably and always had everything she needed at her fingertips. However, whenever bad things happened, she was reminded the cost she paid to have all that she desired. Like right then, she was staring into her own eyes wondering if it was ever even worth it at all. No matter how pretty she was on the outside, Strawberry felt like trash on the inside. She was used goods, and Sir never let her forget it.

Strawberry finished applying her last layer of lip gloss, grabbed a black clutch from her side of the closet, and left the room to show Sir that she was ready. She wore a black velvet strapless dress that embraced every curve on her body. The high bun on her head and the four-inch open toe ankle strap heels set off her entire look. Strawberry's edges were slicked to the gods with a curly *q* on each temple.

"Sir," she said as she walked down the hall, "I'm re—"

She expected to find him sitting in the living room waiting for the girls. Instead, she saw him when she stopped in the doorway of the second bedroom. She was frozen at the scene she was watching. He was perched at the foot of the bed and Spice was on her knees in front of him, sucking his long, hard dick. Bent over on the side of them was Sugar, with her dress hiked up and shaking her ass like he was throwing dollar bills.

Sir had his arm outstretched so he could play in her pink opening while Spice pleased him. He finally took notice of Strawberry standing there and grinned at her.

"You ready, Strawberry Shortcake? Let me bust this nut, and we can be out."

Strawberry turned around before he could see the look of disgust on her face. Biting back her tears, she sat in the living room like an obedient pet waiting for her master. It took almost five minutes to hear Sir's low grunt that signified he'd reached his climax, and another five for the three of them to come from the back.

"Let's go get this money!" Sir was smiling like a new man when he tucked his gun and grabbed his car keys. "I got some ballers lined up for you hoes tonight!"

He wore a True Religion outfit: black jeans and a white shirt with a black emblem. On his feet were a pair of all-black Nike Air Max Classics, and in his pocket there was a wad of cash. His gold chain was what set all of his outfits off. It was something Strawberry bought him long before she was doing what she was doing. She'd used her entire school refund check to buy it for him, and he always rocked it proudly. At that time, Strawberry wanted nothing more than to rip it from around his neck, but she followed him out the door instead. She was the first one in line. She wanted Sugar and Spice to understand that their place was always beneath hers.

Sir was taking them to a newly built nightclub not too far away from the house called Cold Diamonds. It was opening night, and all the ballers and shot callers would be in the mix. When he pulled into the parking lot, it was so deep that he almost wasn't even able to drop them off at the front. The line was out the door, and the music was bumping so hard that the windows in the Cadillac vibrated.

"Listen, this shit is serious. Now that it's four of us, we're gon' need a bigger spot. I need each of you to bring me at least a stack tonight, and I don't care if you gotta work all night to do it, understand?" Sir looked all the girls square in the eyes and waited for them to nod their heads. "If he don't look like he's working with at least five stacks, don't waste your time. Call me if you need me to come get you in the morning. If you come home without my money, I'ma hurt you. Bad. Now get out."

With that, he unlocked the doors to the car, and that was their cue to get going. Strawberry got out of the car first and didn't wait for the other girls. She skipped the long line and ignored all the catcalls she was getting. The bouncer of the club was one she knew well. She'd never slept with him, but he knew what she was about.

"Wassup, Clay!" Strawberry said, smiling big at him.

When he heard his name get called, the big man turned around to see who had said it. When he saw Strawberry standing there, he playfully clutched his chest and gave a playful gasp.

"Mmm mmm mm! Strawberry!" he said, smiling and making his thick mustache turn upright. "You look better every time I see you!"

"Thank you, baby!" she replied. "You gon' let me in this bitch or what?"

"You already know ain't no party unless you add some Strawberry in the mix! You still fucking with that lame-ass nigga you always with?"

Strawberry's smile wavered slightly, giving him his answer. He looked over her shoulder, and sure enough, Sir was still parked, watching Strawberry like a hawk.

"Out of all the niggas you could have in M-Town, you wanna rock with a nigga like that?"

"Mane, Clay, not now, a'ight? I'm just tryin'a have some fun tonight."

"You better than that, Strawberry."

"Yeah, yeah, whatever. Tell these niggas that."

Clay stepped back to let her inside of the club, but voices calling her name stopped her.

Strawberry turned around and rolled her eyes at Sugar and Spice standing on the side of the line. She smacked her teeth and debated on if she was going to let them walk in with her. She guessed they were fly enough, and at least they straightened up after fucking Sir before leaving.

"They with you?" Clay asked, seeing her hesitate.

"Yeah, mane," she said and waved for them to come in with her. "Let them in too."

"Thanks, Johnny," Sugar said, licking her lips at Clay when she walked by.

They followed Strawberry as she made her way through the big group of people until they all reached the bar. Strawberry ordered a drink while the other two sat down, casing the place. Rae Sremmurd's song, "Come Get Her," was blaring through the speakers, and everyone on the dance floor was going crazy to the beat. Every VIP table was sold out, and the occupants looked like they were working with some big money.

"We need to start making our rounds," Sugar said to Spice.

"Girl, I know!" Spice looked around at all the men hungrily. "All this money in here is making my coochie wet! Daddy said he only needed a thousand, but I think I'ma bring him back two!"

"Then I'ma do three!"

Strawberry looked at their eager faces and realized that she too used to look like that. So eager to please Sir and make him happy. All she wanted to do was help him live the life that he wanted, even if that meant giving up her own.

"How old are y'all?" she asked.

She spent all day hating them, and it wasn't until then that it dawned on her that she didn't know a thing about them.

"I'm twenty-one," Spice said. "And she's twenty-three."

"How the hell did Sir find y'all? Are y'all from Memphis?"

"Yeah," Spice answered again. "We met Sir at the hair store two weeks ago. He said he could put us on to some money, and shit, he looked like money, so here we are. We been hoeing on our own for a while, but we wasn't really getting no real bread until we started fuckin' with Sir. That's why he moved us in with y'all. There wasn't any point in us living house to house if he had an extra room for us."

"Right," Sugar spoke up. "Y'all place is real nice. I can tell you was the one who decorated everything in there just by how you dress." Sugar pointed at Strawberry's outfit and gave her an approving smile. "Look, I know you don't really want us there because you've probably been makin' good money without us. But we ain't tryin'a step on your toes or nothin'. We just wanna make some money too. I don't see why we can't just all get along. Like it or not, we all sharing the same dick now."

Strawberry wanted to slap the girl silly, but she was obviously already too silly for words. She shifted her eyes to Spice, who was nodding in agreement to Sugar, and Strawberry just tossed her drink back. There was no point in going to war with people who didn't even know they were in a war. But Sugar was wrong about the reason Strawberry didn't want them there. The real reason that she didn't want them around was because they were the visible proof of all of Sir's lies. She was foolish to think he would ever take her away to Hawaii. The reasons he said no other man would really be with her were the same reasons why he wouldn't either. She was no longer his girlfriend; she was his employee. Strawberry wasn't stupid. She knew what she was, and her fear of Sir and the outside world made her stay in her position. The three of them had a few more shots before Sugar and Spice got too antsy to sit in just one spot.

"We're about to go make some rounds, Strawberry. You coming with us?" Spice said, standing up from the bar stool she'd been sitting on.

"Nah." Strawberry gave her a fake smile. "I'm going to make my own moves tonight. Y'all got my number, though? And a taser?"

"Yup, we got all that."

"A'ight. If I don't see y'all in here again, I'll just see y'all in the morning at home."

When the two of them left Strawberry alone, she asked the bartender for some water. It had suddenly gotten extremely hot.

Javier Jackson was a ladies' man. Not by choice, though. He wore his hair in two long braids and had an eccentric look about him. His jaw structure was strong, and his almond-shaped eyes were almost hazel. His full lips always made girls go crazy as a youngin', and so did his muscular physique. Javier was full black, but his features made him look Native American. They attracted more attention than he would have liked, but then again, what man didn't like attention from women? He just figured that maybe one day the right one would find him, and he would spoil her with all the good loving he had to offer. He knew when he graduated high school that he would be great, he just never guessed that it would be in the illegal distribution of drugs. Javier ran one of the top underground drug trades in all of

Memphis. Most people called him a god, but he was more humble than that. . . . He settled for being called a king.

The past five months, business had been booming, and he hadn't had time to do much if it didn't include a dollar sign. But that Saturday, there was a big party going on at a club that he helped fund the opening for, so his presence was desired. Looking at it as a business matter, he decided to step out; however, not without a small army of soldiers around him. He could never be too careful. A man of his stature was always on somebody's hit list. He dressed casually, in a tan Ralph Lauren button up, a pair of Levi jeans, and a pair of Ralph Lauren loafers. Most times, he was the richest man in the room, but Javier coined the phrase "Money is quiet, never loud."

When he pulled up to the club, he skipped the line and went straight in the large building.

"My nigga!"

Javier grinned because he knew the voice.

"What's up, Clay? How you livin', mane?"

"Can't complain," Clay responded, bumping fists with Javier. "Tryin'a get like you!"

"Shit, I been tryin'a give a little opportunity," Javier said, nodding at the men behind him. "You could probably show these niggas a thing or two! I've heard stories on how Big Clay used to get down, back in the day!"

"Yeah, mane." Clay smiled proudly at Javier's compliment. "But that was back in the day. I'm a simple man now. But go on, head up in there. It's a whole section cleared for you and yo' peoples at the top. Enjoy yaself!"

Javier dapped Clay up one more time and made his way to the party.

"Javier!"

"What's up, my nigga!"

"God! I knew you was gon' show up!"

"What's poppin', King?"

As Javier walked, everyone showed him love, and he realized that he missed the people in his city. He had been holed up working so long, he forgot that they missed him too. When he got to the large VIP section with the soft leather seats, he ordered rounds for the entire club and just vibed out with his people. The strobe lights stalked the club, and everyone was going up. Many women fought their hardest to get in his VIP section, but security was too tight up there. All Javier saw was ass and titties, and he remembered that it had been too long since he last dug deep inside of a woman.

Crazy as it sounded, Javier wasn't the type to just take any woman to bed. He wasn't even the type to entertain just any woman. That stopped a long time ago when he was in high school. His senior year, he learned a lesson from a girl that he always wanted to sleep with. He wanted her so bad. She had the best body in the whole school and a pretty face to match. He liked her because even though everybody made fun of her thick Hispanic accent, nobody would step to her because they knew she could throw hands. Maria Calico was her name, and she'd made him feel like a complete scumbag one night at a party. It was the first time he'd ever seen her outside of school, but the impression he made on her that night was the reason she never spoke to him again. She walked in on him and three other guys getting head from a girl who had drunk too much. Maria didn't try to save the girl, but out of all the boys in the room, Javier was the one she focused on.

"I thought you was different," she said. "You should be more selective on who you let put their mouth on you. She could have herpes."

And she was right. She didn't know it, but she put so many things in perspective for him that night. He even left the room to go find her, but she was already gone. Afterward, Maria wouldn't even look his way, so he never tried to shoot his shot with her. Still, though, years later, she still crossed his mind, and he wondered how she was doing. She was smart and had probably graduated from some Ivy League college, leaving the little people behind.

"I was mobbin' through the beach, yeah the city by the sea, Mama tried to keep me home, but I love the fuckin' streets!"

O. T. Genasis's hit "Push It" blasted through the speakers, and it was almost as if the entire party turned up a notch. He and his right-hand man Teezo stood up on the upper level peering down on the dance floor.

"Aye, mane," Teezo nudged Javier with his shoulder. "That joint over there lookin' kinda right!"

Teezo was pointing his cup of Patrón over at a young woman sitting alone at the bar. Javier had to agree, she was definitely looking right. She was so thick, her entire ass couldn't fit on the bar stool. She was sipping on what looked to be a glass of water, and when she looked up, giving Javier a glimpse of her face, he couldn't believe who he was seeing.

"Aye," he said setting his drink down. "I'll be right back."

"You got that thang on you?" Teezo asked since Javier was going to the lower level with no guards.

"Nigga, I ain't no rookie," he said, lifting his Polo and flashing two pistols on his waist.

"My nigga," Teezo nodded his approval and went back to entertaining the women who had been let in the section.

Strawberry felt that she had wasted enough time just sitting at the bar. She figured it was time to move around. A few men had approached her, but none looked to have the kind of money she was looking to make for the night.

"Maria?"

Just as she stood up in her heels, she heard somebody call her by the name her mother gave her. Whipping around to see who it was, she saw a face and came up blank.

"Do I know you?" she asked, making a face at the man who had approached her.

He was really good looking, but one up-and-down look let her know he wasn't a man she was going to waste any more time on.

"Maybe." He flashed a straight bright smile at her and licked his lips. "Javier. From East High."

Strawberry took the time to study his handsome face in hopes to jog a memory. When she did, her face broke into a smile. She would recognize those eyes anywhere.

"Javier Jackson."

"That's me," he said, still smiling. "You still looking good, I see."

"I've been eating my rice and cabbage, you know," she joked.

"I see. Well, it does you well. Let me buy you a drink."

"Oh no," Strawberry tried to put her hands up to tell him that she needed to go. "I can't."

"I won't take no for an answer." Javier waved the bartender back over to them.

"You still going, King?" the older bartender joked since Javier had spent so much already.

"I'm here to get the club drunk and go home sober, Tim," Javier chuckled. "What would you like?"

"Umm . . ." The banter between the bartender and Javier had caught Strawberry's attention. Reluctantly, she sat back down in her seat and pointed at a bottle of Cîroc behind the cabinet. "Some Berry Cîroc on the rocks would be fine."

"Coo'," Javier told her and pulled out a fifty-dollar bill. "Tim, let me get that bottle, two cups, and a jug filled with ice."

"No problem, King," Tim said, taking his money. "Shit, for a fifty-dollar tip, I'd do just about anything except suck some dick!"

Strawberry's eyes grew wide, and she covered her mouth before her laugh could escape her lips. She couldn't believe those words had just left the old man's mouth, and from the looks of it, Javier didn't either. Tim got them everything Javier had requested and went on his way to get the order of a young couple at the end of the bar.

"Wait," Strawberry said confused. "The fifty dollars wasn't to pay for the bottle?"

"I have a tab open," Javier told her. "For the whole club. So if he made you pay for your drinks, you better get your money back now."

She hadn't, but she had been sitting there wondering why Tim hadn't asked for her to pay.

"What is it that you do exactly to be able to open a tab for the entire club?"

"I'm a street pharmacist, baby," Javier joked, but he was completely serious, and Strawberry knew it, too.

"So that means you probably have a ton of little rats sniffing around your cheese, huh?"

"I'm too real to keep a rat around me," Javier said and licked his lips again.

Every time he did that, Strawberry's stomach did a flip. She didn't know if the alcohol was getting to her, or if the man in front of her was just that fine. He was the kind of fine that gave a girl butterflies in her stomach and her clit at the same time.

"Is that right?" she purred.

"Damn right," Javier replied. "You tryin'a find out?"

"Uh-uh," Strawberry shook her head, giggling. "The Javier I remember is used to bitches chewing the whole crew."

"I left that life behind me." He grew so serious that Strawberry stopped smiling. "I have too much going for me to spend my time degradin' a woman. Shit, I don't even have time to get my dick sucked these days."

"For real? You be that busy, huh?"

"Yeah, I would make time for you, though."

The two of them talked and laughed until the entire Cîroc bottle was gone. It felt like it had only been a short while, but before she knew it, Tim was calling for last drink orders. The entire night had passed, and Strawberry hadn't met a single john.

"So what have you been up to since high school, Maria? You were always the smartest girl in school," Javier was asking her. "What do you do for a living?"

"Strawberry!"

"Strawberry, girl!"

She clenched her eyes shut. Sugar and Spice had chosen the worst time to show up again. She honestly had hoped they'd got their hits for the night and went home. She jumped up from her seat, suddenly embarrassed. They had such a good conversation, drunk or not, and the last thing she wanted was for him to know who and what she really was.

"Umm, I have to go."

"What do you mean? I can drive you to wherever you need to be."

"Strawberry!"

It was too late. Sugar and Spice were already standing right beside her, both with big smiles on their faces.

"We just wanted to say bye and make sure you was all right before we left. You need some blow?" Sugar asked, and when Strawberry shook her head no, pointed at two men not too far behind them. "These drunk-ass niggas already gave us $300 for a hand job! Is this who you're going home with? I thought Daddy said no broke niggas! Come on, Spice."

Spice waved her hand, and the two of them walked away. When they were gone, Strawberry was left standing there with a stuck expression on her face. The music was still loud, but the words sounded mushed together. She kept her head down, not wanting to look into Javier's eyes. She was too ashamed.

"I-I gotta go," she whispered and grabbed her clutch.

"You're a prostitute, Maria?"

"I said I gotta go!"

The disappointment in his voice was too much for Strawberry to bear. She had to get out of there and fast! However, Javier didn't seem to want to let her do that.

"I asked you a question." He placed his hand on her arm, not allowing her to leave.

"Let me go," Strawberry begged and finally looked in his eyes. "Please."

"Not until you answer me."

"Yes," she said snatching her arm away. "OK? Are you happy? Now you can regret the fact that you've spent your night talking to a ho while I try to figure out how to get a thousand dollars. Since I spent my whole night over here talking to yo' ass, I'm probably going to be dead by the morning. Oh my God, Sir is going to kill me!"

Strawberry looked around desperately for a john, but everyone had begun to clear the club.

"Fuck!" she exclaimed and sat back down on the bar stool. She no longer cared about the nice time she'd had with Javier. All she could think about was the gun Sir pointed at her in the car. She knew he was serious about hurting her, and she didn't want to spend another night in a hospital if she could help it.

"Maria."

What am I going to do?

"Maria?"

He's going to kill me this time. I know he is.

"Maria!"

"What?" she finally answered, whipping her neck with an attitude.

"Here," Javier said, holding out a small roll of hundred-dollar bills to her.

"W-what's this for?"

"You said you needed a thousand dollars, right? Or some nigga is gon' kill you. Take it. I owe you for ya time, anyway."

Slowly, Strawberry reached out and took the money from him. She counted it and saw that there was five hundred more than what she needed.

"Thank you," she said, and he shrugged his shoulders.

"You're welcome," Javier replied, turning his back on her. He started to walk away but stopped and turned back to her. "Any nigga that feels that your body is only worth a thousand dollars is stupid. And you're even more stupid if you believe it. Have a good night . . . Strawberry."

He walked away, leaving Strawberry standing alone holding a fistful of cash, and like an idiot, she let him go.

Chapter 3

A cloud of smoke filled the air around Sir, and his eyes were lower than usual. He sat alone in the master bedroom of the apartment, and the intake of the purple haze rolled neatly inside his Blueberry Swisher Sweets had him on his level. He was completely mellowed out as he waited for Sugar, Spice, and Strawberry to return home. He was eager to get the money they were bringing to him, and he had already found the perfect spot to move. The house had four nice-sized rooms, and that meant everyone could have their own, even Strawberry. True, there was once a time where he enjoyed lying next to her, but that was before she'd sampled half of the dicks in Memphis. It was time for him to put her all the way in her place and let her know that she was not superior to anyone in the house. History meant nothing to him. There would be no bottom bitch. They were all just bitches where money was concerned.

And what he was concerned about was that he needed more bitches. Each room in the new house would be able to fit two women, so that meant he could add three more to his roster. Sir figured that if he could turn out Strawberry, who had been a scholar with a strong mind, then he could do it to anyone. She had come from a home with a loving mother and a little sister who looked up to her. When she noticed her daughter changing, Strawberry's mother gave her an ultimatum. Sir, or her family. Of course, Strawberry chose Sir, which made it easier to make her depend on him and only him. She was weak. He didn't even need to taint her body with drugs to control her. All he had to do was remind her that he was all she had. He made her cut all ties with her family, and if he even thought she was in contact, he would beat her with whatever he could find.

Although she was already his property, he would never tell her that he lied about the first time he had her sell her pussy for him. It was true that the dude had wanted to sleep with her, but it wasn't true that Sir's life was in danger. At first, Sir wasn't into sharing pussy, but when he was offered five stacks, he couldn't turn down the offer. He staged the whole thing to make it look like he got beat up because he knew Strawberry wouldn't do it if she didn't feel like it was a need. It was a harsh thing to do to anyone, but he didn't care then—and he didn't care now. He finished smoking his blunt and had thrown the roach in the trash can when he heard the front door open and shut.

"Daddyyy," he heard the singsong voice of one of the new girls call out. "I got some goodies for you!"

He jumped up and followed the voice all the way to the living room. Sugar was standing there, fanning money his way with a big smile on her face. Spice looked like she came right in and passed out. However, the money she brought in was lying spread out on the coffee table. Both women were still in last night's club attire and smelled heavily of cigarette smoke and alcohol. Their hair was slightly disheveled and their makeup was smeared, and Sir made a mental note to have a conversation with them about their appearance. They were to be dimes always, but they had come through on where they needed to, so he would save that conversation for a different day.

"Together, we brought in $4,000," Sugar boasted. "Are you happy, Daddy?"

"Very." Sir took the money from her and scooped up the bills from the coffee table. He counted it, knowing that he already had more than what he needed for the house deposit. He handed Sugar a few bills back and tossed a few at Spice's sleeping body. "Where's Strawberry?"

"I don't know, Daddy." Sugar shrugged her shoulders and yawned. "The last time I saw her she was smiling all up in some pretty nigga's face."

"Was this 'pretty nigga' paying for her time?"

"Not from what I could see," Sugar answered sleepily, not realizing that she had just woken the beast in Sir. "But she was talking to him all night."

Sir's eye twitched, and he felt his high going away already.

This bitch wants to die, he thought to himself. *It's almost noon. If she ain't been out there making my money, where the fuck has she been all night?*

Sir let Sugar go to the room and go to bed, and he sat patiently down at the dining room table to wait for his star ho to walk in the house.

Yawning big, Strawberry trudged up the stairs that led to her apartment on the second floor. She couldn't wait to give Sir his money so she could take a long shower and snuggle deep under her blankets. After the club, she didn't find a john to stay the night with, but with the money Javier gave her, she didn't need to. Instead, she caught a ride to a nearby motel and decided to stay the night there. Except she didn't sleep a wink. She kept thinking about the exchange between her and Javier and couldn't understand how she let him slip away. She hadn't even gotten his phone number. But then again, a man like him would never be interested in a woman like her. Although they had started in the same place, where they finished was completely different.

Using her key to unlock the front door, she peeked inside. The first thing she saw was Spice lying on the living room couch, snoring like a grizzly. She smacked her lips and sighed deeply.

"That's what a bed is for." She told herself she would have a talk with the girl when she woke up about sleeping on her couches.

"Where have you been?"

Strawberry jumped, startled, and swiveled around to find the source of the voice.

"Oh my God, Daddy, you scared me!" Strawberry said, placing her hand over her heart.

"Where you been, Strawberry?" Sir repeated his question, a little louder that time.

"I was out working." Strawberry didn't know why she lied, but still, she hadn't done anything wrong.

The coldness in his voice made the hairs on the back of Strawberry's neck rise. She studied Sir and could tell that he was obviously high as a kite. His bloodshot red eyes were low and watching her like prey.

"Workin', huh?" he asked and looked at the clutch on her waist. "I don't see how you could have been workin' if you was smilin' in the same nigga's face all night."

He banged his fist on the table and got to his feet. Strawberry backed up and fell over onto the couch Spice was sleeping on.

"What's goin on?" Spice grumbled, trying to figure out why she had a body on her.

"Go to my room and get that gold metal belt out of my closet."

"No!" Strawberry screamed and tried to prevent Spice from getting up. "No!"

"Be a good girl, Spice," Sir told her, "or else you'll get the same thing as Strawberry. I gotta teach this ho a lesson."

Spice looked apologetically at Strawberry and did as she was told. Strawberry was shaking so much that she couldn't get a grip on her clutch to show him the money inside.

"No, Daddy! I got your money! It's right here!" She tried her best to twist the knob on the small bag, but she couldn't. The fact that she was still hungover and terrified to death didn't mix very well.

Spice returned with the belt, and Sir instructed her to stay and watch.

"This is what'll happen to you if you ever walk in this house without my money!"

"I have your money!" Strawberry cried, but Sir snatched the clutch and threw it out of the way.

She kept repeating herself, but he ignored her and stripped her completely naked. Tears streamed down Strawberry's pretty face, and her chest heaved. She kept trying to explain to Sir that she had his money, but he didn't seem to care about anything she was saying.

"Bitch!" Sir swung the belt with so much force that when the metal spikes hit Strawberry's face, she got an instant deep gash. He swung again, that time even harder. "Bitch!"

Strawberry's screams filled the entire apartment, and she tried to scoot away. Sir grabbed her by the hair and proceeded to whip her viciously until drops of blood dripped from the belt. Her body had gone limp way before he stopped swinging the belt. Finally, he released her hair, letting her drop to the floor with a loud thud. Spice had been frozen in place watching the horrific scene before her. She had been too scared to move. But when Sir stopped beating Strawberry, she crept to the corner that Sir had thrown Strawberry's clutch and knelt to grab it. Opening it, she choked on her own tears.

"Daddy! She really did have the money, Daddy," Spice told him, showing him the contents of Strawberry's purse.

Truth be told, Sir didn't care if Strawberry had the money. He'd just wanted to hurt her. She'd been too lippy the past couple of days, and he needed to bring her back down to reality. He leered down at the deep gashes on her body and watched as a small pool of blood formed under her, and a sick smile came to his face.

"We have to get her to the hospital, Daddy," Spice's tone was frantic. "Daddy, she gon' die if we leave her here. You gon' go to jail, Daddy!"

Her words must have snapped him out of his daze because the next thing he knew, he was grabbing his car keys and a blanket to wrap her up in . . . so she wouldn't ruin his leather seats.

Chapter 4

Money was something that could do one of two things. It could either make the person with it humble, or it could make them greedy, and for Mike-Mike and Laron, it was the latter. The two boys had been running the streets together from the day they could walk, since their mothers lived right next door together in their public housing apartment complex. They shared just about everything, women being the most common, and when the opportunity arose to be street soldiers for Javier Jackson, the king of Memphis, they jumped at the chance. Straight out of high school, they were making enough money to get their own homes and even take care of their mothers if they had to, but they didn't.

The allure of the fast life was too much for their young minds. In school, although both boys were handsome with smooth baby faces, they were often made fun of for their ragged attire. Mike-Mike's hair was never braided, and

Laron's was never cut, simply because their mothers couldn't afford it. Now, all they cared about was being flashy and having the baddest bitches around them. They often would blow thousands of dollars on material things to keep up with the times, and quiet as kept, the two were always in competition with each other. Who had the newest released shoes? Who had the most expensive Gucci belt? Whose rims were chunkier, and whose car was faster? The mind-sets that both men had were the reason they stayed broke and always available to put in more work. It was nothing for them to pull up and body an enemy of Javier's, and it was nothing for them to flip a brick, but eventually, they knew the little dollars that Javier was throwing wouldn't be enough. And when that time came, Mike-Mike approached Javier's right-hand man, Teezo, about upping the prices for their services.

"You want more money for a job that I could have another nigga do for less? You trippin', mane. Fuck out my face."

Teezo didn't know that he lit a fire in both boys' minds with his answer. It was true that it wasn't wise to bite the hand that fed you; however, what about the hands that prepared the meal? The issue with men in positions of power was that they got so comfortable in their seats that the chair would have an ass cheek imprint if they stood up. Powerful men treated their employees like dirt because they could, and they knew they could replace them in seconds, if need be. It was a never-ending cycle, one that never came with a pay upgrade unless you became the head man in charge. However, that wasn't anything that Mike-Mike or Laron wanted. They just wanted some quick cash that came in a big bulk. What other way to get that than to rob the nigga with the most money?

Mike-Mike and Laron had many jobs under Javier's camp, but the main one was the pickup and drop-off they had to do every Sunday. They were to pick up the product from one of Javier's trap houses in East Memphis and distribute the load among the other street runners to get off that week. But that Sunday, there would be a change in plans.

"Nigga, I can't wait to get that money in the basement," Laron said in the passenger's seat of Mike-Mike's 2016 mustard-yellow Mustang.

"On God," Mike-Mike agreed and glanced in the backseat of the car. "I don't know about that little-ass sledgehammer, though, that you brought. What wall is that mothafucka gon' knock through?"

"Nigga, the walls in that old house are frail as fuck. Trust me, that bitch gon' get through."

"If not, I brought a bigger one in the trunk. Teezo gon' regret talkin' to me like he was fuckin' crazy."

"Mane, that nigga talk to everybody crazy, like he won't get chopped down out'chea."

"He gon' learn, though, after today. That nigga gon' feel me."

Laron studied Mike-Mike's dark face and recognized the look of savagery all too well. It was the look he made right before he ended the life of anyone on the opposing side. Whereas both young men were goons, Mike-Mike was the most ruthless out of the two. Laron had seen him murder an entire family because the man of the house hadn't paid his monthly dues to Javier. If Mike-Mike could do that for another man's business, Laron could only imagine what he would do for himself.

"You gon' body him?"

"Is that a question?"

Laron didn't respond. Instead, he checked the clip in his gun and made sure he had two more in the pockets of his black hoodie. He checked the laces on the new black Air Force Ones he'd just bought that day and made sure they were tied. Feeling the car slow to a stop, he looked out of the window and saw that Mike-Mike had pulled to the back of the house and parked by the garage.

"Hand me a mask," Mike-Mike told Laron, who pulled the black mask from his pocket.

Instead of putting it on his face, Mike-Mike put it in his own pocket and tucked his gun on his waist. He pressed a button and popped the trunk to his whip so he could get the bulky backpack from it and waited for Laron to exit the car too, with the sledgehammer in tow.

"Put that shit in here," Mike-Mike instructed, holding the opened backpack out to his friend, and Laron did as he was told.

Beep! Beep!

Mike-Mike's car was his pride and joy. Although they would probably need to make a clean getaway, and having the doors unlocked would have been a better move, he just couldn't leave his baby wide open like that. Once strapping the bag, he led Laron around the house to the front door and knocked once.

"What's one plus one?" a male voice on the other side of the door asked.

"Shit, a million, if you do the math right," Mike-Mike answered the coded question correctly.

The door swung open and Bentley, another one of Javier's main street goons, stood there with a smile on his face. His low haircut was freshly lined up, and he stood before them in a vintage Coogi fit. The rope chain he wore around his neck gleamed in the light, right along with the big diamonds in his ears.

"What's good, my niggas?" he said, dapping both men up and allowing them entrance. "On time as always."

"Always. Punctuality is a way of life," Mike-Mike said casually. He looked around the house and only saw three other bodies. "Y'all the only niggas here today?"

"For now," Bentley told him. "It's some other niggas supposed to come later. We s'posed to be getting them cameras set up around this bitch today. But aye, let me go grab this shit for you."

He shut the front door when Laron was all the way in, bolting it back up before he headed toward the basement stairs. The basement's entrance was in the living room of the fully furnished house. At first glance, the dated furniture made the house look like it belonged to an old woman. Even the kitchen smelled naturally of fried chicken like a grandma would cook it. Sitting on the couches were three other young soldiers that Mike-Mike never took the time to really get to know. He only knew one of them by name, Roger. He was a cool dude, quiet for the most part, but he got his work done. He was the type of nigga that got in to one day get out, but Mike-Mike couldn't guarantee he would make it out that day. From the smell of the herb in the air and the redness of their eyes, it was obvious that they were high out of their minds, expecting that day to be just another easy Sunday.

"Here you go, my guys," Bentley said, bringing the goods back up the stairs. He noticed that Mike-Mike and Laron hadn't taken a seat, nor had they hit the weed like they usually did when they came over. Another thing that he peeped was that they both were wearing black hoodies . . . like it wasn't almost a hundred degrees outside. "What y'all finna go do, gotta make a move? Shit, do I need to pack a fire and ride out too?"

"Something like that," Mike-Mike told him with a chuckle, opening the backpack to put the product in it.

"Who y'all finna move on?" Bentley asked and watched the sick smile form on Mike-Mike's face.

"You."

Before Bentley could comprehend what he meant, Mike-Mike pulled the small sledgehammer Laron brought out of the bag and hit Bentley on the head. Bentley's body crumbled to the floor with a stream of blood spilling down his face.

"Nope," Laron said when the other three men jumped up from the couch.

Pop! Pop! Pop!

He fired his gun with the expertise of a marksman and dropped all three of the men on the couch when they reached for their fires. He stood over their bodies and put another bullet in each of their skulls for good measure before kneeling and running their pockets.

"Get them gold chains too, my nigga," Mike-Mike said while he was taking the one from Bentley.

"What you want to do with him?" Laron pointed at Bentley's body.

"I can't send him to the afterlife yet," Mike-Mike said, rummaging through the kid's pockets until he found what he was looking for. He held the touchscreen smartphone up and waved it at Laron. "I need him to make a phone call for me. Tie him up!"

"This a stop we shouldn't have had to make," Teezo said to Javier. "I need to tell these niggas they need to straighten up!"

Teezo wasn't just Javier's right-hand man, he was the general of the streets. He wasn't that handsome in the face. Some girls would say his eyes were too far apart, but he still kept an array of them around him. His dark skin and athletic build made him look intimidating, but his ruthless mind-set made him lethal. He did everything that Javier didn't have time to do, like keep the money and product flowing smooth in the streets. The day after the party, Teezo got a call from one of his young goons, saying that two kilos of cocaine were still sitting in the same spot and nobody had come to get them to be distributed. That was unusual, being as everybody knew product wasn't supposed to stay in the same spot for more than three hours. Since Javier was with him at the time, he decided to ride along and see how his streets were moving those days.

"Stop putting these little niggas on and we wouldn't have these problems, mane. Them boys ain't thorough enough."

"The streets period ain't thorough enough anymore," Teezo responded, pushing his all-white Chevy Avalanche through the Memphis streets. "Shit, I remember when a cartel was a family. Now you can't even trust your family."

"True that," Javier said, shaking his head. "Speaking of that, have you talked to Jo about how he fucked your bitch?"

He grinned at the uncomfortable look that crossed Teezo's face. He'd caught his cousin Jo in bed with his main chick Tamera two weeks prior, and his attitude about family hadn't been the same since. It was funny to Javier because he had seen Teezo mess with other girls firsthand, behind Tamera's back. Some of them were even her friends. Yet, the moment she did it to him, he couldn't handle it. It got so bad that he almost put a bounty on his own relative's head, but Javier talked him out of it.

"Man, fuck that nigga," Teezo huffed. "He wasn't real to begin with. He fucked my bitch."

"Mane," Javier shook his head, "the way you were fuckin' around on her, I don't think anybody even knew you had a bitch."

"Here you go, Mr. Captain Save-A-Ho."

"I'm just sayin', my nigga, it ain't hard to make a bitch act right," Javier told his friend. "All you gotta do is keep her happy and make her feel special. Oh, and stop sticking your dick in everything that has a pussy hole."

"That's asking for too much already!" Teezo joked and laughed. "Man, fuck all that. What's up with you and that joint from last night?"

Truth be told, Javier hadn't stopped thinking about Maria since he left her standing stuck on stupid. He felt bad for calling her stupid, especially since she looked so embarrassed already. He wished he would have gotten her number because now he didn't know when he would get to see her again. Why did he want to see her, though? She was a prostitute. For all he knew, she was feeling him out for his money the whole time they were talking. Still, he didn't think that was the case. Instead of telling Teezo the truth, he shrugged his shoulders.

"We went our separate ways," he stated simply.

"*We went our seperate ways,*" Teezo mimicked. "Old soap-opera-sounding-ass nigga. If I were you, I woulda took her home and tore all in that pussy!"

"Nigga, you gon' fuck around and catch something the way you just fuck anything."

"These hoes shouldn't be so easy then. Shit, at least I'm not one of these niggas that gotta pay a joint for some pussy. Ain't no bitch bad enough for me to pay to suck my dick."

"You'd be surprised," Javier said, but his words went up in the air as they pulled into the driveway of the beat-up white house.

There were only two cars in the driveway, but that wasn't suspicious. Teezo hated when there was a lot of traffic at any of the traps because the one thing they didn't need was too many eyes on them. The neighborhood was quiet, as usual, besides a couple of kids playing, riding their bikes up and down the street. The trap house was privately owned by a woman Javier paid to purchase the house. That way, the true ownership couldn't ever trace back to him. Teezo blessed the cracked concrete with each step he took in his True Blues as he made his way up to the front door of the house.

Javier's senses were telling him that something was off, although everything seemed normal. When they walked up on the house, there were no sounds coming from it, which was strange because usually, the young niggas would be on the game hooting and hollering about who was cheating. Without thinking, he pulled his gun out and let it rest at his side, waiting for Teezo to open the front door.

"These niggas tripping!" Teezo said as soon as he was through the threshold.

He and Javier stood in the doorway, peering around at the house. They saw nothing and heard nothing.

"Yo," Javier said and halted Teezo with the back of his hand. "Look."

Teezo's eyes followed Javier's finger, and he instantly drew his gun when he saw what Javier was pointing at. There was a small pool of blood stained in the carpet in the living room, and the wetness of it told them it was fresh. The two men began communicating in low voices to each other.

"I'm about to go check downstairs," Teezo informed Javier, who had taken steps to go check the kitchen.

"A'ight, mane."

The floor of the old home squeaked louder in the silence under Javier's feet with each step he took. Something stank, and it wasn't the odor of the house. Something had happened in the house, but there was no sign of life to confirm or deny it. Whatever it was that was amiss, Javier wouldn't rest until he figured it out.

"Mmm!"

He heard the noise the moment he entered the kitchen. Javier turned and aimed his gun, releasing his hand from the trigger just in time.

"Mmm! Mmm!"

Javier had found Bentley, the young light-skinned kid who was in charge. He was hog-tied in the kitchen with the rest of Javier's young soldiers. The only difference was that Bentley was alive; the others weren't. Javier removed the duct tape from around Bentley's mouth, and then untied him. He needed answers.

"Who did this?" he asked.

"Mike-Mike and Laron."

"Mike-Mike and Laron?" Javier didn't try to hide the shock in his voice. "Why?"

"They had beef with Teezo." Bentley's voice sounded weak and frail. "Said he been paying them pennies to do a Ben Frank job. I tried to give Teezo a subliminal when I called him, but he was too irritated to catch it."

"What did they want?"

"The coke, the money in the walls downstairs, and Teezo."

"Downstairs?" Javier jumped up thinking that he had been a fool to let his brother go to the basement alone.

He ran out of the kitchen and made his move to the basement—but it was too late. The sound of gunfire erupted like fireworks on Independence Day.

"Augh!"

Javier was halfway down the stairs when he heard Teezo grunt in pain. A loud thud followed, like he'd fallen to the ground, but Javier couldn't see him. In order for him to have eyes on the action, he would have to go to the bottom step and look around the corner, but if he did that, he was sure to be made. He didn't know exactly how many people were in the basement, so his best option would be to let his ears be his eyes.

"You greasy mothafuckas," Teezo's voice grunted. Javier heard the quick movements of somebody else in the basement, and then another thud, like Teezo had been hit in the face. "Umph!"

"I thought Javier's niggas was more boss than this. Shit was too easy!"

"Grab the coke, Laron, and see how much money that nigga got on him. I'm tryin'a get a bottle when we leave here. I don't even know why we brought these fuckin' face masks. We ain't even use 'em."

"Mane, Mike-Mike, we hit a gold mine! It has to have been fifty stacks in the wall!"

"It's lit!" Mike-Mike replied. "Let's go drop this shit off so we can put a bug in Javier's ear that the spot got hit before we got here."

"And him?"

Javier was sure they were talking about Teezo, and Javier could still hear him groaning on the ground. That was good. It meant he was still alive, but for how long was the question. He raised his gun preparing to go in, guns blazing.

"Fuck 'em," Mike-Mike answered after a few moments of thinking. "That's a fatal blow to the stomach. Let him bleed out. Bitch-ass nigga. Let's go."

The two men rounded the corner . . . only to be met by the nose of a gun pointed in their faces. They were caught like deer in a pair of headlights. Javier was the last person they expected to see.

"On the wall, scum," Javier's voice drenched with malice. "Drop ya guns—now!"

Laron was in front of Mike-Mike, and that was the moment that Laron learned that Mike-Mike was never really his friend. He pushed Laron into Javier, causing him to pull the trigger and catch Laron in the chest at close range. He was dead before he even hit the floor. Mike-Mike tried to push past Javier to get up the stairs but was caught in the back of the head by the butt of Javier's pistol. Mike-Mike refused to go down without a fight. He tried to aim his weapon, but Javier kicked his wrist and made him drop it.

Thump! Thump! Thump!

The gun bounced down the stairs, and that left Mike-Mike defenseless to deal with the Grim Reaper himself. Javier was so angry at the blatant disrespect that he tucked his gun back in place and proceeded to beat Mike-Mike with his bare hands.

"You come in my spot and kill my little niggas? Huh?" Javier yelled in Mike-Mike's face as he plummeted it with his fists. "Mothafucka! You thought you was gon' rob me, little nigga?"

Javier stomped Mike-Mike's head into the hard wooden stairs so viciously that his body began to thrash. Not caring about the seizure he'd sent Mike-Mike into, Javier continued his ferocious attack until the kid moved no more. Javier's fresh white Adidas now had streaks of blood on them, and he wished he could bring Mike-Mike back to life just so he could kill him again. His chest heaved, and he held on to the rail of the stairs, waiting for the adrenaline rush to calm down, but a call from his right hand told him there was no time for that.

"Javi!" Teezo's voice was weak. Life was leaving him with each second that went by. Javier appeared by his side and scooped him up in his arms. "Get me to the hospital, nigga."

"Nah," Javier huffed sarcastically, helping Teezo get his footing, "I'ma take you to the mall."

"I can't believe that little mothafucka shot me!"

"Now maybe you'll listen to me when I tell you to stop putting these little niggas on so quick."

Chapter 5

"You need to leave that boy alone, Maria! He ain't gon' do nothing but hurt you! Oh, Dios mio!"

"Mommy!" Maria ran around her small bedroom, throwing clothes in the overnight bag she had on her shoulder. "I'm a big girl, I can handle myself!"

Mary Calico sighed heavily at the fact that her daughter just wouldn't listen. The two women were in Maria's small bedroom, and that night, the bright pink wallpaper seemed dull. Mary stood in the bedroom door with her hands on her hips. She was staring at her twenty-one-year-old daughter as she bustled around the room getting ready to leave yet again. Her hands were on her hips, and she was prepared to block her daughter from getting out. That night, Maria even went as far as to take down the family photos that were taped to the wall and put them in her bag.

"Y-you're not coming back?" Mary asked softly.

"Sir and I are moving in together, Mommy. We've been together for a while now."

"It's only been a few months, though, mi amor. I just don't think that's a good idea! How well do you really know him?"

"I know he loves me, Mommy."

"Love?" Mary scoffed. "What do you even know about love? And why are you worried about love? What about college?"

"Mommy, what are you doing?" Maria said with an exasperated tone. "Come on, stop playing. Sir is outside waiting for me."

"'Sir is outside waiting for me. Sir is hungry, I have to buy him some food. Sir doesn't have any gas in his car, I need to go pick him up.' Don't you see? You're losing yourself behind a no-good-ass man! You're supposed to be being a role model for Marisole, and instead, you're chasing dick!"

Maria turned on her mother and put her hands on her hips. She looked in her mother's face and ignored the pain there and just focused on her words.

"What would you know about what a good man is? Before Daddy died, he treated you like shit! So don't tell me anything about what a bad man is when you lived with one for twenty years!"

Mary gasped and put her hand over her heart like Maria had stabbed her there. She couldn't believe the words that had come out of her oldest daughter's mouth, but she was more hurt that Maria didn't look like she regretted her words. Instead, she just continued packing her things. When Maria was finished, she used her shoulder to brush her mother out of the way so she could get by. As she walked to the front door of the small one-story house, she saw her little sister Marisole standing in the hallway by her room door.

"Maria, are you coming home later?" Marisole asked. "You told me you would help me with my math homework, remember?"

"I'm sorry, mi amor, I have to go now."

She had completely forgotten that she had told Marisole that she would help her with her eighth-grade algebra assignment. The look of disappointment on Marisole's face wasn't even enough to keep Maria from walking out the front door. She grabbed Marisole and pulled her into a hug, planting a soft kiss on her cheek.

"I'm sorry, sis," she said pulling away. "Mommy will help you. I have to go now."

If Strawberry would have known that was the last time she would see her mother and sister, then maybe she would have been more sensitive when she left. But if she had known that five years later, she would be in a hospital bed fighting for her life, she would have never left in the first place.

"Stay with us, Maria!"

"Her vitals are dropping! She's lost so much blood; we need to do a blood transfusion *now!*"

Strawberry felt as if she were moving faster than light. She didn't know where she was, and she didn't recognize the voices speaking around her. Every time she tried to open her eyes, they rolled to the back of her head. Everything around her was a big white blur, and her body was in more pain than it ever had been. Maria was sure that she was about to die, and if that was the case, hell was sure to welcome her. She hadn't done anything good or worthwhile in her life. Everything had been for the sake of money, money that wasn't even hers to keep.

It's over. I'm about to die. I didn't even get to tell Mommy that I was sorry. Strawberry didn't have any fight left in her. Her mother's smiling face flashed behind her eyelids, and that was the last thing she saw before she gave up.

"We're losing her! Get her in the room, now! We need to find somebody in this hospital who has the same blood type as her. Go! Go! Go!"

***

Javier sat in the lobby of the ER of Baptist Memorial Hospital waiting to hear how Teezo's surgery had gone. His friend had lost a lot of blood by the time he finally arrived at the hospital, and Teezo was going in and out of consciousness. The doctors had taken him for emergency surgery as soon as they were told that there was a gunshot patient. Javier told them that he wasn't leaving until he was sure his friend was all right, so he'd been waiting for over an hour. He was sitting with his elbows on his knees and his face in his hands, trying to force himself to stay awake.

"Mr. Jackson?"

Javier looked up when he heard his name being called and hurried to his feet when he saw that it was a surgeon.

"My name is Doctor Nola," the tall, white man shook Javier's hand. "The bad news is that your friend lost a lot of blood and will need to stay overnight. But the good news is that it looks like the gunshot wound was only a flesh wound. Terrance is expected to make a full recovery."

Javier let out a big sigh of relief and shook the surgeon's hand again.

"Can I go back and see him?"

"He's out like a light right now, and the nurses are doing a few more tests, but once they are finished, yes, Terrance may have guests."

"OK, thank you for everything, Doctor Nola."

"My pleasure."

The surgeon walked away, and Javier prepared to sit back down and wait until he was able to go back and see his friend, but he was almost knocked to the ground by a doctor and two nurses. They were running while wheeling a patient whose blood had drenched the white hospital sheets of the bed.

"Stay with us, Maria!"

The name instantly caught his attention, but he just knew they couldn't be referring to the same person that was at the club last night.

"We're losing her!" The blond female doctor shouted. "Get her in the room now! We need to find somebody in this hospital who has the same blood type as her. Go! Go! Go!"

"Maria?" he asked himself, feeling his feet move faster to keep up with the doctor and nurses. He got a good look at the woman on the bed, and although she had been knocked up pretty badly, he recognized her. "Maria! What happened to her?"

"Beat up by her pimp. Again!" Maria was pushed into a room that the doctor wouldn't let him get through. "I'm sorry, sir, I can't let you back here."

Javier strained his neck to get another look at Maria and saw how lifeless she looked. She was hooked up to a heart monitor, but her heartbeat was only beating faintly. He had to do something. He looked at the doctor's name and held the door with his hand so she couldn't shut it in his face.

"That's my friend, Doctor Lawson," Javier told her. "My name is Javier Jackson, and I have type O blood. If she needs it, take it from me."

"We don't have much time, Doctor Lawson. She's going to die if we don't move now!"

Doctor Lawson looked at Javier, and then back at Maria. All the times that the girl had come to the hospital bruised up and hurting, no one had ever poked their nose around, claiming to be her "friend." Especially not Javier Jackson. She recognized his name and face as the man who'd made generous donations to the hospital over the past years, and as skeptical on how he and her patient were connected, still, the look of genuine concern in Javier's eyes made her believe him, so she made a split-second decision.

"Get her up to an operating room! Tammy, I need somebody to poke this man's finger and make sure he can give this girl some blood. Now!"

The young Asian nurse with short hair, Tammy, grabbed his arm and yanked him in the room with them. She poked his finger and ran out of the room with the sample of his blood. Moments later, she ran back in the room nodding her head frantically.

"He's a match!"

"Javier!" Doctor Lawson said his name while he was brushing Maria's hair out of her face. He looked back up just in time to see a set of scrubs being thrown toward his six-foot-one frame. "Put those on and follow Tammy to the operating room!"

Am I dead? Strawberry asked herself when her eyelids fluttered open. *No. I'm in a . . . a hospital room? How did I get here?*

She squinted because although the room was dimly lit, the little bit of light there hurt. She shifted her gaze from the ceiling to her arm and saw that she had an IV in it. It was connected to a machine that was monitoring her heart rate. She tried to move her body in the soft hospital bed, but she ached so badly that she couldn't. She willed herself to remember what had happened, and once the memories flooded her brain, she wished she hadn't. Flashes of Sir's hateful face plagued her mind, along with the sight of his belt coming down on her.

"Mmm," she moaned softly, and her lips pouted. "You're finally awake."

The voice to the left of her shocked her, and she jumped. Swiveling her head, she was confused to see Javier sitting beside her bed. She opened her mouth to ask him what he was doing there, but he shook his head, silencing her.

"Save your energy, shorty," he told her. He stood up and went to a cart that wasn't too far from her bed. "They told me to try to feed you some crackers when you woke up. You think you can eat something?"

Although Strawberry wanted to bombard him with questions, she didn't. She watched him pick up the small two packs of saltine crackers and open it for her. There was some apple juice, too, that he put the straw in for her. He then scooted the chair he'd been sitting in closer to her and fluffed her pillows before pressing a button that made the bed go into a sitting position.

"Tell me if I'm hurting you," he said softly while the bed was still moving. When she didn't complain, he sat back down in his seat and held the juice to her lips. "Here."

Her lips quivered when she opened them
as he put the straw to her mouth. It hurt to
swallow, but the juice tasted good going down.
She released the straw from her mouth and tried
to bite the cracker he put to her lips, but she was
too weak to chew.

"I-I'm sorry," she croaked in a whisper.

"It's all right. We can try again in a little bit."

"Why a-are you here?"

"My friend was hurt, and I was up here when
they brought you in. You almost died," Javier
told her. "Twice. You needed a blood transfusion, and me being the Good Samaritan that
I am, let them poke into me to get you the
blood."

Out of every reason he could have said, she
didn't expect to hear that one. He'd saved her
life, but why? He was being so kind to her. She
didn't get it. If what he said was true, then that
meant that she had his blood coursing through
her veins. She blinked back the tears that had
rushed to her eyes due to her realization of
how pitiful she must look to him. Strawberry
lowered her head, feeling embarrassed that he
was seeing her like that, battered and bruised
because she was a prostitute.

"Don't do that, shorty," Javier placed a strong hand on her chin and forced her head back up. "Chin up. You're too pretty to cry."

"I'm not pretty right now," Strawberry shook her head. "I look like shit. I can't believe he did this to me."

"Your pimp?" Javier asked bluntly, and Strawberry nodded her head yes. "Has he done this to you before?"

"Yes."

"Then why would you think he wouldn't do it again?" Maybe he was being a little harsh. After all, she'd just woken up. But that didn't change the fact that they were words she needed to hear. "You need to leave that nigga alone. You are better than this."

"You don't even know me to tell me what I'm better than." The tears streaming down her face were hot. Javier had every right to judge her, but that didn't mean she was in the mood to listen to what he had to say. "Did the doctor say how long I have to be in here? I need to go home and straighten some things out."

"What?" Javier couldn't believe the words that she was saying. "Go home to *him?* The nigga that put you in here, Maria?"

"You wouldn't get it," Strawberry told him. "It was just a misunderstanding. He loves me."

"I guess the thirty cuts and that big-ass gash under your eye is a misunderstanding too, huh? *Pshh!*" Javier tried to collect himself, but it was too late. He had been watching her throughout the whole night. He was the one who heard her whimpers and who had held her hand through her shudders. He didn't know what kind of shit she had gone through with Sir, but he sure had a good visual. "Are you stupid? Do I need to get you a mirror so that you can see what you look like right now? That mane don't love you."

"He loves me," Strawberry said again, that time not sounding so sure.

"Who are you trying to convince—me or yourself? Love ain't gon' put you in the hospital, and from what the doctors were sayin', you've been here ten times this year alone. Love ain't gon' have you selling your pussy every night. Do you even keep the money?"

Strawberry wanted to scream at him and tell him to leave, but she couldn't. He was telling the truth, a truth that she'd known for a long time. In all honesty, she was just too scared to come to terms with the facts. She had tried to leave Sir in the past, but she always came right back like a fiend who needed a fix. She was too afraid to live without Sir because for so long, he had been her life. Without her, who would take care of him and make sure he was OK? But then, again, did he make sure she was OK? She stared at her arm and saw the purple bruises through her blurred vision.

"I know," she said clenching her eyes shut. The sob that expelled from her lips made her sore rib cage hurt, but she couldn't stop crying. "I don't have anywhere else to go. I am what I am, and I've been this for a long time. I don't know how to be anything else anymore."

"Have you tried to be something else?"

"Not in five years."

"What do you know how to do?"

"I'm-I'm good with kids," Strawberry wiped her tears. "I was in college years ago. I never graduated, but I was going to be an elementary school teacher."

"What if I told you that I can get you a job? Not as an elementary school teacher, but close to it."

"Really?"

"Yes." Javier's tone was serious as they stared into each other's faces. "But you gotta let this life go, shorty. Dead this shit. I ain't gon' tell you what to do like your pimp did. You gon' always have a choice with me. But I'ma let you know that whoever this Strawberry person is, she can't roll with me."

The room went silent, and Strawberry pondered her thoughts. She'd left everything she owned at the apartment, but all she really cared about were her family pictures. However, if she went back to get them, Sir would just put her in the hospital again for trying to leave—or worse. She couldn't go back. Javier was right. Sir didn't love her. How could he? Look at what he made her do. . . . Look at how he treated her. He put her in the hospital all the time and then would make her catch a taxi when she was released.

"I'ma let you think on it a little longer," Javier said, preparing to leave the room, but Strawberry caught his hand.

"No." She couldn't hide the plea in her voice. "Please don't leave me."

He looked down in her face. Even tattered and beaten, she was one of the most beautiful women that he'd ever seen. He couldn't put his finger on it, but there was just something about her that tugged at his emotions in a way no woman ever had. If she didn't want him to leave, then he would stay.

"OK."

"Javier," she said still clutching on to his hand, "I haven't seen my family in almost five years. I don't even know where they are. I won't have anywhere to go when I leave."

Javier kissed the back of her hand tenderly and wiped the tears from the corner of her eyes before they dropped.

"Yes, you do."

Chapter 6

Over the next month, Javier took some time from being the governor of the streets to be a real friend to Maria. He could tell that she was standoffish at first when it came to allowing him to get close to her, but soon, he could see the wall around her slowly wearing down. He moved her into the large home he owned in the suburbs in Collierville. Not counting the security and housekeepers, he lived alone, and it was nice to have some company for once. Maria was given her own room, next to his, and free reign of the entire property. He also kept his promise and got her a job at a daycare he owned once she healed up well enough to move around. It was true that Javier was responsible for the poison circulating in the city, but he figured that would be there with or without him. He didn't see why he couldn't have any kind of business he wanted. Growing up with a single mother, he had always stayed house to house with whoever she could find to keep him.

His mother, Nia Jackson, couldn't afford to put him in daycare. Every extra penny that entered their household went to a bill. His daycare, Children's Place, was one of the first businesses he opened, and he put his mother in charge of it. It was targeted to low-income families who didn't qualify for assistance and couldn't afford to pay for childcare out of pocket. Since he owned it, he could hire anyone he wanted to, and he felt that Maria deserved a fair chance. So far, she seemed happy, and for now, that was all he could ask for. Since she'd been working at the Children's Place, his face had been seen around the daycare more than usual, and his mother let him know that she noticed.

"You've been sniffing your nose around here quite often lately," Nia told him with a raised eye.

The two of them were in the cafeteria area, and Javier was helping her prepare lunch for the kindergartners to third-graders. Children's Place was always busier in the summer since the kids were out of school, so the kids' lunchtimes were split by their age.

"I can't come see how my mama is doin'?" Javier asked and finished setting the table he was working on.

"You know I love seein' my baby, but I don't think you're here tryin'a see how *I'm* doing."

Javier opened his mouth to protest, but at that exact moment, the doors to the cafeteria burst open, and a class of fifteen kindergartners ran in. Their laughter was contagious, and their teacher walked behind them instructing them to get in a straight line. A few of the kids ran to be the only ones to hold her hands, and Javier found himself smiling at how well Maria controlled her class. She looked radiant in the coral maxi dress that made her full figure look heavenly. The skirt of the dress came down and covered the gold gladiator sandals she had on her feet, and her new asymmetrical bob haircut bounced with every step she took.

"They say when a girl cuts her hair, she's about to change her life," she'd told him when she asked to be taken to the hair salon. And changed her life she truly had.

"Mmm-hmm," Nia smirked and nudged her son's arm with her shoulder. "I see why you like her. She's very pretty."

Nia was a beautiful older woman. She was a tiny woman, and her short, curly hair was completely gray. However, that was the only indication of her age. Her face was as smooth as the skin on a newborn baby, and she had a smile that could brighten up a room. Javier had gotten most of his features from her, including his defined cheekbones and eyes. She'd taken an instant liking to Maria, but the second she saw the way her son gazed at the girl, she did what any mother would do. She dug. The information she found on Maria almost knocked her off her feet. She would have never pegged a woman as well versed as her for a hooker, but then again, everyone had a past. She herself had once been addicted to the drugs that Javier sold. She had been young and living a fast life filled with bells and whistles. Getting pregnant by a complete stranger was what slowed her down and made her rethink her life completely. She thanked God every day that He gave her a healthy baby boy and not a disease that she couldn't get rid of. The fact that she didn't know who Javier's father was made her love him all the more. It was why she raised him to not be as judgmental as other people, because at the end of the day, everybody had demons in their closet. Blessed were the ones who could clean them out. She didn't know everything that Maria had been through. All she knew was that when she first came to work, she had the eyes of someone who'd lost the world. It was a wonder what being around good people could do for the soul, because now when Nia looked in her eyes, she saw a girl with some hope.

"I don't like her, Ma, I'm just helping her get on her feet."

"Boy, did you forget I pushed you out? I can read the look in your eyes from a mile away whenever you see that girl! Now, lie again! Talkin' 'bout you don't like her . . . Well, *I* do. How about that?"

"You crazy, Ma," Javier laughed and brushed her off.

"Crazy my ass." Nia gave her son a knowing look. "Go on. Go over there and talk to her. You know that's what you want to do anyways."

She handed him a handful of silverware and left him to set up another table. Javier took his leave and headed over to where Maria had just sat her class down at.

"Hi, Javi!"

"Javi!"

All the kids bounced in their seats, excited that their table was the one Javier had stopped at. He hugged a few of them and gave a few of the little boys daps. He handed them all their eating utensils before he reached the head of the table and stood by Maria. She gave him a curious look but waited for the kids to dig into their burgers, corn, and fries before she spoke.

"You've been here a lot this week. Is something wrong?" Her voice dripped with concern.

She'd seen him across the room speaking to his mother, and she wondered if Miss Nia had told him something. "Am I doing something wrong?"

"Nah, chill out, shorty," he calmed her nerves. "I've just been checking up on you, that's all."

"All week?" It was Maria's turn to raise her eyebrow. "Don't you have shit—I mean, stuff to do?"

"See, look at you, cussin' around the kids," Javier playfully shook his head. "This is why I gotta hang around here and make sure you aren't teaching these kids bad habits." He instantly regretted his words. Although he was just joking, Maria's expression changed noticeably.

"I'm sorry," she said sadly and looked at her hands. "I've been trying. I shouldn't even be teaching these kids nothing, let alone be around them, period."

"Aye, chin up, shorty." Javier lifted her head back up and gave her a genuine smile. "I was just kiddin', Maria. I wouldn't have hired you if I ain't think you would be good to these kids. They love you. My mom likes you, too."

"Really?"

"Really," he told her. "She thinks I like you."

"Do you?"

"Do I what?" He played dumb, and she smacked her lips.

"Stop playin', Javier. Do you like me?"

"I guess I do," Javier told her and then turned away from her to face the kids. "A little bit. You got an attitude problem, though."

Maria studied him and felt the sides of her lips twitching. If he was telling the truth, she couldn't tell. Since she'd been staying with him, she'd caught him staring at her a few times when he saw her walking around the house, or sometimes at work. He never made a move on her, though. She thought that maybe he was just genuinely trying to help her get to where she needed to be. The only thing was, that was what was attracting her to him. Since she'd been under his wing, she, of course, heard all of the gruesome stories about how he moved in the streets, but as far as she was concerned, he legitimately was a good dude. That day, he was looking delectable in a pair of joggers, all-white Huaraches, and a white Ralph Lauren T-shirt that had a navy blue emblem. There was something about his dressed down look that made her want to fall into his chest and inhale his cologne.

"You don't like me."

"Why would you ask me a question if you were just gon' disagree with the answer?" Javier asked and crossed his arms.

"Because somebody like you would never like somebody like me," she told him, stretching her hand out to play with one of his Cherokee long braids. "We come from two different worlds."

"How can that be possible when you're here with me right now?"

"You know what I mean," she shrugged, releasing his hair. "My past and your present just don't mix."

"I like mix-match shit. People would look at you crazy if they saw you with me. If I was the type of man that cared about what other niggas thought, those niggas wouldn't be my employees," Javier said briskly. "And if I cared what them other niggas thought, I wouldn't be standing here now, askin' you to come to Hawaii with me."

"What?" Maria was paralyzed. "Say that again."

"You heard me," Javier cast a serious look down at her. "This weekend. I saw all the pictures of the ocean you put up in your room, and I'm due for a vacation. We can leave tomorrow and stay for four days, until Sunday. I can get someone to fill in for you while you're gone."

"Javi, I—"

"I'm not taking no for an answer." Javier leaned down and kissed her cheek. "After everything you've been through, you deserve it, shorty."

"They kissin'!"

"Ooohh!"

"Miss Maria, is Javi your boyfriend? Javi, are you her boyfriend?"

Maria's face had turned beet red, and Javier left her side before she could get another sentence out. She watched him walk away with a swagger that said he knew he was the man. She bit her lip to contain her giggle and turned back to the kids to settle them down.

"Y'all need to mind your own business!" She tried to sound stern, but she couldn't.

"You going to Ahwowee, Miss Maria?"

"It's Hawaii, Justice," Maria corrected her. "And I guess I am. Wow . . . Hawaii."

It was seven o'clock in the evening when Maria got back to Javier's three-story home, and she went to work packing everything she needed. Javier had taken her shopping a few weeks prior and told her not to look at the price tags. She had gotten so many clothes and shoes, more than she'd ever had with Sir. Everything was going great. She hadn't seen or spoken to Sir, and she had even blocked his number. There was no way for him to get in contact with her, and it was refreshing. Javier treated her like she was an actual person, not property, and that was something that she appreciated. He helped her throw Strawberry away and called her by her given name. He was kind to her and didn't expect anything in return but her happiness. The two had grown close in a month and could talk about almost anything. If they didn't have anything else, they had a solid friendship, and she was OK with that if that was all they would have. Still, she knew that soon, the wave would subside and she would have to go her own separate way, but in the meantime, she would enjoy the time they spent together.

Her bedroom in his home was the size of both of the bedrooms in her old apartment, combined. Her long walk-in closet was to die for, and she had never felt a carpet so soft on her feet. She even had her own connecting bathroom, and her room was the guest room. The bedroom set was a mahogany brown, and it went well with the pale yellow drapes over the window and the pale yellow comforter. Splayed across on the bed were at least twenty outfits that Maria couldn't choose between. Sighing, she flopped on her bed and looked at the white walls in the room. They were so empty without her family pictures there. Since she hadn't spoken to her mother and sister in years, they were the only things she had left of them. The last Maria heard, they had moved to the other side of Tennessee and didn't leave a forwarding address. Sadness threatened to take over her demeanor, but when she heard a knock on her door, she straightened up.

"Our flight leaves at eight in the morning," Javier told her from the doorway. "I wanted to grab some food after you were done packing. That coo'?"

"Yeah," Maria told him, forcing a smile. "I'm still just tryin'a decide what I even want to take."

"You all right?" Javier noticed a look in her eyes that he hadn't seen since the first day he brought her home with him. "You still wanna go?"

"Yes!" Maria answered quickly, a little too quickly. "I'm just thinking about my family. The only thing I had left of my mom and my sister were the pictures I left at the apartment. And we both know I can't go back and get them."

She looked so devastated that Javier gravitated toward her. Sitting on the bed, he placed his arm gently around her shoulder, pulling her toward him.

"You ain't never even *tried* to reach out to them?"

Maria shook her head. She wanted to tell Javier that she was ashamed to, but for some reason, she felt he already knew that. She was so ashamed and embarrassed, mostly because her mother had been right about Sir. She didn't want to come home to a big "I told you so."

"You gotta put your pride aside sometime, shorty. I don't know what I would do if I didn't have my mom."

"Eventually I will. I just want my pictures for now." Maria sighed, looking at the empty walls again. She shook her funk and changed the subject. "Have you ever been to Hawaii before?"

"I've been there once or twice."

"Alone?" When Javier didn't answer, she tried to pull away from him. "You're taking me somewhere that you've taken other women?"

"Yes, I've been there with other women," Javier explained, pulling her back to him. "But it was never anything like this."

The way he said "like this" made Maria stop fighting and lean into him. She looked into his eyes and saw something in them that she'd never seen before. Not lust . . . more like he was yearning.

For her?

"What do you mean 'like this'?"

"Come on, shorty," Javier said to her. "We gon' keep playin' this cat-and-mouse game like we aren't feeling each other? I felt it the first moment I saw you in the club."

"Javier," Maria breathed deeply, "you can't feel that way about me. Look at me. Look at what I am."

She went into a rushed Spanish spiel that he didn't understand, but he waited for her to get done venting to speak.

"I see what you are, Maria," he moved a piece of hair that had fallen in front of her eye to the side. "A beautiful, hardworking woman. You're smart, sweet, and you actually listen to me when I talk to you. You're my friend, and the more I get to know you, I can't help what I feel for you. But I'm not going to keep doing this if you don't want the same."

"Doing what?" she breathed.

"Wanting you." He leaned in until their noses touched. "Thinking about how your lips taste. Wondering how your voice would sound screaming my name."

"Javi . . . I'm tainted."

"Nah," he shook his head. "Not to me. I don't care about who had you before me, because I guarantee you, they won't have you like I will. Now, as for me, I won't take away your choice."

"Oh, kiss me, Javi," Maria whispered, finally giving in. "Fuck me, Javi. Please fuck me, baby."

She didn't need to ask him a third time. Javier plunged his tongue in her mouth, and the two shared a deep, passionate kiss. He pulled down the dress she was wearing and broke the kiss on her lips to plant soft ones along her neck bone.

"I'm not going to fuck you, Maria," he said softly between kisses. "I'm going to make love to your body. Has anybody ever done that to you?"

She shook her head no and let him undress her completely. With one swift motion, he knocked all of the clothes that were on her bed off of it and positioned her head comfortably on a pillow.

"I want you to just lie there and let me take care of you. Submit to me."

His lips found her right nipple while he rolled the left one in his fingertips, pinching it ever so slightly. She wriggled underneath him. It had been awhile since she'd felt the kind of electric shocks of pleasure he was sending rippling through her body. She moaned and reached down to swirl her finger around her clit, but he gently hit her hand away.

"Don't touch my pussy," he commanded. He began licking her stomach, heading down south.

"OK," she moaned.

"OK what?"

"OK, Daddy—Ahhh!"

Javier took her swollen clit in his mouth and sucked it like a rare berry. Her love spot was already drenching, and it only got wetter as he pleasured her with his mouth. He kissed, sucked, and licked her pussy until she was on the brink of insanity. Her bedroom door was still open, so she knew all of the help could hear her screams of passion, but she did not care one bit.

"Open these fuckin' legs," Javier demanded when she tried to close them.

"Daddy, I can't take it," she gasped after she'd been brought to her third orgasm. Out of all the sex she'd had, none had felt as good as what his mouth alone had done. "It feels too good!"

"I thought you said you submitted to me?" Javier said, standing to his feet and undressing. "It's my job to make that pussy feel good."

He dropped his boxers and revealed that he was blessed. His dick was so thick and long it hung halfway down his leg. At the mere sight of it, Maria's pussy walls began to throb in high anticipation to meet their new friend.

"Javi," she moaned. "Touch me, Javi."

He did what she asked for and massaged her gushy center between her fat pussy lips. He pumped his fingers in and out of her opening, all the while standing over her and admiring her body. She still had a few fading bruises, but that didn't take away from how sexy she was. He wanted to kiss every inch of her a hundred times.

"You are so beautiful, shorty," he told her, stroking his long manhood. "Do you know that?"

Maria felt a surge of emotion for Javier and just wanted to please him. He was making her feel so amazing that she wanted him to feel the same way. She removed his fingers from inside her, even though she was almost to a fourth orgasm. She could wait. She brought his fingers to her mouth and sucked her own juices from them before sitting up on the edge of the bed. Grabbing his erection, she pulled him to her, and before he could stop her, wrapped her lips around it. If there was one thing Maria excelled in, it was the art of giving head. She slurped and spit all over Javier's dick, opening wide so that he could fuck her face when he wanted to.

"Fuck! Maria!" He threw his head back, gripping her by her hair.

She deep throated him to the point that she gagged, but that didn't stop her from trying to swallow his monster cock. She was sucking on him so good that he eventually had to pull away from her, not wanting to bust before he sampled the pussy.

"Turn the fuck over," he demanded, and when she didn't move fast enough, he flipped her over himself. "Grab that pillow, Maria. I'ma be one hundred with you. I don't think I'ma be able to take it easy on that pussy."

"OK," Maria moaned, twerking her ass in the air, enticing him even more. She felt the bed dip when he climbed on and positioned himself behind her. "OK!"

"That's OK with you?"

"I want you to dig into me however you want, Daddy. This is your pussy."

Her words were music to his ears, and the first thrust inside of her sent ripples of bliss all the way to his toes. He stroked her long and hard, just like that for thirty minutes. Her arch never wavered, and her screams did nothing but get louder and louder. Every stroke he pitched, she caught like a pro, and when she felt his dick start to throb, she hurried to catch his nut on her face and her voluptuous breasts. She rubbed his tip all over herself and kissed it until the last drop was out.

"Damn, shorty," Javier grinned down at her. He had never seen a drawing so beautiful than the one she sketched on herself, using his dick as a pen. "You a freak."

"Too much?" she asked, smiling up at him.

"Hell nah!" He told her, getting off the bed and scooping her in his arms. He picked his shirt up off the ground and wiped the come from her face before kissing her. "I love this shit! Go get cleaned up. I'll be back in a few hours so we can go to dinner."

"Where are you going?" Maria pouted, not wanting him to leave her so soon.

"I just got some business to wrap up real quick. It won't take me long, I promise." He put his boxers and joggers back on before leaning down and kissing her on the forehead. "Yo' ass better be packed by the time I get back, OK, baby? I'm about to show you the time of your life!"

"Promise?"

"I'ma a man of my word, shorty."

He left her sitting there naked, with come still dripping from her body, but strangely, she'd never felt more appreciated.

Chapter 7

The sound of the cheering that filled the two-bedroom apartment snapped Sir out of his thoughts. He had a controller in his hand and was sitting in his living room playing 2K with his partners, Slime and Cory. Their team had evidently just scored a point, but Sir hadn't been paying attention at all. It had been a month since he'd seen or heard from Strawberry, and it was starting to wear on his mind. He'd called the bitch multiple times, but none of his calls were getting through. He'd even made some moves in the streets to see if anyone had made any noise about her, but she was like a ghost.

The last time he'd seen her was when he dropped her off at the hospital, barely breathing. Usually when he beat her up, he would make her catch a cab home because he didn't want to risk anyone seeing his face and putting two and two together. However, that time, he decided to be gracious enough to come scoop her from the hospital, knowing that she would be ready to grovel at his feet. Imagine his shock when he was told that she had already checked out and gone home. Except she couldn't have gone home because her home was with him. He couldn't grasp it. Where could she have gone? She didn't have anyone, and he had banned her from making any kind of friends because he was the only friend she needed. The only thing she knew how to do right was lie on her back with her legs open, so maybe she'd gotten a new pimp? If that was the case, he would be sure to kill him and her on first sight.

"Yo, homie, what's the word?" Slime, a short, dark-skinned man with more hair on his face than anywhere else on his body, said. "You in the game or not?"

"Yeah, mane, we almost twenty points up on these weak-ass, li'l niggas."

"Yo, fuck you, you old-ass mothafucka!" A voice came in through the headsets they wore on their heads. *"Why y'all old asses on the game anyway? Where y'all jobs at?"*

"Ya moms is my job," Slime taunted the kid. "She said if I let her put her mouth on my dick, she would pay me a band."

"Nigga, you a bitch!"

"Yeah, yeah," Slime laughed at how mad the kid had gotten. "You just mad 'cause you losing. Take it like a man, li'l punk mothafucka."

His last statement must have really gotten to the kid because he forfeit the game. Cory looked at Slime like he wanted to kill him and threw his hands in the air, letting out a sound of frustration. He was a buff dude with a bald cut that looked like he could break the game system controller in two with his bare hands.

"Nigga, your shit talkin' keep fucking up our ranking!"

"Yo, my bad," Slime shrugged still laughing a bit. "You know how I get when a nigga gets to shit talking."

"You always bullying these kids and shit," Cory said putting his controller on the ground and turned to Sir. "And *this* nigga got his head in the clouds and shit. How many threes did you attempt and fail?"

"He still hurt that he lost his main bitch," Slime shook his head. "Did you love that bitch or somethin'?"

"I don't love nobody but my money and my pistol, my nigga." Sir set his controller down on the glass table in the living room and stood up to head to the kitchen. "A bitch don't mean shit to me."

"Well, tell the game that!" Cory stated, still fuming at the thrown game. "We was about to win!"

"Shut the fuck up about that game!" Sir barked and shot Cory a look that silenced him immediately. It was no secret that Sir was the leader out of the three of them. "You finna piss me off. That li'l nigga was right. Fuck is y'all doin' playin' a game when you could be gettin' some money."

"Last I checked, you was playin' the game with us too," Slime said, not appreciating his boy's hostility.

"Yeah, and I got hoes out there selling pussy for me. That's a guaranteed ten stacks a week between the two of them."

"Still must not be enough, since you still in this small-ass apartment!" Cory joked. He and Slime laughed and dapped each other up. "Come on, mane, we all know Sugar and Spice ain't bringin' in the money that Strawberry did."

Truth be told, Cory was right. He was hurting since Strawberry left, and it read all over his face. It even showed in his actions. He was flat bitter, mostly because he truly never thought Strawberry would leave him, so he never prepared himself for her absence. She did everything for him except wipe his ass, and now with her gone, everything around him was going to turmoil. Spice and Sugar had good pussy, but that was their only good quality as women. They couldn't cook to save their lives, and when he made them clean up, they half-assed it. Strawberry had been the glue that kept everything together for the past five years. It had crossed his mind that bringing Sugar and Spice in wouldn't please her, but he never thought it would be the reason that she left him, either.

He just knew he had Strawberry wrapped so tight that she wouldn't dare betray him, but there he was—alone with two of the dumbest hoes in history. In a week, together, they could barely bring in what Strawberry did alone in two days. Sir was used to being able to splurge, but now with two more people in his home and the fact that he wasn't getting as much money, he had to tone down a bit. They were forced to stay in the apartment because he couldn't afford a bigger house. Every day, he seemed to take his frustration out on Sugar and Spice, not caring about the bruises he put on their faces.

"Cover that shit up with some makeup and make sure you don't come back with less than a thousand," he told them whenever he saw the black and blue bruises.

Sir had both women selling pussy from sunup to sundown to accommodate for the lost person.

He had gone from waiting on Strawberry to come home to plotting on what he was going to do to her when he found her. Sir ignored the words from his partners and grabbed a glass from the cabinet. His nerves were getting the best of him, and the only thing that calmed them was a glass of his favorite drink, Hennessy on the rocks.

"You stay drinkin' that hood shit," Slime told him, pulling a small bottle of Rémy out of his own pocket. "You need to fuck with what the big boys do."

"Nigga, you talking about big boys, but you got that small-ass bottle!" Cory ridiculed him for flexing with such a small bottle.

Sir took a big gulp of his drink, welcoming the cold feel of it going down his throat until he felt the burn in his chest. He was about to go sit back down on the couch in the living room and tell them to start up another game, but a knock at the door made him do a quick detour. When he looked in the peephole to see who was banging on his door like the police, he saw the last person that he would ever expect on the other side.

"Can I help you?" he asked when he opened the door. He took another swig of his drink and mugged the newcomers. "Or are you niggas lost?"

His tone was hostile, and maybe it was the liquid courage talking, because no man had ever taken that tone with Javier Jackson and lived to tell the tale. Behind Javier were three men, all wearing black button ups and nice dress slacks. They looked like nice church boys, or like they'd just gotten off work, but Sir knew better, and the bulges on their waists gave them away. The stony expressions on their faces never changed, and all four men matched the mean mug Sir was throwing their way.

"May I come in?" Javier's voice was patient yet firm.

He asked the question, but for some reason, Sir knew it wasn't a question. He wanted to hit Javier with a big "fuck you" but figured that wouldn't be wise. Especially since his gun was all the way in his bedroom. He stepped out of the way and granted the men access to his home. Slime and Cory stared at Javier like he was a dead man that had come back to life, and then at Sir with questions all over their faces.

"Can I ask what I did to deserve the presence of the King of Memphis?" Sir asked again when Javier stopped in the dining room and looked to be giving the apartment a once-over.

"I see you know who I am." Javier finally stopped looking the house over to face Sir. The two men stood the same height with the same build, but his presence was more lethal. "Because the hostility in your voice made me think you didn't recognize me. Sir, right?"

Sir didn't understand why Javier had so much hatred in his eyes. He'd seen him in passing a few times and heard about how he moved in the streets, but they had never been formally introduced. But there Javier was, standing in Sir's home, looking at him like *he* was the guest. How did he even know where he lived, let alone his name? His tone was even icier than Sir's, and that didn't go unnoticed by Slime and Cory. Naturally, they'd put both of their hands on their waists, preparing themselves for whatever was about to happen.

"Yeah, that's me," Sir replied. "And since you know who I am, I'm sure you know what I do. I never pegged you as the type of man to pay for pussy."

"Because I don't." Javier's lip threatened to curl. "And I don't need bitches to sell it for me, either."

"Well," Sir looked at Javier like he was a fool, "if you ain't here to buy no pussy, and excuse me if this is rude, *King*, what the fuck is you doin' in my house?"

"I'm here for a friend," Javier answered. "Maria."

Hearing the name made Sir's blood run cold. He now knew how Javier had gotten his address and name, but now the question was, how did Javier know his top ho?

"Strawberry!" Sir forced a slimy smile. "Now, what business do you have with her, mane? She ain't shit but a ho with some good pussy."

"Maria," Javier accented her name, "left some of her things here. Pictures of her family. She wants them. And you gon' give them to me so that I can leave and go on about my night."

"I tell you what," Sir said, taking a step closer to Javier. "You tell that ho to come home and get the pictures herself. Yeah, tell good ole Strawberry that a few of her old clients have been asking about her."

"Her home is with me." Javier didn't move or look intimidated when Sir got closer to him. "And her name is Maria. Strawberry is dead. Now, the pictures?"

"Damn! I know her pussy is good, but if I had known it was good enough to pocket the king of the streets, I woulda put you on her roster a long time ago!" Sir laughed and looked over at his homies who chuckled too. "Look, mane, how about this: Since you seem to know where that bitch is, tell her to come on home, and I'll pencil you in as one of her regulars. Shit, I'll even throw you a cheaper rate."

"I'm not here to body you, and after what you did to her, I shoulda aired this bitch out when I first walked in here. You living like a fuckin' peasant," Javier's voice dripped with contempt. "But if you call her anything other than Maria again, I *will* paint these walls with the blood from ya stomach."

Sir, always the kind of man to pull the horse's tail, didn't heed the warning. Instead, he nodded his head, placed the glass of alcohol on the kitchen table, and walked to the back room like he was going to get what Javier was asking for. In all actuality, he was going to grab his fully loaded pistol. The liquor coursing through his blood was causing him to act illogically, and he was furious. Not only was Strawberry giving his pussy away for free, she'd sent another nigga to his house, unwelcome. Images of Javier lying dead on the floor plagued his mind, and he wanted to get to that future sooner than later.

"Yeah," Sir said, coming back down the long hallway. "I got what you lookin' for, right here, my nigga. Like I said, fuck that ho! And fuck you too, nigga!"

He entered the dining room again, with his gun raised, ready to start popping off at any moving body, certain that Slime and Cory would follow. He was met with a surprise, though, and it sent his heart to the pit of his stomach. Both Slime and Cory were lying facedown on the ground. Both were staring aimlessly with smoking holes in the middle of their foreheads and pools of blood forming around their heads, staining the carpet.

"I'm not here to play no games with you, my nigga," Javier said, not sounding even a little worried about Sir's weapons. "Put that little pea-shooter away and go get what the fuck I asked for. Ya homies had to pay for ya insubordination. You got three seconds before I let my nigga fire off on you, too."

Behind him, not too far away from the dead bodies, one of the men let his arm fall to his side. In his hand was a still-smoking gun with a silencer screwed at the top. Sir was so shocked that he lowered his own weapon. They'd murdered his friends. He looked from them to Javier's hard face, and then back to them again.

"Now," Javier said when it was apparent that Sir knew he wasn't playing, "the pictures."

Chapter 8

The four days Maria spent with Javier in Hawaii were pure bliss. She had never seen a place more beautiful, and being there with the man she was falling in love with made it all the more peaceful. When they weren't making love, they were sightseeing. The people were amazing, and the food blew her away. She was having such a great time with Javier that their last day in paradise snuck up on her too quickly. Javier decided to surprise her with a moonlit dinner on the beach, listening to the waves and watching the stars form in the sky. She wore a two-piece black swimsuit with a black and pink floral kimono cover-up. Her new short haircut blew slightly with each small breeze, and her hands played with the soft sand underneath the blanket they were on. Javier wore only a pair of shorts and let his muscular top half gleam in the moon. He was so sexy, the kind of man that women looked twice at, but he seemed to only have eyes for one woman. Back home, it was rare to find a woman more stacked than Maria, but there in Hawaii, almost every woman had curves for days. Still, Javier let Maria know with words and actions that she was the one he wanted.

"I want to live here," Maria sighed, watching the ocean. "I have never been more at peace in my life."

"I guess my crib just ain't up to par," Javier joked, pulling a warm kabob from the basket they'd brought with them.

"You know what I mean," Maria giggled. "It's just amazing here. Nobody knows me. I can walk down the street without anybody giving me those looks, you know?"

"I told you, shorty," Javier stroked her face tenderly before holding the kabob to her lips, "you ain't gon' have those problems back at home no more."

"Since I got the Big Bad Wolf to protect me?"

"That's right! Now taste this shit. I had some of these back at the hotel. Fire!"

She bit into the meat, making sure to get a piece of shrimp too, and moaned at the flavor.

"Ooo, *Papi!* That *is* good!"

He puffed his chest out and gloated. "Have I steered you wrong yet?"

"You did last night," Maria leaned in to him and gave him a wet kiss on the lips. "Right off the bed!"

"Shouldn't have been running," Javier lowered his eyelids sexily at her. "Round twenty tonight when we get back?"

"Or round twenty right here," Maria straddled him and licked the flavor from the kabob from his lips.

At first she was hesitant to unleash her inner freak, afraid that it would remind him of her past. But Javier let her know quickly that he appreciated her experience. It meant she could keep up with him. He'd gone so long without having a consistent sexual partner that Maria was his perfect match.

"Damn, shorty," he said, feeling his erection grow as she ground down on it. "Slow down. Wait."

He gripped her hips to make her stop and leaned back so that he could look into her face.

"What, Papi? You can't be lookin' all good with your shirt off and stuff and expect me to not want it right here. Right now!"

"Yo, chill!" He laughed at the serious pout on her face. "With your horny ass, you gon' get Daddy's dick for sure. But first I got a surprise for you."

"Surprise?" Her face lit up instantly at the word.

"Yeah," Javier said with a look of mischief. "In the basket."

"Is it that necklace I saw at the jewelry shop when we went shopping yesterday?"

Maria clambered off him excitedly and dug instantly in the basket. At the bottom of it, her hands touched something that felt like a folder, and when she pulled it out, she saw that she was right. She peeled back the seal and peered inside it before pulling out the contents.

"Oh my God, Javi," she breathed as the tears welled up. What she held in her hands wasn't the necklace she wanted, but she wasn't even thinking about the diamond-encrusted thing anymore. What Javier had gifted her with was priceless. "Oh, Javier."

She glanced down at her family pictures and kissed the faces of her mother and little sister Marisole. She thumbed through all of them and saw that all the pictures were there, even the ones that dated back to when she was a baby.

"Does that make you happy, Maria?"

"Yes! I can't believe these are my pictures!"

Javier watched Maria's face light up every time she looked at a different picture. He could tell she missed her family and couldn't understand why she hadn't even tried to find them. She was scared, and that was OK. But he knew from experience with his own mother that no matter what, a mother's love prevailed over all.

"There's something else in there for you." Javier nodded to the envelope. "Pull it out."

Maria put her hand back in the envelope and pulled out a folded up piece of notebook paper. When she unfolded it, her hand flew to her mouth and she gasped. "Is this . . . ?"

"Your mom's number," Javier told her. "And her address. It pays to have friends in high places. I thought having those would be useful, but the choice to use them is yours. I can tell you miss them. It's time for you to make up for lost time."

"Oh, Javi," Maria said again and clutched the piece of paper to her chest. "But how? How did you get the pictures?"

"I have my ways," he answered briskly.

She wanted him to go into more detail because the only way to have gotten the pictures was to go to Sir's place. But from the temperament in his answer, she figured it could wait. Plus, she almost didn't even care. She was just happy that he'd gotten them before Sir burned them.

"I love you, Javi," she said and wrapped her arms around his neck. "You are the best thing God ever blessed me with."

"You mean that?"

"Yes." She pulled away and kissed his chin. "Nobody has ever treated me the way you do. You are truly a blessing."

"Nah," Javier's expression was serious as he looked down at her. "I mean, do you really love me?"

It had only been a month, but Javier burned a fire so fierce in Maria that she couldn't explain. All she knew was that he completed her. She wasn't quite over all of the emotional strain that Sir had put on her, but Javier had put Band-Aids over all of the pain with his kindness. He was the reason that she was healing, and she would forever appreciate him for that. Javier had taught her what it felt like to be a woman and how she was supposed to be treated. With him, she felt a security like none other. She knew that no matter what happened, she was safe now. When he wasn't around, she yearned for his presence and wanted him around. At night when she said her prayers, he had snuck in through the backdoor somehow, and she asked God to keep His angels around him at all times. It was at that moment, there on the beach, that she realized what all those emotions were equaling to.

"Yes," Maria breathed up at him. "I do. And I never want to let you go. I love you, Javier. I love you because you have never judged me, and you have always been kind to me. I love you because you make me remember what it's like to be a lady, and I'm proud to walk by your side. I love you because when you're inside of me, Papi, I'm the happiest I've ever been in life because you're mine. And for that moment, I don't have to share you with the world. I love you—"

Javier didn't need to hear anymore. He pressed his lips on hers and kissed her slow and softly. He relished in the feel of her lips and cherished the taste of her tongue. Placing his hand on the back of her neck, he gently lay her on her back and got on top of her. He didn't care who saw them, and whoever was watching was sure to get the show of a lifetime. He wanted to hear her tell him she loved him in his ear over and over with each deep thrust he gave her. That was his only focus for the rest of the night. Removing her swimsuit bottom, he positioned himself in front of her pretty pink opening and licked his lips.

"I love you too, Maria Calico," he told her before he dived in, face-first.

***

It took Spice and Sugar four days to clean up the blood from Sir's fallen partners while his demeanor grew darker with each of the four passing days. Anybody else would have turned the other way and run if they came home to two dead bodies in their home, but not Spice and Sugar. They both had seen their share of murders, even helped set some of them up. Since they were Sir's property, it was only right that they make sure that the murder scene looked like, "What murder scene?" When they finally finished, they took the bloody rags downstairs to deposit them into the Dumpster of the apartment complex. They got back in the house and saw Sir in the same spot they'd left him in, on the couch throwing back bottles of alcohol. Instead of disturbing him, the women went quietly to their room and closed the door to a crack.

"Have you thought more about what we talked about?" Spice asked Sugar, who had taken a seat on the bed.

"Yeah," Sugar replied looking at her hands. "This ain't what I thought it would be, Spice."

"Tell me about it. All the pussy we sell to still be having to share a room! What the fuck does he do with all the money?"

"I don't know," Sugar shook her head. "But for all this, I could be fuckin' for me and me only!"

"Yeah, Daddy ain't been the same since Strawberry left."

"The way he beat her, I'd be surprised if she ain't dead somewhere. And now this nigga got mothafuckas getting murdered where we lay our heads at. I'm from the hood, and I done seen some shit, but, Spice, this is gettin' to be too much. I think we should move around."

"Yeah," Spice agreed. "But I think we should wait a few weeks and save up secretly. It's too many bitches sellin' pussy in Memphis now. I think it's time we take our business global."

Sugar nodded her head and motioned her hand to the door. "Let's go get cleaned up. I ain't had to get rid of a dead body since I was sixteen. I need to wash all this shit off me."

She left the room, and Spice followed her when she heard the shower water running. Both women stripped completely naked, put their shower caps on, and got in the wide bathtub together. The water coming from the big showerhead hit them both, and they instantly went to work cleaning each other off, scrubbing vigorously.

"Mmm, girl," Spice said, eyeing Sugar lustfully as she rinsed off. "I love watching water fall off that ass."

"Shut your gay ass up," Sugar said, but bent over so Spice could get a better look.

"I'm only gay for you." Spice reached her hand out and cupped Sugar's pussy from behind. "I love this fat pussy."

As she played with Sugar's pussy, she felt herself growing moist between the legs. She and Sugar didn't have sex often, but it was no secret that she enjoyed plunging her tongue in her friend's pussy every now and then. Truth be told, they both would have loved to play with Strawberry's pussy if she had stuck around long enough, but unfortunately for them, that never happened.

"Get on your knees, bitch," Sugar instructed, hiking her leg up and resting her foot on the soap holder. "I want you to eat this pussy like I'm paying you for it."

Their profession fit them both perfectly. They were both very sexual and loved coming until they couldn't take it anymore. When Spice got on her knees, Sugar gripped the back of her head and forced her face into her pussy lips. Spice's tongue did things no man's ever had, and she loved it. Sugar threw her head back and played with her own nipples as Spice pleasured her clit.

"That's a good bitch," she moaned. "Yes, baby, eat this pussy!"

Back in the living room, Sir heard the fun the two women were having. Spice's moans carried, and usually that made him want to get in on the action. Not that time, though. Her moans carried all the way to the front room, and instead of arousing him, they made him want to get away. Far away . . . and he knew the perfect spot. He stood up, clenching the bottle of Hennessey in his hand, and walked out of the apartment. He was no longer buzzed. He was drunk out of his mind, and thinking logically was nowhere in his plans.

When Javier had come to Sir's house, he not only disrespected Sir, but he bruised the man's ego. Sir let the bodies of his friends lay there for days before he made his whores clean up the mess. He was empty and completely defeated, something that he couldn't cope with. Something he *wouldn't* cope with. He wanted revenge. Through the grapevine, he learned that Javier and Strawberry had left town for a few days and were coming back that day. Because of what Javier had come to get, he was positive that he knew where Strawberry's first stop would be as soon as she touched down. He was just going to be the one to get to them first.

***

Four days truly wasn't enough when it came to paradise. The moment Maria stepped off of the plane, she wanted to beg Javier to book another flight back.

"Every day will be paradise from here on out," Javier told her when he practically had to drag her to the car. "I promise."

"Yeah, yea. Whatever!" she pouted.

"For real!" he laughed, shutting her door and hopping in the driver's seat. "Plus, you have things to do. Remember what we talked about."

Maria nodded her head to let him know that she had heard him. While they were in Hawaii, she reached out to her mother. Her heart was enlightened when Mary began to cry on the other end of the phone. Maria didn't even have to say who it was. Mary recognized her voice. When Maria tried to apologize for everything, her mother would hear nothing of it.

"We all learn lessons; some of us later than others. But as long as you learned yours, you are welcome to come home anytime!"

That was music to Maria's ears, and she knew Javier was right. She couldn't hop on another trip to Hawaii, but when she did, she wanted her entire family to be with her. The couple touched down in Memphis at around eight in the morning. Javier had business to attend to once they got home, but he gave her the keys to one of his vehicles and told her she could go wherever she wanted. Her plans were to take a nap and go across town to visit her mother, and she was looking forward to it. Javier pulled up to his home and unloaded all of their luggage. They weren't even there for twenty minutes before he had to hit the streets, promising to be back before sundown.

Maria was so antsy that even though she was tired from the flight, all she wanted to do was hit the road and see her mother. Mary wasn't expecting her until late that evening, but Maria thought it would be fun to surprise her. She hopped in the shower in Javier's room, soon to be the room they shared, and got dressed comfortably in jeans and a V-neck cotton shirt. The keys Javier had given her were to the gray Jeep Grand Cherokee he'd just added to his collection.

"I'm on my way, Mommy," she said to herself, pressing the "Push To Start" button in the Jeep and zooming away from the house.

The drive was almost an hour, but Maria enjoyed the solitude of it. On the drive, she thought deeply about Javier. He loved her, he really loved her, and she could tell. There was no time frame on love, and she appreciated him so much. Not just for everything he did for her, but for everything he let her do. Like drive his car and give her freedom like he trusted her. He *did* trust her, and although they had just been together nonstop, Maria couldn't wait to get back to him. Next time, he would just have to come with her.

"Next time," she smiled to herself because she knew there would be a next time.

Javier wasn't going anywhere, and she for damn sure knew that she would never let him go. She pulled into a quaint neighborhood and looked for the address her mother sent her until she finally found the house. Maria parked and gave herself a once-over in the visor mirror and groaned at her reflection. She looked like shit, and she hadn't even taken the time to properly do her hair.

Fuck it, she thought and got out of the car.

She was so excited to see her family that she didn't notice the familiar Cadillac parked on the street. Clearing her throat, she knocked three times on the door and straightened her shirt. She heard footsteps scurrying inside the house, and she smiled, wondering if it was Marisole coming to let her in. When the door opened,

Maria stood up straighter and prepared to jump into the arms of whoever was on the other side—but who she saw was not who she expected.

"What's good, Strawberry?" Sir slurred, pointing a pistol at her chest. "How nice of you to join us. Get in here."

Chapter 9

Being huddled together in a basement corner was not how Maria envisioned being reunited with her family. The happiness that she hoped to be in her mother's eyes was overcome by the fear in them. The basement was full of boxes and furniture that nobody sat on anymore. There was one lightbulb hanging in the middle of the room, giving them all dim lighting, but enough to see around them. It smelled like laundry since the washroom was down there, but the pleasant smell had nothing on the sinister energy in the room.

Sir sat on the arm of one of the old couches, staring at the three women holding on to each other like their lives depended on it. He's stripped them all of their electronic devices and made Maria leave her car keys on the kitchen table upstairs. Maria watched him turn his nose up at her new haircut, but still, he said nothing. His eyes lingered on her younger sister, Marisole, a little longer than they should have. She was the spitting image of her older sister, except her brown hair was long. She knew what he was thinking, and she wanted to throw up. What had she gotten her family into?

"Mommy, I'm so sorry!" Maria said into her mother's hair. "This is all my fault."

"Now is not the time to be placing blame," Mary said and cupped Maria's chin with her hands. "I have been wishing that God would send you home to me, and here you are. No matter the circumstance, I love you!"

"Oh my God, shut the fuck up with all the sentimental shit." Sir finally spoke up. "Strawberry is the one to blame for all this shit!"

He was drunk out of his mind, and that made him all the more dangerous. He waved the gun around like a wand, and the women ducked whenever it was pointed their way. He got to his feet and went to the corner they were crouched in.

"I want you," he said, grasping Marisole's arm. "You look like ya sister. I wonder if the pussy is the same."

"No!" Mary yelled and tried to push him back. "You stay away from my daughters! Demon!"

Bang!

When his gun went off, he ignored the screams of Maria and Marisole at the sight of their mother clutching the bottom of her stomach. Blood spilled through her fingertips, and her eyes were wide in shock. Sir didn't shoot Maria, but he hit her hard in the temple with the butt of his gun.

"That wouldn't have happened if you wouldn't have run from me, bitch!" he shouted and hit Maria again. "You shoulda stayed home like a good bitch. A *good bitch!* Now your sister is about to pay the price of you being a disobedient ho!"

"No! Mommy! Mommy!" Marisole screamed as Sir dragged her away and back up the basement stairs. "Maria! Maria!"

Her screams broke Maria's heart. Her head was throbbing, and she was seeing blurred doubles of everything, even of her stout mother laid out on the ground.

"Mommy," she said. "Mommy, I can't-I can't focus. I can't see!"

"Ma-Maria," Mary panted. "Follow my voice and focus! I forgive you. Do you hear me? I-I forgive you, my dear child! I should have been more of a mother to you and maybe this wouldn't have happened. Bad people attach themselves to good hearts and turn them black. But not you, *mi amor*, you found your way back home. You are still good. You are not used goods. You are a queen, and right now, you need to save your sister from that man. P-please. Save your sister."

"I can't leave you, Mommy!"

"I got stabbed four times when I was your age and lived to tell the tale. Maybe I'll live to tell this one too, now . . . *g-go!*"

A bloodcurdling scream filled the air, and Maria didn't wait to hear her mother tell her again. She struggled to her feet and blinked a few times to clear her vision. On her way upstairs, she grabbed a piece of scrap metal behind the staircase. It was sharp at the bottom, sharp enough to plunge through that piece of shit's heart. She held on to the wooden rail and, with some difficulty, got up the stairs. Marisole's screams were coming from a room in the back, and they were now mixed with hopeless sobs.

"Please don't do this! Please! I'm a virgin! Please!"

"Nah," Maria heard Sir respond. "Your pussy is going to pay for the negligence of your sister. Do you know how much money I missed out on because of her? Huh? She's my property!"

"No, she's not! You sick bastard! You ruined her life and took her away from the only people who loved her!"

Slap!

"Shut up! I didn't bring you in here to listen to you talk. By the time anyone finds any of y'all, you'll be stinking. Unless you want to take Strawberry's place on my team."

"Fuck you! And her name isn't Strawberry, it's Maria!"

Hearing Marisole defend her like that, although they had been apart for so many years, gave Maria newfound strength. The metal in her hand no longer seemed as heavy, and her eyesight focused a little better. She walked in the small bedroom and saw that Sir had Marisole pinned down with her dress hiked up to her neck. He'd ripped her bra and panties off and thrown them to the side to give himself full access to the young girl. He slapped Marisole a couple more times so hard that she looked to be on the brink of passing out. All of the fear that Maria ever had in her heart for Sir went out the window as she watched him beat Marisole like a bitch off the street. She didn't just see Marisole, she saw herself. She had put up with it for so long, and now her baby sister was paying her debt to the devil.

Never again.

"Get your hands off of her," Maria growled from behind him and ran with the pointed side of the scrap metal facing him.

Sir turned around just in time to be met with the metal being pushed through his stomach. His body began to twitch violently as his lips moved feverishly, trying to inhale air. Maria couldn't have that either. She grabbed the gun he'd set beside Marisole's body and pointed it at him just as he reached for her.

"Go to hell," she said, looking into the face of the man she once worshipped and feeling nothing but hatred. "You son of a bitch! Just go to hell!"

She pulled the trigger and felt her shoulder knock back from the power of the gun. Her first bullet caught him in the chest, but her second one caught him in the head. Blood and brains sprayed the television behind him, and the look of complete shock was frozen on his face. Maria didn't wait for him to fall to the ground to tend to her sister. She pulled Marisole's dress back down and patted her face gently.

"Marisole? Marisole!"

"Please stop smacking my face," she groaned. "It hurts already."

Maria gave a relieved laugh and pulled her sister up into a bear hug. She cried in her neck and apologized over and over, until finally Marisole leaned away.

"I love you, Maria," she said with tears in her own eyes and tenderly kissed Maria's hands. "You'll always be my sister."

In the hallway, there suddenly was a loud sound of somebody walking toward them. Maria turned the gun to the door but quickly dropped it to the ground when she saw her mother lean in the doorway, clutching her wound. She had tied some sort of sheet around her waist to slow the blood flow, but slowly, her blood was starting to drench that too.

"Mommy! We have to get you to the hospital!" She got up as fast as her throbbing head would let her and rushed to give her mother a hand. Marisole did the same.

"Yes, that would be good," Mary said, glancing at Marisole's bedroom floor, and spat at Sir's dead body. "I never liked him. I hope your new boyfriend is nothing like him, Maria. Otherwise, I'll kill him at the front door."

"I'm surprised the police haven't showed up yet," Marisole said while she and Maria helped their mother walk through the house and out-side to the Jeep.

"These people don't give a fuck about nobody but themselves. But it's all right. The next time I hear Mrs. Buxton's husband beating her ass, I won't intervene. And when Mr. Winslow's badass dog runs away again, I sure as hell won't help him look for that motherfucker!"

Maria rolled her eyes. Her mother hadn't changed one bit. She thought about calling Javier and telling him about what just went down, but she figured she would do it while at the hospital.

"You OK, Mommy?" Marisole asked, looking at the wound in Mary's stomach.

"Yes," she said. "I saw a bullet hole in the basement, so that means that drunk motherfucker shot straight through me. I think it's only a flesh wound, but it hurts like hell! But I'll be all right."

"Thank God," Maria said, driving a few miles to the nearest hospital. "I have a question, though, Mommy."

"W-what is it, *mi amor?*"

"Did you *really* get stabbed four times when you were my age? And don't lie! Because that's what you said when you were dying in the basement."

Mary looked at each of her daughters and contemplated fake passing out right there in the backseat. Sighing, she leaned her back on the door and tried to ignore the pain in her stomach.

"Yes, it's true," she started and saw the surprised looks on her daughters' faces. "Before I tell you this story, I want you both to know that I wasn't always this straight-shooting woman that you know to be your mother. As you both have learned firsthand . . . some crazy shit happens in the hood."

The End

Payback

by

Paradise Gomez

Chapter 1

The Past . . .

I loved him. That's why, through all the pain, I stayed. In my eyes, Demarcus "Marco" Lancastor could do no wrong. Maybe it was the sex that kept me so submissive, or maybe it was because he was the King of the South. Shoot, maybe it was the fact that he had deep brown eyes that could peer into my soul and make me feel like I needed him. His eyes accented his muscular, caramel build nicely . . . and that eight inch thick dick? I was a goner way before our story even began. Demarcus was the son and street general to Antonio Lancastor, the King of Houston. Antonio had the whole state on lock, which meant Marco was the rightful heir. Maybe that was why I just felt lucky enough to be the one he called his girlfriend. Me, the poor girl from Houston whose parents kicked her out when she was fifteen. The girl who had to lie and say she was eighteen just to swirl on a pole in front of greasy old men for wrinkled dollar bills.

Surprisingly enough, I didn't meet Marco in the strip club. We met at the library, and I was just intrigued that a nigga like him liked to read. I had been sitting cross-legged in a big orange plush chair in a corner by myself when I felt a presence looming over me. Now me, I have always had a bad attitude. I hated when people approached me without being invited, especially if they didn't have at least a hundred dollars to give me. I looked up, preparing to go off on whoever had interrupted my reading session . . . until I saw that I was staring up at the sexiest man I'd ever seen in my life. He was smiling down at me with those straight white teeth, and that day, he must have been fresh out of the barbershop because, ooh . . . wee! That boy was fine. His taper fade and beard had been lined up and were sharper than a chef's knife. I was so startled that I couldn't do anything but stare at the man.

"Do you know where I can find a biography on Nelson Mandela?"

Those were the first words Marco ever said to me, and after that, it was a wrap for the next two years. I was his, and he was mine. The first year was amazing. He spoiled me rotten, moved me out of the hood, and I was able to kiss my job good-bye. I moved in with him in his big home in the suburbs and lived life like a modern-day Cinderella. I just knew he was going to marry me. Couldn't nobody tell me I wasn't going to be Jackie Lancastor. But then . . . everything changed the second year.

He changed.

I was used to Marco running the streets. I knew what he did, and I respected my place. I was never intimidated by the drugs or the guns, and I never asked questions when he came home with bloodstains on his clothes. Instead, I would go out and buy him another one of whatever he ruined. When his late nights turned into days of him being gone, he just told me he was away "handling business out of state." When he started to leave the room to answer the phone, I believed him when he told me it was his best friend Tommy talking about their next move. But when our love life started to dwindle and I began noticing purchases in our account that weren't for me, my mind began to wander. There was once a time where I couldn't keep Marco's arms from around my 32-inch waist. He loved using hands to squeeze and slap my plump behind. He used to have to dive into my ocean at least two or three times a day when he was home, but suddenly, I was only getting it once a month. And when I got it, it wasn't the same. He was boring with his strokes and didn't even care if I got mine off too. Being naïve, I thought that maybe he was just tired and his business had him off his game.

It wasn't until Marco started disrespecting me that I knew something awful was wrong. No longer was I "baby" and "honey." Marco called me "bitch" so much I almost started to think it was my real name. It was hard because outside of him, I had no life. I moved in with him so quick because I never thought he would turn on me. My main goal was to keep him happy, because, truth be told, he was the only thing I had in the world. So I put up with the bullshit. Even when I caught him texting other girls, I believed him when he said he never slept with them.

"Those hoes ain't shit to me, Jackie," he told me. "I just need them to move the pack for me. I can have any bitch in the world, so just be happy it's you for now. You need to just mind ya business. Be happy I'm not one of these niggas out here slapping their bitch around."

So I did just that because he was right. There were a lot of things about our relationship that made me unhappy, but he hadn't put his hands on me the way I'd seen his friends do their girls.

One weekend, he told me he was going to be gone from Friday to Sunday, so I decided to surprise him. Because my name was on all the accounts, I found out that he was going to be staying at a Hilton in California. It didn't dawn on me then that *all* of his "business trips" had been to California, and he stayed at the same hotel every time.

I packed my sexiest lingerie, hell-bent on pleasing my man and making things the way they used to be. I had never been to California before, so I was looking forward to him showing me around, maybe even taking me to the beach. When I got off the plane that Saturday and caught that taxi to his hotel, I soaked in the daytime scenery. It was just like the movies, and I was so excited to get to Marco. I got off the plane dressed to impress, OK? I had on a skintight, nude, short sleeve Marc Jacobs dress complete with a pair of blood red, ankle strap, closed toe four-inch heels. I accessorized accordingly, wearing the thick, gold rope chain necklace he got me for my birthday, along with the gold ruby-studded tennis bracelet he bought for Christmas. The hotel he was staying in was amazing, but I wish I would have paid attention to the bellhop's face when I told him who I was there to see.

"Mr. Demarcus Lancastor?" the young white man said. His name was Joe, and he didn't look to be more than twenty and had a clean bowl haircut. His face was riddled with acne, but he had a nice smile and cleaned up well in his work uniform. He checked the computer again when I confirmed that we were talking about the same person. "They just got back and headed up to the room."

"OK, great. I just need the room number so I can head on up too," I told him.

"Um," Joe hesitated, "is he expecting you?"

"No. I'm here to surprise him on his business trip. He's only here for one more day before he comes back home, so I figured, when in Rome, right? Might as well come see what my baby is up to!"

That poor child looked so confused, and I swear I saw him swallow his spit, but I didn't care. I was too anxious to make Marco happy. Joe checked in his system, and then looked back at me.

"May I have your name again, please?"

"I'm Jackie Stewart," I told him, setting my small overnight bag down to get my ID out of my purse. "It says it right there, plain as day."

"OK," he said, taking my ID and matching it with a name on the screen. "Yup, umm. There you are. I see your name on the reservation. Let me get a key ready for you."

It took Joe all of thirty seconds to hand me the key in a hotel envelope and send me on my way. He had almost gotten on my bad side, but I let it ride. He was probably new and just getting a hand on the job. My experience with him washed away quickly when I got to the floor Marco's room was on. The smile on my face when I got off the elevator said it all, and I almost ran to his room. I didn't realize until then that I missed him so much and I just wanted things to be the way they used to be.

I put the key in the door and entered the luxurious suite. It was set up like a one-bedroom apartment, except that there was a hot tub in the living room. On the ledge of the hot tub were candles that needed to be lit and an unopened bottle of champagne. I smiled when I saw the rose petals that went from the front door to the hot tub and floated peacefully on top of the already-run water.

He knew I was coming, I thought to myself. *I knew I shouldn't have used the card to our main account to book this flight!*

Well, so much for the element of surprise. I threw my overnight bag on the couch of the suite and made my way to the closed bedroom door, where I was sure to find him passed out asleep. I wrapped my hand around the doorknob to make my presence known, but what I heard next made my blood run cold.

"Marco, you said you were going to leave her and move me out to Houston with you!"

I was so thrown off guard by the woman's whiny voice, I froze with my mouth open slightly. I had never heard that voice in my life, but it was apparent that she knew my Marco. So many thoughts were rushing through my head at once that I couldn't grasp even one of them. He was there with a woman? He told her he was going to leave me and move her to our home? How long had this been going on? Is *this* what he did whenever he came to California?

"You have to be patient with me, baby," Marco's voice replied. His tone was low, sexy, and sure of himself. It was the tone he'd used to get me, and also the tone I hadn't heard in a long time. "But I promise you'll be my queen soon."

"How soon? We've been doing this for months now! I love when we're here because I can have you all to myself, but I hate that when you take me to Houston we have to hide like we're a secret! Why is it so hard for you to let that bitch go? It's not like she's your wife!"

"It's not as easy as you think, ma," Marco told her.

"Do you love her?"

"No. I love you, Brina."

I felt my heart drop to the pit of my stomach at how quickly he responded to her. He didn't love me? Since when? Did he *ever* love me? Tears welled up in my eyes as many emotions surged through me. What was I going to do? I didn't have a penny to my name. I never thought Marco and I would end, especially not so soon.

"Then leave her! I know her pussy ain't better than mine. Otherwise, you wouldn't be jumping on red eyes to come get this ooey gooey. Stop playin' with me, Marco." Her voice was demanding, and I heard Marco's laugh.

"This is why I'll always choose you, ma," he said, and I heard a sound like he kissed her. "You aren't submissive like that bitch. I like the fire in you. I like *this* too." I don't know what he did to her, but her moan let me know it was sexual. "Give me a week to kill ties. She just knows more about my business dealings than I would like her to. But I promise I'll move you in with me as soon as all this is deaded. With this good pussy, you deserve to be the queen of Houston."

"Okay!" she moaned loudly. "Okay, Daddy! Ohhh, Marco, I love you!"

I'd heard enough. I let the doorknob go and turned to walk out the same way I came. Just like that, my world had come crashing down at my feet. No wonder he'd been treating me the way he was. He didn't want me anymore. No wonder why he was never home, and no wonder why he never had the energy to make love to me. I felt like the greenest of all shits, and all I wanted to do was curl up in a ball and cry. Where would I go? Would he *really* just throw me out on the streets, knowing I didn't have a penny to my name? I could empty his accounts, but his reach went around the world. He would just find me and kill me. I was only twenty, so I was still young and vibrant, but I never started college. How would I find a good enough job to live the way that I was used to? My heart was heavy as I passed through the room and all of our memories flooded back to me. Lies, they were all lies. Marco had taken the last two years of our lives together and wiped them away for a bitch named Brina.

Soon, the sadness was overcome by anger. I knew what he did to those who crossed him, but deadly or not, how dare that nigga do me bad like that when I did everything I could to make his home a home and keep him happy! How dare he plot to have another bitch lay her head on the silk, thousand-dollar pillows *I* picked out for our bed? No. Just no.

Before I left the suite, I felt my feet make a detour in the kitchen. Beside the refrigerator was a set of knives in their wooden holder. From it, I grabbed the biggest one and headed back toward the room. Brina's screams of pleasure had gotten louder, and I heard the sound of Marco's balls slapping her ass cheeks.

"You greasy motherfucker!" I shouted and entered the room.

Marco looked like a deer caught in a set of bright lights when he saw me standing in the doorway, holding the knife. He was sitting upright with his knees on the bed, with a woman my age bent over in front of him. I turned my nose up at her. She was cute, but nowhere near as fine as me. The only thing she had on me was a bigger butt. Other than that, homegirl was trash. She was short and had skin a little darker than my brown complexion. Her eyes were too close together, and the weave on top of her head didn't blend well with her leave out. I could tell that she was shorter than me and slightly on the plump side; however, my beef wasn't with her. It was with the piece of shit with his dick still in her pussy.

"So *this* is what you've been doing when you aren't home?"

"Jackie, I can explain," Marco said, finally removing himself from inside of Brina. He pulled his boxers back up around his waist and put his hands out like he was trying to calm me down. "Put the knife down."

"What? Mr. Gunplay is scared of a knife," I taunted him with a scowl. "Fuck you! How could you do this to me?"

"Jackie, it's not what it looks like."

"Oh, it's not?" Sabrina sat up on the bed, exposing her naked body. There was no shame in her game. She didn't even attempt to cover up as she gloated in my direction. "Marco is in this pussy almost every weekend. He even bought me my own crib, and it's his name on my car note. Ain't that right, baby?"

Marco's eyes were still on the knife that I was holding on to for dear life. His eyes shifted to where his pile of clothes were near me, and I already knew what he was trying to get to. I hurried up and kicked them out of the room, not daring to give him a chance to get to the gun.

"Is that true, Marco?" I shouted trying to sound tough, but my voice betrayed me and cracked. "After everything, you cheat on me with a bitch with a bad weave? Do you love me?"

I expected him to console me. I thought that since he was caught in the act, he would do like the niggas in the movies did and kick Brina out so that I could yell at him, and then forgive him. He should have, he really should have. He walked up on me slowly, with his arms out.

"Jackie, I'm so sorry, baby," the expression on his face was regretful, and the arm holding the knife waivered slightly. When he got to me, I thought he was going to wrap me in a tight hug to comfort me. Instead, the regretful expression changed to one of disgust, and he put a hand around my neck. "I *never* loved you."

His right hand squeezed my neck, choking the life out of me, while the other held the arm with the knife, keeping it at my side.

"Mar-Marco. I can't bre—*ckkk! Ckkk!*" I tried to beg him to stop choking me, but my airway was cut off.

"How did you get here, bitch? Did you use the money in my account to pop up on me?" Marco sneered in my ear. "Guessing by your outfit, you probably thought I would be happy to see you. But now, since you wanna come in here on some rah-rah bullshit, let me tell you how I *really* feel about you. You were just supposed to be a bitch to pass my time. It was never supposed to go this far, but I felt sorry for you. You didn't have shit, so I gave you everything. But now? You gotta go. I thought it would be nice having some live-in pussy, but you can't even do that right. I'm a king, baby girl, and you were always just a peasant to me."

He released my neck right before I passed out, and punched me to the floor. The blow was so hard that my lip busted and my nose leaked with blood. I didn't have time to get my wits together before Brina jumped from the bed, using me on the floor as her chance to attack me. She riddled my body with her fists and hard kicks to my stomach. The bitch even dragged me around the room by my long hair. Now, don't get me wrong. I could fight, but I was too weak from oxygen loss to defend myself. Every time I tried to, Marco would come to her aid with another blow of his own. It was at that moment, as the two of them were beating me, that I truly believed him. He didn't love me. Not if he could do me that bad behind a girl he'd only been screwing for a few months.

"Grab my gun," Marco huffed. "I was gon' just put the bitch on the streets, but now I'ma put her underneath them."

I lay on the ground, bloody and in pain while Brina stepped over me and went to where I'd kicked Marco's clothes. From where I was, I could see underneath the king-sized bed in the room, and my eyes fell on a black square plate.

The lines of coke there let me know why both of them were so hostile, and it also made me realize that Marco was only partly in his right state of mind. He was ruthless sober, so high, I had no doubt in my mind that he would really kill me. The knife had fallen out of my hand, but it wasn't too far from me. I grabbed it when Marco wasn't looking and put it under my stomach. While Brina was still out of the room, Marco grabbed me by my hair, pulling me up from the ground into a standing position. I hurried to put the knife behind my back and stared into his eyes using the one eye of mine that wasn't swollen shut.

"It didn't have to be like this," he told me and spat in my face.

"I know," I said weakly. "I really loved you."

With that, I used the last of my strength to shove the knife in his stomach and watched the look of shock ripple over his handsome face. I pulled the knife out of him, and he released my hair to clutch his stomach.

"Oh my God! What did you do?" Brina had come back in the room, and there was a loud thud.

I gathered my wits and saw that she had dropped the gun he'd sent her to get. Instead of waiting around to see what would happen next, I limped out of the room with my purse and overnight bag in tow. You all probably think I went out pretty gangster, huh? You probably think I went back home, emptied his accounts, and kept it pushing. I could tell that lie, but then this wouldn't be a very interesting story. I didn't do any of that. I didn't even make it back to the airport. Turns out that Joe the bellhop had a feeling that something was about to go down since he'd seen Marco enter the hotel with another chick. Not only did he send the hotel security, but California police met me right at the entrance of the hotel. But get this . . . They didn't believe a word I said. They didn't care that I was beaten to a pulp and had blood running down the front of my dress. All they cared about was that there was a man with a stab wound to his stomach.

Magically, the drugs and gun disappeared from the suite, and I was painted to be a monster who had premeditated the murder of my ex-boyfriend. They didn't look at the fact that my name was on the reservation. When money talked, money won. Marco didn't put me underneath the earth like he had wanted to. What was done to me was way worse. Using Brina as a witness, he got me locked away for fifteen years for attempted murder and use of a deadly weapon. But that was the past, and if prison taught me anything, it was to never dwell on that. Let's bring y'all back to the present so you can see how I made this nigga pay . . .

Chapter 2

The Present . . .

"What makes you qualified for this position?"

The voice caught me by surprise, and I forgot where I was for a second. Glancing down at the grandma-looking, two-piece pantsuit given to me by my halfway house coordinator, Trudy, I remembered where I was.

"I'm sorry, can you repeat the question?" I asked, and the woman giving me my interview, Linda, furrowed her brow.

"I said, what makes you qualified for this position, Miss Stewart?"

I couldn't help it. I looked at her old, white, Betty White-looking self like she had poo all over her face.

"I thought I was interviewing for a janitorial position, not to be the CEO of this Fortune 500 company. What do you mean, what makes me *qualified?* Can't everybody clean toilets and take out the trash?"

Apparently, that was not the answer she was looking for because she pushed my résumé to the side and made a motion with her hand toward the door.

"Maybe this is not the job for you, Miss Stewart, or maybe you just don't need the money bad enough. Have a nice day. I have three other people interviewing today."

I should have asked her for another chance because she was wrong. I definitely needed the money. However, I wasn't about to grovel at her feet and beg her to hand me the plunger so I could clean up somebody else's shit either. I grabbed my résumé from her big desk and walked out of her nice big office with my head held high. If you didn't know any better, you would have thought I got the job, or maybe even owned the whole building. I glanced down at the tattered black flats I wore on my feet and shook my head. OK, maybe not the whole building, but perhaps a corner of it. I didn't want to wait inside the building for my ride, so I stood outside the tall building in downtown Houston and called Trudy to come pick me up. I knew she wasn't going to be happy if I told her I was coming home jobless yet again, but I had been out all day, and it was obvious that nobody was looking to hire an ex-con.

"Hello?" Trudy's high-pitched voice came through the other end of the phone.

"Hey, Tru, I'm ready to be picked up. I'm at Advanced Marketing, that place downtown."

"All right, Jackie," she said, and I thought that she was just going to disconnect the telephone without saying anything further, but, of course, that was too much like right. "Did you find a job today?" My deep sigh answered the question. "Jackie! You know one of the requirements of your release is for you to find employment within sixty days. You know you are on probation for the next year! I don't want them to come and take you away."

"I know," I said into the gray flip phone. "And I have been trying every day, you know this! Nobody wants to hire me because of my background."

"I know you're trying, but maybe you aren't trying hard enough. Maybe you need to tone down your attitude, just for the interview, to secure a spot."

I opened my mouth to snap at her, but I bit my tongue just in time. She was right. Things weren't the same as they were before I went to prison. There was no man to foot all of my bills and provide me a lavish home. And even if there was, I was sure to not trust them again.

"I know, Tru," I said. "But I'm tired and done for the day. Will you please come get me, and I will try again tomorrow."

"Fine," Trudy surprisingly gave in. "But the only reason I'm agreeing is because your aunt Patricia came by the house lookin' for you."

"My aunt Patricia?" I asked, wanting Trudy to confirm what she'd just said.

"Yes! That's what I said, ain't it? She's still here in the front room waiting for you to come on home. She said she ain't leaving until she talks to you. I'm on my way now. Be waiting on the street!"

"O-okay," I replied before Trudy hung up the phone.

It had been a good seventeen years since I'd seen my aunt Patricia. She was my father's sister but was significantly younger than him. She was like a mother figure to me when my parents were always out partying and doing God knows what else. It was Aunt Patricia who was the one who helped me with my homework. Aunt Patricia was the person who wiped my tears and made me feel better when I felt alone in the world. I never understood why she abruptly stopped coming around when I was sixteen. All I knew is that she and my father, Orlando Stewart, got into it pretty bad, and after that, I just never saw her again. It was a year before I'd gotten kicked out of the house, and sometimes I wondered if Aunt Patricia would have been around, would things have played out differently?

It took Trudy half an hour to pick me up in her 2016 Chevy Malibu and another half hour to get us back to the house. Trudy was a fifty-year-old woman with a head full of gray hair that she kept cut in a bob. I learned not to let her size fool me because she was a strong little lady when need be. A million and one thoughts played a game of tag with my brain when she pulled up to her two-story white house that we lived in with five other women. After I was released from prison, I just knew they were going to put me in the sleaziest halfway house known to man. However, the first time I walked through Trudy's front doors, I became aware that it wasn't like the nightmare other inmates said. We all called it Trudy's Place because it was the most well kept spot on the block. She took pride in having a clean home, and she treated us all like her children. We all had chores, mine being watering Trudy's beloved petunias that she kept in a small garden at the front of the house.

Petunias? Why was I thinking about flowers at a time like that? My heart was beating fast, just like it had when I stood before the judge and got my sentence. I got out of Trudy's car and walked hesitantly to the burgundy front door of the house. I didn't know what to expect when I walked through the threshold, so I just stood in the foyer for a few seconds. Well, until Trudy came through behind me and pushed me forward.

"Girl, if you don't go in that living room!" she told me in a hushed voice. "It's women in here that wish they had family to visit them. And when you're done talking to her, take my damn suit off and put it on my bed! I'm about to go make sure Hannah and Bernie cleaned the hallway bathroom like I told them to!"

She shut and locked the front door and headed toward the staircase to go upstairs to check on the girls. I looked down at myself, suddenly embarrassed by my appearance. At age thirty-five, I was definitely nothing to sneeze at. My body was still intact, and I had curves that would put girls ten years my junior to shame. Still, I was ashamed because I had gone from living like royalty to having to answer to someone like a child. I sighed deeply before making my way to the living room down the hallway. The lights were on in there, and I heard the voice of Steve Harvey coming from the flat-screen television Trudy had on her wall. When I rounded the corner, I saw that it was a rerun of his hit show, *Family Feud,* playing quietly in front of a woman sitting on one of Trudy's flowered embroidered couches.

"I was starting to think you weren't going to show up."

I swear I had entered the living room quiet as a mouse, but somehow, she'd sensed my presence without even looking at me.

"Aunt . . . Aunt Patricia?" I asked, moving closer to get a better view of her.

She turned to face me, and her lips spread into a wide smile on her round, caramel face. She had to be at least in her mid-fifties, but she didn't look a day over forty. She was beautiful, and although she was seated, I could tell that she was in good shape. She should have been a poster child for the phrase "Black Don't Crack," because she was over there giving me a run for my money. Her skin was smooth, and she looked as vibrant as a model on a magazine. She rocked a neat, wand curled sew-in with a middle part closure, and she was dressed casually in a black Gucci T-shirt, a pair of light blue jeans, and a pair of all-black Nike Roshes.

How is she older than me, but is looking way better? I thought to myself, suddenly wishing that I'd gone upstairs to change first.

"Jackie!" Aunt Patricia stood up and rushed to wrap me into a tight hug. "Oh my God, baby, it's been too long!"

"Fifteen years," I said, trying to muster up a smile, but I couldn't.

"Yes, indeed. Fifteen *long* years that I'm *so* sorry about!" she pulled away and looked me up and down. "Well, I don't know why you have on this granny suit, but you're looking good, girl. I guess you ain't have much to do in prison but eat and work out, huh?" She motioned for me to have a seat beside her on the couch, and I obliged, sitting on her right side.

"Actually, now that I think about it, I haven't seen you since you and my dad got into it a long time ago."

"Yeah, that mean devil kept me away from you. You and I, we were so close." Aunt Patricia's round brown eyes grew dark for a split second before coming back to the light. "He knew I couldn't have kids, so you were always the closest thing I'd get to it. He got mad at me and removed you from my life completely."

"And then he threw me out," I finished.

"He always had such a mean side," she shook her head. "He's probably the devil's favorite demon in hell right about now."

I didn't have to speak to let her know I agreed with her. I hadn't seen either one of my parents since the day they threw me to the streets, so when I was told he was dead while in prison, it didn't move me very much. Word on the streets was that when he died, my mother really lost it to her drug habit and had gone missing. Good riddance, because I wasn't going to be the one to find her.

"Why did you and my dad fall out in the first place?"

"Money issues," Aunt Patricia sighed and shrugged her shoulders. "I was in a position where I was making money, a lot of money, and he wanted some of it. See, I already had honed in on his drug problem and the fact that he and his wife were treating you badly. I knew if I gave him a penny, he would spend it on a rock before he spent it on you, sooo, I told him that. I told him to tell me what you needed and I'd get it myself. Well, he didn't like that. Felt like I was looking down on him, so he took you away from me. Told me that you didn't need me and filed a protection order on me filled with bogus lies."

"Wow."

"Yup. And you did. You needed me a whole lot. If he hadn't thrown you in the streets, you would have never met that slimy mothafucka that got you locked up! Fifteen years of your life down the drain!" Aunt Patricia turned to me and took my hands in her soft, cocoa butter-smelling ones. She looked deeply in my eyes with tears welling up in her own. "Oh, Jackie, it broke my heart to know you ended up where you did. It was my guilt that left all the money on your books, but it was also my guilt that kept me away. Do you forgive me?"

So that's where all the money I had in prison came from. That was always the biggest mystery to me. Aunt Patricia looked so miserable sitting beside me. Maybe I wasn't the only one who had suffered the past fifteen years, but I had to wonder. If her guilt was what kept her away, why was she here now?

"Aunt Patricia," I said kissing her hands, "it's nobody's fault but my own that I ended up in prison. Regardless of how my parents did me, those were the cards I was dealt, and I just played them all wrong. I lost the little that I did have left behind a nigga, and you know, maybe that was because of some daddy issues I had buried deep inside of me. But if being locked up for fifteen years taught me anything, it taught me to stand behind my decisions. It taught me that nobody *made* me stab that nigga. I did that on my own."

"That's my baby," she said and pulled me into a deep hug. "You get your smarts from your auntie, did I ever tell you that?"

"All the time when I was little," I smiled, drawing back from her, and she stood up like she was preparing to leave. "Are you leaving already? What time is it . . . five o'clock? We eat at six. You're welcome to join us if you'd like."

"Yes, I'm leaving," she said grabbing up her Gucci tote from the table beside the couch. "And that brings me to the meaning of this visit."

"What?" I didn't understand.

"I have a question to ask you before I leave, and it is a question that will determine your future."

"Okayyy," I said raising my brow at her. I hoped she hadn't started doing the same stuff that led my father to an accidental overdose.

"Do you hate him?"

"Hate who?"

"Demarcus Lancastor."

"Yes," I answered without having to think about it.

I didn't need fifteen years to tell me that. Although my time allowed me to accept my fate, it was one that I would never forgive Marco for. While I was in there rotting away, he was on the outside getting richer and richer. He'd caught a few cases for drugs, extortion, and money laundering, but he beat them every time. I used to be in the cafeteria of the prison seething in anger whenever he walked out of the courtroom wearing a glorious smile. With each passing day, my loathing for that man grew until it turned to a passionate hatred—a hate that burned a hole so deeply in my heart that love could never grow again.

"Do you have any regrets?" she asked, looking down at me.

"Yes. Only one."

"And what is that?"

"That I didn't kill that son of a bitch when I had the chance."

"Good answer." Patricia gave me an approving smile and nodded her head before reaching in her purse, pulling from it a large stack of money. "Now, let me go pay dear Ms. Trudy so we can get you out of here and into some clothes that suit you. My niece can't be walking around looking like she got dressed from a grandma's closet!"

"W-what?" I asked, trying to grasp her words.

She leaned down and kissed both of my cheeks before placing her hands on them.

"Twenty thousand dollars for your freedom." She was so close to me that I could smell the minty freshness on her breath as she shined her white teeth in my face. "I would have paid ten times that, because, you, my dear, *are* priceless. Go upstairs and grab anything you need, then meet me in the black Maybach parked at the end of the street. We have much to discuss."

Chapter 3

If anybody would have told me that my aunt Patricia was the head of an underground drug cartel, I would have laughed in their face and called them stupid. But that was *before* I rode in the back of her Maybach with her, and way before I pulled up to her mansion in Towne Lake.

"Auntie, you live here?" I asked in amazement.

"Yes," she said proudly as the driver pulled into her half circle driveway in front of her tandem garage. She grinned and grabbed my hand to pull me out of the car when the driver opened her door. "This is my two-story, four-bedroom, four-bathroom, 4,000 square foot home. Correction, this is *our* home. Come on so I can explain some things to you."

Without a question, I followed her to the front door, but not before getting a peek at the other houses in the neighborhood. Everybody who lived there *had* to be millionaires or something, because I'd never seen houses that big before.

The one I lived in with Marco all those years ago could fit *inside* one of those houses, and that was saying something, because his house was big. The moment I stepped foot inside Aunt Patricia's, I mean *our,* home, I felt my stomach drop. She had a fountain with a naked angel spewing water from his mouth into water filled with—

"Are those fish?" I leaned down and saw live fish swimming carefree in the clear water of the fountain. "Oh my God, Auntie. You have to be rich to have some shit like this in your home."

"Come on," she told me. "Let me show you around before I take you upstairs to your room."

She gave me a quick rundown of the house and introduced me to the help. Her main housekeeper's name was Gloria, and she was a nice, chocolate-skinned older woman who looked to be in her upper sixties. Aunt Patricia then took me to the basement and showed me her home theater and the dance floor she had built next to it.

"I always wanted a dance floor in my house," she admitted to me when she showed me the bar room in the basement. "And now I have someone to shake my old ass with!"

"I'm old now, too," I giggled and sat on a bar stool, while she was on the other side acting as bartender. "Or at least I feel like it after being holed up with all those old drug heads."

"Girl, stop!" she exclaimed, pulling out a full bottle of Patrón from the fridge. "You don't even look a minute older than twenty-five!"

"That's practically how old I was when I got locked up," I said, watching her pour both of us shots of the liquor. "Like you said, I didn't have much to do but work out and eat. I put on some pounds but curved them out. I guess I do look good for my age, huh?"

"Damn right! And once we get you out of those clothes, you're gon' show these little heffas what you're working with. But right now, you look like somebody named Edna!"

"Anna Mae!" I joined in on her clowning me. It was like no time had passed between us. I felt like I was a teenager, and she was my cool-ass aunt all over again.

"Girl, shut yo' crazy ass up!" she said, howling with laughter. "Take this damn shot so we can celebrate you finally being back home!"

We took one shot, and then followed it by three more. Before I knew it, we were both on the dance floor stepping to R. Kelly's "Step in the Name of Love" like two best friends finally reunited. We danced and laughed until finally, the song went off and we sat along the mirrored wall, worn out. I figured that would be the best time to ask her the questions swarming around in my mind. The last time I saw her, she was living in a one-bedroom apartment not far away from our house in the hood. How could she afford all of this? Not only that, how was she able to pay Tru $20,000? She had held the stack of money in her perfectly manicured hands like it wasn't nothing. Also, how had she pulled the strings to get me out of the halfway house without anyone sticking their noses in my business?

"Auntie, how can you afford all of this? And what did you mean when you said we had business to discuss?"

"I guess it's time for me to do some explaining, isn't it?" she said, leaning back on the wall behind her. "I wish you would have asked me this before I had all those damn shots, child."

"Auntie—"

"OK," Aunt Patricia said. "I'm going to give it to you straight, just like that Patrón. I got all of this," she waved her hands around, "because I am the widow of a drug kingpin. The best drug lord to ever bless the state of Texas."

"Who?" I asked, trying to think of any other names that I knew of, but drew up a blank. I could only pinpoint one. "The only kingpin I knew of was Antonio Lancastor, Marco's father."

"*Ding, ding, ding!* Boy, you are bright, aren't you?"

"W-w-what? Auntie, you were married to Antonio?"

"Yes," she answered, and her face became dreamy. "I was. We were just getting to know each other around the time your father started his mess, and although it hurt me to stay away from you, I had my own life to live. We were married five years after that, the same year you went to prison. I kept my last name, though, only because his ex-wife was spiteful enough to keep his. He was the best thing that ever happened to me. He was loyal, honest, and always took care of home. It never bothered him that I could not have children. He always said it didn't matter to him, and that he could have me all to himself." She stopped to smile happily to herself before continuing. "He was a good man, and I just wish I could say the same about his son."

"So you guys were together while Marco and I were?"

"Apparently, but I found out about your relationship with Marco too late," she said, nodding her head. "But around that time, Marco had many different women, and I'm sorry to say, that house he had you living in was not his only home. His outrageous spending habits were one of the many things that used to drive Antonio up a wall. Marco was supposed to inherit the throne, but every day, he showed his father that he was not ready. When the cancer hit, Antonio had just remade his will. Nobody knew it, but he had appointed someone he knew in charge of his empire."

"Who?"

"Me. You see, I was more than a housewife. Yes, I could clean, and cook the best chicken that man ever tasted in his life, but I knew how to flip a brick too. I have always been good with math, so the drug game was nothing to me. My innovative business ideas marketed his product in ways he never thought possible. I helped him bring in more green than he'd seen in his whole career as a dope man, and the fact that I have the aim of a marksman was an added bonus. That's why when he died last year, I became the queen of Houston. It wasn't the most desired lifestyle, but I would ride to the moon and back with that man if he needed me to. You would have loved him."

The look on her face was such a happy one that I was sure she was telling the truth. The smile she had on her face as she went down memory lane was the same one she wore when she saw me for the first time in fifteen years.

"I bet Marco wasn't too happy about his father choosing you over him."

"No." The smile wiped instantly from her face. "And that brings me to why we're here. That boy is like the tack in the elephant's foot, too small for me to reach. His father wasn't even in the dirt for three months before he started a war with me."

"War?"

"Yes," she said. "I know y'all had the news in prison and in the halfway house. There is a new gang running around, wreaking havoc on the city, called DBD."

"Yeah, I watched a few stories about them while on the inside. 'Death Before Dishonor,' right?" I nodded my head. "The stories were always running while an episode of some ratchet reality TV show was on, so I never saw too many of them. But last week at the house I saw they held a couple people hostage at a hair salon."

"Just Right."

"Just right what?"

"That's the name of the hair salon. I know because I own it, along with the six other businesses they terrorized. They killed five people at the salon that day, trying to send a message, one of them being one of my closest friends, Tamika.

DBD is a gang full of handpicked soldiers whose sole purpose is to shut this empire down."

"Handpicked by who?"

"Demarcus Lancastor," she said, looking me square in the eyes. "He is a cold, bitter man who will stop at nothing until my husband's empire is in shambles at my feet."

"Oh my God, Auntie," I said and put my hand on her shoulder. "I'm sorry."

"I have to be completely honest with you about why you're here, Jackie," she told me, wiping away the tears at the corners of her eyes. "I did get you out of there, and Trudy is to pee for you and also report that you are working for the next year. I have also paid off your probation officer, Dan Roberts, to make false records of your progress. Although you won't be free by law for a year, I have granted you the livelihood to do whatever you want forever."

"That sounds to me like you *have* been completely honest with me, then," I said, but she shook her head.

"As I said before, you, my dear niece, are priceless. Whereas I can still handle the professional side of this business, I am too old to move in the streets like a soldier. Which is why I will be asking this of you, versus demanding."

"Asking what, Aunt Patricia?" I was growing antsy now. The look on her face read one of determination and malice. "What do you need?"

"I want you to finish what you started. I cannot get close to Demarcus, but you can. I want you to kill him, Jackie."

Chapter 4

OK. I know what you are all thinking, and it probably goes something like, "Jackie, you just served fifteen years for trying to kill this man! Steer your lifeboat straight. It isn't your war to fight." And if that *is* what you're thinking, you're completely wrong. It *was* my war to fight as much as it was my aunt Patricia's. The best years of my life were wasted all behind a moth-afucka who could have left me where he found me. Aunt Patricia didn't have to do much per-suading after she popped the question. I won't lie and say I didn't think about the possibility of going back to jail, but with the way my aunt's reach was, I didn't think that would be a prob-lem. Still, Aunt Patricia told me she would give me the night to sit and think on her request. She warned me that it would not be a simple task, and the job would entail me getting my hands more than a little dirty.

The next morning, I sat in my new bedroom on the California king-sized bed. The foot of it was round, and the headboard had my initials carved big in cursive. The wood of the bed was black, much like the rest of the furniture in the bedroom, and looked darker in pigment along the snowy white walls. I had a sixty-inch TV on the wall in front of my bed, and don't get me started on the walk-in closet. It was the size of another bedroom, and Aunt Patricia had taken the liberty to go shopping for me. There were many of the same pieces, just different sizes in there, but I assumed it was because she didn't know my size. I wasn't complaining, though. It had been so long since names like Marc Jacobs, Fendi, and Gucci blessed my body, so I was thankful, if anything. My bathroom was to die for, and I mean that in the figurative sense. The light fixtures above the long mirror looked like crystals and lit the room up brilliantly. The shower had an overhead faucet with a gray and black tile decoration that matched the ledge of the hot tub in the far corner. I'd woken up before the sun had even come out, just to spend two hours in the bathroom. It had been so long since I took a lavish bath like that, I even used one of the purple bath bombs Aunt Patricia had under the sink to accent the mood.

I sat on my bed, contemplating the outfits I had sprawled out on it before I finally settled on a long pink sundress with a slit in it that came all the way up to my thigh. The low cut V-neck showed off the cleavage caused by my soft breasts, and it nicely displayed my ass. My ass looked so big that even *I* wanted to squeeze it—both cheeks. Slipping on a pair of silver thong sandals that matched the silver hoop earrings in my ears, I decided to make my way downstairs to give Aunt Patricia my final answer.

As soon as I opened the door, the delicious aroma of bacon being fried blessed my nostrils and led me to where my aunt was. Sure enough, there she was, right beside Gloria, whipping up a big breakfast. Aunt Patricia was wearing a silk peach blouse and a pair of ankle capris that were tight on her big butt and thighs. Naturally, I headed toward the counter by the stove, where a pan and a carton of eggs sat. Before I could even crack one open, I felt a hand swat the back of my arm.

"Girl, sit your ass down and let me make you breakfast!" Aunt Patricia pointed for me to sit down at the dining room table. "You aren't about to mess up my eggs."

"I know how to cook," I laughed.

"Well, you don't have to in this kitchen, chile," Gloria said, wiping her hands on her apron. "Go on in there and sit down like your auntie said."

"You clean up nice, by the way," Aunt Patricia added over her shoulder.

Reluctantly, I did as I was told and waited until Gloria placed a hot plate of food in front of me. She set another one down right across from me, and Aunt Patricia sat down. Gloria came back with two tall glasses filled with orange juice before taking her leave to another part of the house. I waited for Aunt Patricia to get settled, and the two of us held hands, like we used to do, and said our grace before digging in.

"Oh my God, this is so good!" I moaned with a mouth full of hash browns and bacon.

"Girl, you better slow down before you choke!"

I paid her no mind and kept on stuffing my face like nobody's business. It took me all of six minutes to scarf down the entire meal, and when I glanced up, I noticed that she still had half of her food on her plate. Smiling sheepishly, I just shrugged my shoulders.

"I guess that prison mind-set hasn't completely left me just yet."

"You can say that again," she said, chuckling, and handed me a napkin from the center of the table. "Did you give my request some thought last night?"

"I honestly didn't even need a whole night to think on it," I replied after I wiped the grease from my mouth. "The answer was yes the second you asked the question."

"I need you to understand what this means." Her fiery eyes were on me, and her expression was serious.

"I know. It means you need me to put a bullet in the middle of his head, right?"

"Yeah and no. It means I need you to put a bullet in his head, but before you do that, I need you to learn how my soldiers move."

"What do you mean? You want me to be a soldier?"

"No, definitely not," she chuckled again. "You're royalty compared to them. I want you to lead them. I want you in charge of all drug trade in the state of Texas. The job Marco should have taken instead of gallivanting around the city like a fucking crybaby."

Now that was new to me. I thought she just wanted me to body Marco and keep it pushing. I didn't think she was asking me to be a part of a drug cartel. I took a long swig of my orange juice, trying to buy myself time. Her eyes pierced my expression, looking for any indication of what I might be thinking, but I think I did a pretty good job holding a poker face.

"Auntie, I don't even know how to shoot a gun."

"You'll learn."

"I don't know how to flip a brick. I don't even know the difference between good and bad product."

"I'll teach you."

"Who's going to teach me to shoot a gun?"

Ding! Dong!

The sound of the doorbell ringing interrupted our conversation, but by the sparkle in Aunt Patricia's eyes, she must have known who was at the front door. Gloria must have let the person in, because the next thing I knew, a newcomer had entered the kitchen. I was thrown completely for a loop because I was suddenly staring at what had to be a chocolate god. The man was about six foot two with a muscular build. He had a smooth baby face and bright, mahogany-colored eyes with fans for eyelashes. He had juicy lips that I wanted to suck just to see what they tasted like, and a jawline that would make Idris Alba jealous. He was dressed simply in a navy blue Nike sweat suit, complete with a pair of all-white Air Max 90s.

"Braxton, this is my niece—"

"Jackie," he finished.

Ohhh! His voice was deep and sensual too. He held his hand out to me, and I placed mine in it and tried to tell my pussy to calm herself down there.

"How do you know my name?" I asked.

"Pat Pat has been talking about how you were moving in with her for the past month now," he told me, then gave me a slick smile, showing off a small gap between his front teeth that made him even sexier. "Plus, I'm the one who had to drop off the payment to your probation officer. You was locked up for stabbin' a nigga, right? I gotta watch you."

My mouth dropped open, and I made a sound that not even I recognized. The two of them seemed to enjoy my reaction because they burst into laughter. I hurried to close my mouth and regain my composure.

"He put his hands on me," I told him. "I did what I had to do."

"Good," he said, giving me his approval. "That means you'll do what you have to do on the streets."

"The streets?" I asked, and Braxton looked at my aunt with a raised brow.

"You ain't tell her what's up for the day?" he asked my aunt.

"We were actually just getting to that part before you got here," she told him and focused her attention back on me. "Jackie, this is who is going to teach you everything you need to know about how to move in the streets."

"How to be a street general," he corrected her.

"Same thing!"

It dawned on me that I had never given her an official answer. I looked back and forth between the two of them and thought about what I wanted to do. I didn't know the first thing to being a "street general," as Braxton put it, but then again, I wanted Marco dead as bad as I wanted to breathe. Whatever I had to do to make that possible was OK with me.

"All right," I told them. "When do we start?"

"Now," he said and nodded his head toward the front door. "Your car is still running outside."

"My . . . car?"

"Yeah, come on, ma. I put your tank on full, and we wasting gas," he said, grabbing me by my hand again and throwing up a peace sign at my aunt. "All right, Pat Pat! I'ma fuck with you later."

I didn't even have time to grab anything, not even a purse, before I was already outside. But once I saw what was waiting there for me, I didn't care about a purse.

"This is *not* my car."

"I look like a liar to you, ma?" Braxton asked and got in the driver's seat of the bright red

Porsche. "911 GTS. I think she fits your swag. What you think?"

"Hell yes!" I eagerly hopped in the car and ran my hands all over the interior of the vehicle. "Oh my God. This is really mine?"

"Yes," he said, putting the car in drive and speeding around the circle driveway and away from the house. "Unless you want me to take it back to the dealership."

"You picked this out?"

"Yes," he said. "Pat Pat showed me a picture of you a minute ago." He averted his eyes from the street to look me up and down. "I mean, you were a little younger in the picture, but I thought this would fit you."

I rolled my eyes at him and called him an asshole under my breath. He turned on the radio, and I let my window down to feel my long hair blow in the wind while he drove.

"You from here?" I asked even though I knew he couldn't have been. His accent was one I hadn't heard before.

"Nah," he said. "I'm a Midwestern boy. Detroit."

"What you doing here, then?"

"No opportunities where I'm from," he answered simply. "I can be a king here freely. Where I'm from, it's too many niggas after the same position, and nobody wanna make money together."

"I guess I can understand that. How old are you?"

"Twenty-nine. Why? You wanna get your cougar thing on with me?"

"No!" I said and couldn't hold the laugh that spurted from my lips. "And I'm only six years older than you, so I don't think that qualifies me as a cougar."

"I was just fuckin' with you." He shot me a look I couldn't read, but his eyes lingered on my small waist. "But real shit, you look way younger than that."

"They used to tell me that when I left prison, I would look like I aged double my time, and I saw it happen right before my eyes while I was in there. But I always told myself that wouldn't be me."

"Why?"

"Because I knew eventually I would get out, you know? And when I did, I wanted to be just as bad as I was when I got there. I want a husband and a normal life." I paused and grinned at him. "Well, as normal as I can get it."

"What was it like on the other side?"

"At first, the bitches up in there tried to fuck with me 'cause I'm pretty. I got cut up a couple of times, but soon they learned that these hands ain't shit to play with."

"You can fight?" he asked and looked at me like I was lying.

"Niggaaa," I raised my eyebrow at him. "I gets *down!*"

"OK," he said, laughing, "Miss Get Down, tell me somethin'."

"What?"

"You was down for fifteen years. Were you eating pussy?" he asked, and the serious expression on his face is what made me lift my lip in disgust at him.

"No, nigga," I said, then turned my face out the window. "I had them licking on my pussy, though. I busted so many times in those bitches' mouths I lost count."

I didn't turn back to face him to see his reaction, but the fact that he had no further questions told me all I needed to know. We were quiet for a while until he started to explain that day's game plan. He told me that he was taking me to one of the hood spots to introduce me to some of the young niggas that would be under me.

He took me to a neighborhood about five blocks away from the one I grew up in, but it looked the exact same. Some of the owners kept their homes up, while some had let them go to complete turmoil. I smiled at the scenery because it was all too familiar. A group of girls who looked to be about twelve were posted on the sidewalk with their bikes, probably talking about boys. A few teenagers were walking their pit bulls, and, of course, there were the junkies posted outside a family-owned liquor store, arguing over who drank the last of the bottle. As we drove, everybody's eyes went to the red car rolling down their block. Strangely, it didn't make me feel awkward. In fact, I even nodded my head at a couple of people as we passed.

"We're here," Braxton said, pulling in to the back of what looked to be an abandoned house.

"You sure?" I asked. "It looks like there are boards over the windows."

"Lesson one," Braxton said, reaching over me to get into the glove compartment, "never be deceived by the 'look' of something. Everything ain't always what it seems." He handed me something, and I peeped quickly that it was a small firearm. It was small but fit perfectly in my hand. "That's a nine millimeter Glock. You know how to work one of them?"

"Nope."

"Don't trip," he told me, cutting the car off. "Nobody taught me how to shoot or aim. My OG just gave me a gun one day and let me have at it. Now, I don't think there's a nigga around who could fuck with me when it comes to gunplay. Just aim. Shoot."

He gave me a little tutorial before he got out of the car.

"Wait!" I called. "You never told me why I would need a gun!"

He was too far away from the car to pay attention to me. I had no choice but to jump out after him and follow him around the house to the front door. He waited for me to get there before he did something that I didn't see coming. He kicked the door down.

Bang! Bang!

His gun sounded off before I could register what was happening. In the house, there were a few fiends passed out, high, on the filthiest mattress I had ever seen in my life. The other people in the house were the distributors who scattered like roaches once the door burst open. Braxton's bullets caught one of them in the back, and he dropped instantly. The sight of his blood made me realize that this was really happening.

"DBD *who,* niggas?" Braxton shouted, pulling his trigger.

Gunfire filled the entire house. I jumped to the side, behind an old couch, when a bullet whizzed past my head. The dress I wore made it hard to maneuver, but with my life at stake, I made it do what it do.

"Nigga, this DBD over everything! Opp-ass nigga!" one of the little niggas shouted from wherever they were perched.

"Watch out!" I yelled to Braxton when I peeked over the couch.

He was doing his thing without me and had already killed two of the four DBD gang members. He was taking cover behind a desk and didn't even know a scope was making its way up his back all the way to the back of his head. I followed the scope with my eyes until I found the source. The nigga holding the gun didn't look to be older than twenty-one, but it was him or Braxton. I opted for the latter.

Bang! Bang!

The power from the gun made my shoulders jerk when I stood up and fired at the kid, but I kept my footing and didn't fall.

"Umph!" the kid groaned and fell to the ground from the bullet wound in his chest.

There was one last shot and a loud thud that filled the air before everything ceased. The two fiends that had been passed out on the mattress were now asleep forever. They must have gotten caught in the crossfire because they both had multiple bullet holes in their backs. Slowly, I walked up to the person whose life I was responsible for taking. His eyes were still open, and his gun still hung loosely in his hand. I thought I would feel something, anything. I was not God. Who was I to take a life? But surprisingly, I felt . . . nothing. Nothing at all. I had a choice to make, and I knew I made the right one.

"Let's go," Braxton said and grabbed my arm. "Come on!"

We ran out of the house, me gripping the bottom of my skirt, all the way back to the car behind the house. Everything had happened so fast, I was still trying to process it in my head. I was confused, but even more so, I was angry.

"What the fuck!" I yelled when we were already back on the main street. I couldn't help it, I punched his arm as hard as I could. "What the hell was that!"

Braxton threw my fists back at me so I would stop hitting him. He was quiet, like I hadn't just asked him a question, so I cocked my gun back and put it to his temple while he drove.

"I said, what the fuck was that?"

"Practice," he replied, not bothered at all by the fact that I had a gun to his head. "Put that thing down before you hurt yourself."

"Practice?" I yelled. "*Practice?* I could have been killed!"

"Exactly," Braxton said, hopping on the interstate. "No better way to practice than in a real-life situation. Now, put that gun down . . . please. I'm on your side."

"How are you on *my* side when you want to see me dead?" I asked, slowly lowering my weapon.

"I knew you weren't going to die."

"How?"

"You have Pat Pat's blood in you. I saw the fire in your eyes the moment I met you. You don't even know it yet."

"Know what?"

"You were bred for this. You killed a nigga, and I bet you don't even feel bad about it. Word of advice, though, if you plan on getting close enough to Marco to kill him, head shots only, ma."

I was silent for a second because he was right. I killed somebody, and the only thing I felt was a growl in my stomach because I was hungry again. I shook my head, trying to get the dead kid's face out of it.

"How did you know they were there?" I asked. "DBD, I mean."

"They been around setting up shop in all our old trap spots," he said. "And the only reason they know the locations of them is because—"

"Marco is telling them where they are," I finished for him. "Damn. That nigga is older than me and still being childish."

"We used to be coo'," Braxton told me. "He asked me to join his little movement, teach his people everything I knew."

"Why didn't you?"

"You don't bite the hand that feeds you," he answered simply. "Pat Pat always been like a mom to me. She took me in when I was twenty-one and new to the state. She found me asleep at a bus stop the day after I got into this savage brawl. I broke a nigga's neck with my bare hands. To this day, I don't know what made her stop for me, but she asked me if I wanted a job. I asked her what she needed me to do, and she said 'protect me.' Ever since then, that's what I've been doin'. I'll body an entire group of niggas behind Pat Pat."

"That's deep."

"As fuck," he agreed, getting off the interstate. "That's why when she asked me to train you to take her place, it wasn't a question."

"Wait, train me to take *her* place? That's not what she told me."

"I know," he said, pulling into the parking lot of a business. "But if she would have told you that she was training you to be the new Queen Pin of Houston, I guarantee you that you wouldn't be in this car with me right now."

"If she would have told me that she was sending me to put in work already, I wouldn't have been in this car with you either." I cut my eyes at him, and he shot me back a sly smile.

"Actually, she don't know that I took you on that hit with me. I was supposed to handle that before I pulled up on y'all."

"What?"

"Yeah, so don't tell her that," he said, opening his door.

"Where are we now?"

"Where I was supposed to take you, the gun range. Put that 9 back in the glove compartment. The registered guns are in the trunk. I hope you're ready, because you're not leaving here until you're a pro."

"Can we go get some food first?"

"You think Marco is going to wait for you to get some food when he has an automatic pointed at your head and an extended clip?"

I sighed deeply and put the gun back where I pulled it from. It was going to be a long day.

Chapter 5

"Oooh, Daddy! It's been forever since you fucked me like that!"

The woman lay her head on her man's shoulder, whirling her fingers around the short hairs on his chest. She was in love, and the feeling that he gave her was a blissful one. Sabrina Tillman looked up into Marco's sexy face and sucked his bottom lip one more time.

"Girl, you better stop before Daddy gives you round four," he joked and kissed her forehead.

"I won't complain," she said, lowering her eyes at him. "You know I'm always down to fuck."

"I wish I could slang this dick for you one more time," Marco said, sliding over so her head hit the pillow, "but I gotta go. There's a few things that I need to tend to today, and I already took half the day off to lay up with you."

Brina pouted and stuck her bottom lip out. The high she still had from the two lines of coke she'd snorted was still on ten, and her pussy was throbbing to get hit one more time. Marco had always been the only man who was able to fulfill all of her sexual desires. Since she'd met him all those years ago, she could honestly say he was the only man to dive into her sea of gooey love since. Well, besides her own fingers occasionally, when he was out handling business.

"OK, baby," she said and sat up in the bed to watch him get himself together.

Marco was like wine. He was the kind of man that got better with time, and she couldn't help but to twirl her finger on her clit, watching him throw his clothes back on. She loved when he didn't take a shower after they fucked. She enjoyed when he left the house with her scent still on him. It made her feel like she had left her mark.

"Mmm," she moaned as her fingers worked magic between her thick brown thighs. Her pussy was a little hairy that day, but Marco never minded a little hair in his food. "Marco, you are so sexy."

"You still think that way after all of these years?" Marco paused to watch her. He thoroughly enjoyed when she pleasured herself.

He was starting to regret that he was fully dressed. He could see that her already-wet pussy was starting to soak. She nodded her head to his question and stroked her own clit until her back arched on the bed and a stream of juice shot from her pussy. Her loud moan filled the room, and he felt his manhood grow. Quickly shaking the thoughts of diving back in her to see what her new ocean felt like, he completed getting dressed.

"Marco," Brina whimpered to herself with her eyes shut.

When she opened them, she expected to see Marco still standing there, but instead, she was looking at a wall and an open bedroom door. She hated sharing her husband with the streets; however, she loved all of the money he brought home. She enjoyed living without a worry, so the streets were the only bitch that she was willing to share Marco with. Sighing, she got out of her comfortable bed, grabbed her Victoria's Secret robe from her closet, and put it on. She hadn't even stepped out of the master bedroom of the home she had made with Marco before she felt someone run straight into her legs.

"Mommy! Mommy! Can I have lunch now? Daddy just left and told me to ask you for a sandwich."

Brina scooped her five-year-old pride and joy, Demarcus Jr., into her arms and hugged him tight. In her entire life, Little Marco was one of the things that she had done right. After what she and Marco had done to his ex-girlfriend Jackie, she couldn't say she felt bad about fighting for her man, but she knew that the woman getting fifteen years in prison wasn't right. But she shrugged it off because at the end of the day, she was her own priority. Marco kept his promise to her and moved her to Houston, Texas, and loved on her ever since. When Little Marco was born, it was the best day of their lives. Marco finally had the heir he always wanted. She looked into her son's eyes and smiled at how much he looked like his father. Little Marco was still in his pajamas, which she was OK with since she didn't plan on going anywhere that day. When she placed a kiss on his forehead, she inhaled and smelled the strong scent of maple syrup.

"Smells like you tried to make yourself something to eat," she said and blew on his neck, making him cry out in a fit of giggles. "Come on, so I can make you a sandwich. Peanut butter and jelly, like always?"

Marco held his cellular phone to his ear and listened to the other end ring. While he was beating down Brina's walls, he had missed several calls from his partner, Roy. He was in the car on his way to his second house that he used as his place of business. It was also the place that he did his dirt without Brina knowing. It was actually the house that he lived in at one point with Jackie. He told Brina that he'd gotten rid of it, but truth be told, he never put it on the market to be sold. The phone rang three times before he heard the deep voice of his best friend answer the phone.

"Where the fuck you been at, bro?"

"I was handling some things at the crib, what's poppin'?"

"Nigga, somebody got us."

"What?" Marco felt the alarm well up in his chest.

"The house you just set up over there in the old hood, nigga. Every soldier in that bitch is bodied. I don't know who got us, but—"

"Nigga, what the fuck you mean you don't know who got us? It could only be one person! That bitch Patricia is tryin'a get back at us for that salon shit."

"That's what I was thinkin' too, but ain't shit been proven yet, boss."

"It don't gotta be proven," Marco snapped with boiling blood. He didn't realize how hard he had suddenly started to grip the phone until his right hand began to throb. "It's only one other person besides me and my dad who knew of the trap's existence. Tell everyone else who set up shop in my pop's old spots to pull back for now. We need to regroup."

"On it, my nigga."

"All right, I'ma get at you later."

He disconnected the call and tossed the phone on the passenger's seat. Gripping the steering wheel, he let his memory drive him because in all honesty, he didn't see anything that was in front of him. He saw nothing but red. Patricia had done nothing but stand in his way since the day his father met her. Antonio had fallen victim to the pussy, when he was the one who always told Marco how dangerous it was to fall in love. Maybe that was why Antonio brought her from his bed and made a seat for her at his table. It wasn't until Antonio died that Marco knew that he was not the heir to his father's empire anymore. He found that out at the repast, when the lawyer came to read to them Antonio's will. His father had left him a small fortune, but Antonio had left his entire estate to his wife, Patricia. That meant *everything*. The businesses, the stocks, the houses, the cars, and that also meant she was in charge of the cartel. Her. A woman who he hadn't even known half of his life. It infuriated him to the point that he stormed out of the home he was raised in and hadn't been back since.

The war was started out of spite. There could only be one ruler of Texas, and it would be a king, not a queen. Marco formed DBD to show everyone what happened when the wrong hand was bitten. At first, they started off with petty crimes against her, like robbing and setting up people in her camp. But then the crimes got bigger and more malicious. When they took over the salon, Marco counted on the fact that the last thing Patricia wanted to do was get the law involved. The salon was always the final drop of the week for all her illegal funds. That hadn't changed since Antonio was alive. When Marco made DBD raid the building, it was before any of those funds had been removed, and that made it the perfect setup. Because of the hostage situation with her employees, Patricia had no choice but to allow law enforcement access to her establishment when people lost their lives. Marco figured for sure that he had her where he wanted her. His thirst for power and reclaiming his rightful place on the throne caused him to suffer the worst loss in the war so far, however. Somehow, someway, the illegal drug money wasn't there when the building was searched. All they had were a couple of thugs who had just thrown their lives away for nothing, and the dead bodies of the innocent.

He should have known that Patricia wasn't going to let that situation fly, and should have been standing on ten toes. All he knew was, he would be smarter next time. He'd gotten the message that Patricia was trying to send, loud and clear. But he didn't care. He wouldn't stop until her heart did.

"I'ma kill that bitch," he said, pressing harder on the gas pedal of his BMW. "If it's the last thing I do."

Chapter 6

Six months later . . .

"Let me see what the fuck these niggas talkin' 'bout in this bitch," I said to myself, stepping out of my Porsche.

I was in a spaghetti strap black crop top that showed off the huge diamond in my belly button with a long flowy black skirt. On my head was one high, jumbo braid that came all the way down to my hip. Burgundy peep toe heels stabbed the concrete as I made my way into the hotel that I was at to meet a potential new connect. With me were four men from my camp, who were there to simply ensure my safety. One of them was carrying a briefcase as we all walked to the elevators together. I personally didn't like the venue for the meeting, simply because I naturally went into every situation with no trust. If I needed to pop off, I couldn't without being seen. The risk of being thrown back in jail for some bullshit was just not something I was willing to risk.

In the months that had gone by, my mind was given time to catch up with my body. Things weren't the same on the streets as they were when I was just a girlfriend. Back then, kids respected their OGs just off their title. Now, you had to brandish your pistol for a mothafucka to hear you.

"Jackie, I'm going to teach you what I had to learn by myself," Aunt Patricia had said to me after I'd been working the blocks for her for a few months. "You're a woman, but not only that, you're an older woman. A lot has changed, and the streets don't move the way they used to. Don't be scared to body *anybody* for disrespectin' you, understand me? These niggas feed off of *weakness,* and they'll try to get you before you get them."

At the time, her words were just that . . . words. But with each day of me moving around in the streets, I found the truth in what she was saying. If Braxton hadn't been with me during a couple of drops, Lord knows what would have happened to me. I was still learning the game and getting a grip on how it went, but being in a sea of sharks meant I had to learn fast. However, it only took me six months to get used to my newfound position. My presence was one that brought chills, and the way I viewed the world was completely different. Gone was the timid girl who let everyone walk over her, and welcomed was the grown-ass woman that would put a bullet in the brain of anybody who tried her. The streets knew me as JO the Ruler, because that was exactly who I was. No product entered the city unless it went through me first. Houston was such a hot market for drug trade right then, and anyone with some work wanted theirs to be distributed throughout the city. That's why I was at the hotel that night. It was kind of like a job interview. In these interviews, I would test the product presented to me, and if it was good, I'd put an offer on the table.

Bzzz! Bzzz!

I took my cell phone from my burgundy clutch and answered it when I saw who it was.

"Hello?"

"You inside?"

"Just walked in. Getting on the elevator now," I told Braxton. "You positioned?"

"Yup," he responded. "My snipers have the perfect view of the balcony, too. If anything goes wrong, we'll start droppin' 'em like flies. How you feelin'?"

I pressed the button that would take me to the seventh floor, where Leon Sanchez's presidential suite was. When he asked his question, I instinctively glanced in my clutch to check on the two extra clips I had in it. My pistol was strapped securely on the inside of my left thigh, waiting patiently to be unleashed from its holster.

"I'm coo'," I said. "I'm just trying to get this shit over with. Can we get some Chinese tonight? I'm starving."

"You've been talkin' about Chinese food all week," he laughed.

"I know, and after tonight, I'm sure I'm going to deserve some."

"Yeah, yea. You just make sure that you secure that bag."

"And if I do, what you gon' get me?"

"I can *show* you better than I can *tell* you," his voice lowered with his words, and I smiled.

"Uh-huh. We gon' see," I said, still smiling when the elevator doors opened. "I'm up here now. Showtime."

I disconnected the phone and put it back in my clutch. Then I stepped off the elevator with my goons, and we walked down the hallway toward room 736. Even if I didn't know where to go, it would have been obvious. A Mexican security guard stood on either side of the door, wearing black suits and sunglasses. If I didn't know this was real life, I would have burst out laughing. They looked like the CIA or some shit, and when they saw me, the hard expressions on their faces didn't change.

"Business?" one of them asked me and eyed my security.

"JO. Leon is expecting me."

When I stated my name, both men shot each other confused looks. The same look that always came across a nigga's face when they found out JO was a girl. Like I said, in six months, I put in so much work, I'd surpassed the people who had been in the game years before me. Aunt Patricia would joke and say I was a natural-born hustler, but in all actuality, the streets were all I had. She breathed new life into me when she got me from Trudy's, and at first, I was intimidated. But after that first day with Braxton, everything just came naturally. The goal was not to only secure the bag, it was to secure the entire empire.

"Welcome," the other security guard finally said and granted me entrance to the room.

When I entered, I didn't pay attention to any of the bells and whistles of the suite. I wasn't there to drool over how nice the kitchen area was or to take a selfie in the bathroom mirror.

I was there for one reason, and that reason was out on the balcony, sitting at a table waiting on me. I walked with my head high, ignoring Leon's goons glaring at me when I passed them. Only two of my men came on the balcony with me, while the other two kept an eye on Leon's people. It was almost nine o'clock, but that night, Houston was still warm. There was a table for two outside on the huge balcony, and I saw that Leon was sitting there, smoking a Cuban cigar.

"Leon," I greeted him by flashing a smile with my perfect teeth. "Pleasure to meet you."

Leon was a stout Mexican man with a thick mustache and thick eyebrows. The gray designer suit he wore made his skin look dull, but brought out his sapphire-colored eyes. He was not handsome in the least bit, but the three diamond rings he sported nonchalantly proved that he reeked of money. He stood to his feet respectfully, and I saw that he was exactly my height . . . without heels.

"JO!" he said with a thick Spanish accent. He took my hand in his and kissed it with his rough lips. "The pleasure is all mine." He motioned for me to take a seat, and I did. "And when I say that, believe me. It has been a long time since

I even entertained the thought of allowing my work to be pushed through Houston. But, with Antonio dead, I have been more open to the possibility."

"Excuse my ignorance, but what do you mean 'with Antonio dead'? He was a man whose name wasn't just respected worldwide, he was worshipped."

"To those who took a chance on him, not me. You see, with me, I don't just pay attention to the face that is sitting before me doing business, I pay attention to the faces of those around it as well. The last time I was sitting across from somebody brokering this same deal, it was Antonio's son, Demarcus, who I spoke to. I knew, from just that one meeting, that he would be a problem. Not just for me, but for Antonio as well."

"How?"

"When Demarcus met me, it was on the strength of his father's name. He was there to be conducting business for Antonio, but still, he was only thinking of himself. Demarcus tried to barter a deal for himself on the side, one that Antonio knew nothing about."

"He was going to cross his father?"

"Yes," Leon nodded his head. "But what he asked me for, I could not give."

"Because that deal would have surely started a war. Well, the war that we're in now, but way sooner."

"That, my dear, is a bad thing for you and him. But it is a good thing for you and me."

"How is that?"

"You can thank your current connect, Alfonzo, for running his mouth about how much product is moved through Houston a week. That is the type of business that we need for distribution."

"Before we continue this conversation, Leon, I need a sample of your work first. If you don't mind."

"Of course," he said and motioned for one of his men to come out onto the balcony. The tall Mexican man brought Leon a brick of cocaine with a small knife on top of it. Leon used the knife to poke a hole in the coke and pull some out on it. "Here you go, *mi amor*."

I took the knife and brought it close to my lips but not letting it touch them. When I stuck my tongue out and tasted the product, the tip of it instantly got numb.

"Mmm," I said and handed him the knife back. "That's some good shit."

"I wouldn't be wasting your time if it wasn't. Now let's cut to the chase, shall we? I got thirty of those bad boys for you. They're usually fifteen a pop, but for you, I'll do it for ten each."

"That's a pretty good deal, Leon, but I have to know," I clasped my hands on the table and looked him square in the eyes. "What's the catch?"

"No catch, just business. In order for us to seal this deal, at that price, you must cut off all business with Alfonzo. And you also must dispose of Demarcus."

Slowly, I opened my briefcase and pulled out three hundred of the five hundred thousand dollars from it, placing it in the center of the table.

"Done," I said and waited for his men to hand mine the two duffle bags. Standing up, I smiled and held my hand out for him to kiss before I left.

"Nice doing business with you."

"I should be the one saying that." I had one foot in the suite and the other still on the concrete of the balcony.

I winked at him and left. I didn't need to tell him that I'd kicked Alfonzo to the side weeks ago and that we already had plans to kill Marco. I just kept it cute and kept it pushing, smiling the entire way from the suite back to the elevator.

Bzzz! Bzzz!

"You done already? My men said you just left the balcony."

"You sound surprised, Brax," I said. "I learned from the best, remember? Didn't even have to pull out Sheila on 'em."

"I don't think we ever cleared that name for your gun, ma."

"Because *we* didn't have to. All *we* have to do is go get some Chinese. I'm already dressed up and everything!"

"Here you go. Just hurry ya ass up and get out of there so we can get this food."

Beep!

I glanced at my phone and saw that Aunt Patricia was trying to call me. I ended the phone call with Braxton, telling him I would see him in a few moments.

"What's up, Auntie?" I said.

"Hey, baby," her sweet voice came through the other end. "How did it go?"

"You already know I got that locked in, Auntie." I popped the trunk to my car and had my men toss the bags in it. "Leon asked for us to do something, though."

"And that is?"

"Eliminate our threat. He wants us to take Marco out."

"Figures. Especially with this war going on. But that task is easier said than done. Marco has been ghost for months!"

"I know," I said, getting in the car, starting it, and zooming away from the hotel. "DBD hasn't turned up on us in minutes, but I feel like this is the quiet before the storm. Marco is going to slip up, and when he does, I'll be there to watch him fall."

"I believe you," she said. "It's all about timing; don't rush nothing. Anyway, I wanted to talk to you about something else. As you know, my birthday is coming up next Saturday."

"How could I ever forget!"

"Oh, hush up," she laughed. "I don't need your smart mouth, girl. Any who, I was thinking about having a big party. Like a big-ass party, Jackie, and I want *everyone* to come out and enjoy it with me."

"I think we can make that happen, but next weekend is pretty short notice."

"Then we need to start getting the invites out now, don't we?"

"OK, we can start once I get home. I'm about to go eat with Braxton."

"He finally asked you on a date, huh?"

"No!" I laughed because I was pretty sure she put her phone closer to her ear just to hear what my response was going to be. "We're just going to grab a bite of food together, but it is *not* a date."

"Listen here, Jackie, y'all are both too old to be playin' them games now. You better hurry up and get to that man before one of these nappy-headed hoes do! You need to have a baby before your eggs dry up!"

"Auntie!" I exclaimed, checking my rearview mirror and seeing that Braxton was right behind me. "You know that I gotta let you go on that note."

"Uh-huh, whatever. Don't forget to come home in the morning. I love you, Jackie."

"I love you too, Auntie. Bye."

Braxton did what he promised to do and took me to get my Chinese food. Along the way, he also bought me two bottles of champagne to celebrate a good day's work. We didn't pop the bottles until I somehow ended up back at his house. The fact that I'd found him attractive since the first day we met didn't mix well with the buzz that had snuck up on me. We sat next to each other on his dark brown suede couch in his living room, and I was trying my best to focus on the movie we were watching. It was hard to keep myself in check because my pussy jumped whenever he did something simple, like smile.

"This shit ain't even scary, man," he said, picking up the DVD cover from his coffee table. "Who the fuck are these actors?"

"You think you could do any better?" I teased. "Come on, you gotta give it to them. They did a pretty good job for it to be a low-budget movie."

"Well, it's obvious you should have been in this movie," he said, downing the rest of his drink.

"Why is that?" I asked and inhaled deep when he scooted so close to me that I could smell the cologne on his neck.

"Because you sitting here acting like you were watching this movie, when you and I both know you've been watching *me* this whole time, ma."

And there I was thinking that I was being low-key about my lustful stares. Fuck it, I was already caught up, and the champagne had already had a long talk with my pussy. It had been too long since a man had been inside of me, and I would be lying if I said I didn't want Braxton to be the one to knock out my cobwebs.

"It's because I think you're so sexy," I told him, scooting closer so that way, our lips brushed against each other with every word I spoke. "You wanna know what I've been wondering since I met you?"

"What?" His tone matched mine, soft and seductive.

"I find myself wondering, at least five times a day . . . how big your dick is. Is it thick and long like I pray it is? I wonder how it tastes and if it can make me scream. I wonder if you're the kind of nigga who would want to nut in my pussy or on my face. I'd let you do either . . . or both."

"Damn, ma," his hands began to fondle my body. I licked his bottom lip when his hands got to my breasts. "You're turning me on. Jail turned you into a freaky bitch."

"Can I be *your* freaky bitch?" I asked right before I felt his tongue swim inside of my mouth.

We tongued each other down hungrily and let our hands do the talking. I didn't care about the fact that he ripped the fabric of my outfit and snatched off my bra. I wanted him to see my naked body. I wanted him to explore every piece of it. Gently, he picked me up and carried me to the master bedroom. Everything we passed on the way was a blur to me, except him. He lay me down on his soft, king-sized bed, climbing in shortly after on his knees. He was naked. When did he take off his clothes, and how had he done it so fast? The questions I was asking myself stopped when I got a good look at what he was working with.

"Oh my God," I said and looked into his face with my eyes wide in shock. "Braxton, I—"

"Shhh," he said and put a finger to my lips. "I'ma take it easy on you. You probably ain't think the first dick you would take in a long time would be a monster dick."

And a monster dick it was. Braxton wasn't just packing, the man was *blessed*. His dick looked like a chocolate rod from heaven. It was long and thick with veins popping out, just like the men in the pornos. I always thought Marco had a big dick, but he didn't have nothing on Braxton's anaconda. My pussy throbbed harder when I felt the cool of his hand touch it. He rubbed my wetness, flicking my clit whenever his thumb passed it.

"Uh . . . Uh . . . Uh!" I moaned.

"Yeah . . . Daddy gon' give you what you like. Don't worry about it. I'ma stretch that pussy out." He stuck two fingers inside of me and dug as deep as they could go. I humped down on his hand whenever he plunged, and he licked his lips at the way my face was turned up. "You wanna know what I've been wondering?"

"W-what?"

"I've been wondering why it's taken you so long to give me this pussy!"

I screamed when he dipped his head down and took my fat, swollen clit in his mouth and began sucking on it like a Now or Later. I gripped the back of his head and let my fingers swim in his waves while he took me on the ride of a lifetime. The only sounds that filled the air were his slurping and my moans. I lost count of how many orgasms he brought me to, but when he finally resurfaced, his chin was dripping with my juices. I tried to get up to return the favor, but he pushed me back down, shaking his head.

"Just lie back and get fucked," he told me, gripping the backs on, my thighs and pushing on them until my knees were at my shoulders.

"Ahhhh!" I screamed and gripped his blue sheets. Or were they green? It was dark, and this man was pounding my lights out. "Braxton!"

"I'm sorry, baby," he said as he looked down on me. "I know I said I would take it easy on this pussy, but I can't. Who told you to get this wet and be this tight, huh?"

At first it hurt because he didn't even try to ease his way in. He just dove in headfirst. But that was a good thing because once the pain subsided, it was pure bliss from there on. He was touching places nobody else had ever even tried to, and before I knew it, I was screaming things that didn't make any sense.

"Stop! Oooh, Daddy, stop! No! Please don't stop, don't ever stop!"

"Which one you want?" he asked, pulling out. "You want me to stop?"

"No! Please, Braxton, fuck me!"

"That's what I thought." He flipped me over and put my face in the pillows.

I arched my back, giving him a perfect view of my round ass and pink, wet pussy. Reaching under, I played with my own clit and looked back at his entranced face.

"After this, you better never give my pussy away."

"Oh . . . This is your pussy now?" I bit my lip to show that I was happy at his choice of words.

"Yeah, that's what I said, ain't it?"

"Show me that you're the only nigga this pussy needs, then."

Those words must have challenged him, because he plunged into me with every inch. All of the sensations my body had were screaming his name, and I didn't know how to act. I threw it back at him for as long as I could before it got too much for me to handle. Then I kept my body still and let him have his way with me until I felt him jumping inside of me.

"Ahhh!" I heard him yell from behind me.

When he pulled his dick from my pussy, I collapsed on the bed, weak from every orgasm he had brought me to. He fell next to me, and we stared into each other's eyes. No words needed to be spoken. We were one. What was understood didn't need to be explained; it was embedded in us. I snuggled under the covers of his bed and got as close to him as I could. I was weaker than I'd ever been in my life, but that didn't stop me from wanting more.

"You done?" I asked.

"Girl, you want some more?"

Bzzz! Bzzz!

"You must got one of your other women fiending for your nut," I said, shooting him a knowing look.

"Stop," he said, grabbing his phone and looking at the caller ID. "This is Pat's security. Hello?" I watched his face go from exhausted to alert in a matter of seconds. "What! Hello? Hello? Hello!"

"What's wrong?" I asked, not understanding why he suddenly had just jumped up from the bed. We had been relaxing so peacefully.

"Somebody just hit Pat's spot. I gotta get there now!"

"What!" I asked sitting up in his bed. "Who?"

"I don't know! This nigga's phone cut off when he was talking to me. Hurry up and get dressed so we can go."

"Who all knew where she stayed?" I asked, hopping out of the bed and throwing on a T-shirt of his and a pair of basketball shorts.

"Only the people closest to her," Braxton said.

"Including Marco," I said, thinking about the fact that the house I lived in with my aunt now was the one that Marco grew up in. "Hurry up. We have to go!"

Chapter 7

I drove my own car to Aunt Patricia's, and I got there faster than Braxton, but it didn't matter. I was still too late. The moment I pulled up, all I saw was blood. Nobody was manning the entrance of the home since all of Aunt Patricia's security were lying bloody and dead at the front door. I eased my way inside of the big double doors and walked through the house, trying not to make a sound. I was sad because I knew all of the fallen soldiers had families, and I didn't know how to explain to them that they were dead.

"Where is the safe?" I heard a voice say.

It had been years since I heard that voice, but it was one that I would never allow myself to forget. Marco's voice had gotten deeper and much more menacing since the last time we'd seen each other. Although I was hiding in the den while they were upstairs, I couldn't believe that I was so close to the man responsible for sending my life down shit creek. If it were not for him, I would have no dealings in the street, and I would be content.

I followed the sound of him yelling and the sound of him breaking things. I had underestimated my enemy. I did not think he would be bold enough to barge in Auntie's home like he did. I treaded lightly because I was positive that he wasn't alone. My gun was drawn, and I ducked low as I made my way up the stairs toward my aunt Patricia's bedroom.

"I said, where's the fuckin' safe?"

Smack!

He slapped her so hard that it echoed throughout the house, and I heard her scream out in pain. I reached the top of the stairs and stopped right in my tracks when I saw that there were three DBD members standing in the hallway outside of her room.

Shit! Think, Jackie. Think!

"I have nothing for you here," Aunt Patricia's feeble voice said. "You must have fallen on hard times if you're trying to rob me, of all people."

"What do you expect, bitch? You've taken all of my business. And that little stunt that you pulled some months back at the trap house got the feds hot on my ass. I've been waiting for this exact moment. And guess what? The look on your face is better than I imagined. Now, I'm going to give you one more chance to tell me where the safe is before I put one in your dome."

"Go to hell."

"I'll see you there."

I had to act. Fast.

Bang! Bang! Bang!

I came out of hiding, firing my gun immediately. The element of surprise was my best friend in that moment because Marco's men didn't even have time to draw their weapons. One of them was still writhing around on the floor in pain. I ended it for him by putting a bullet neatly in his forehead. Walking in the master bedroom, I saw Marco with his arm around Aunt Patricia's neck, and he had a gun to her head. My aunt was wearing the silk pajamas I got her with the matching robe. She must have just gotten ready for bed before she was ambushed.

"Who the fuck are you?" he demanded as he held my aunt hostage.

"Oh," I told him, never lowering my weapon. "You don't remember me now?"

We both studied each other's faces. His was full of hate and resentment. . . . That was what aged him so much to me. Gone was the young, ambitious man I first met all those years ago.

Greed had taken hold of his heart, and there was no coming back from that. It was what made him so ugly. His eyes stalked my face until I saw recognition in them; then came the confusion.

"Jackie?"

"In the flesh, you son of a bitch! JO to you, though."

"*You're* JO? The nigga that's been running around the city shutting down my shops?"

"Yup, that would be me. Now let my aunt go."

"Aunt?" He looked from Aunt Patricia back to me, and then laughed. "That's crazy. I woulda never guessed. You look real good by the way, Jackie. Jail did you some good."

"Are you slow or something, nigga? Let her go and I'll let you live."

"Jackie . . ." Aunt Patricia tried to say something, but he squeezed her neck harder.

"You gon' let me live?" He looked at me as if I had just said the dumbest thing ever. "No. How about I kill her so you and I can finish where we left off?"

Bang!

"Nooo!" I screamed. "Nooo!"

The bullet went straight through my aunt's neck as Marco smiled sinisterly at me. He threw her to the side, and when I tried to run to her body, somebody snatched me and my gun up from behind.

"I heard your voice and thought to myself, nah, it can't be this bitch!"

I looked over my shoulder into the face of a woman that I knew I would hate for a lifetime. It looked like Brina had done the prison time, not me. She already had dark bags forming under her eyes, and her cheeks sagged a bit. She was wearing a baby-blue two-piece designer suit, and her hair was pulled back into a ponytail, showing off all her grays in the front.

"All that coke done caught up to your ugly ass, I see," I said, pushing her off of me. "You wanted this nigga so bad. Now look at you."

"You mean look at *this*." She flashed her left hand in my face, showing off a big stone on her ring finger. "I got the ring, something you could never do. We have a family, a son. Do you have kids? Oh, wait . . . you were too busy licking pussy in prison."

"Fuck you, bitch!" I said and swung my fist as hard as I could. It connected with her jaw, and I heard a loud crack. "After this, I'll be sure to kill your son, too!"

She fell back, and I only got one more good hit in before I felt Marco grab me. He tossed me like a sack of pennies, and I hit my head hard on Aunt Patricia's dresser. Struggling to sit up on shaky arms, I blinked rapidly to clear my vision. I saw my aunt's body not too far away from me, lying still and in a pool of blood. My chest was tighter than it had ever been before, and I ripped my eyes away, not wanting to see the horrible sight anymore. Aunt Patricia was anything but a saint, but she had a good heart, and she didn't deserve to go like that. I knew if I didn't think of something, and quick, I would be next.

"I'm going to do it right this time!"

Marco kicked me in my ribs several times in the same spot until I felt them crack. I cried out in pain, but that didn't stop him. Then he grabbed the back of my neck, forcing my face in the carpet, and pinned my arm behind my back. While he was holding me, I felt another set of fists beating on me. I was helpless and feeling pain shoot up and down my body. It was happening again. I felt then exactly how I felt years ago—helpless. My gun was too far to get, and I was positive that they were going to beat me to death if I didn't do something.

"Hand me her gun," Marco instructed. "I'ma put her whole clip in her skull."

"OK, baby," Brina said and stopped hitting me. "Let me put a bullet in her, too."

"She was going to take my father's empire and give it to *you*?" He kissed the side of my face, and I couldn't pull away. I had to lay there and feel the wetness of his tongue as he licked my cheek all the way up to my ear. I felt the humidity from his warm breath and closed my eyes. "I heard of JO, but I never thought it would be you, Jackie. The same thirsty bitch I found broke in a library. The same bitch I used to stick my raw dick in any way that I liked. You? What the fuck can *you* do that *I* can't? Nothing. And that's why you have to die."

I felt him release me, but that was only short lived. Next, I felt the gun on the back of my head, and I clenched my already-closed eyes even tighter. I didn't want to die, especially like that. But maybe I hadn't done enough good with my time on earth, and now it had run out. Maybe I could say a quick prayer to at least *attempt* to get into heaven. I did say a quick prayer and ignored the shit talking Marco was doing behind me. He had won, and he knew it. He was relishing in his victory so much that I didn't think he would ever pull the trigger . . . until it happened.

Bang!

I jumped, but I didn't feel the bullet enter my body. Because it *didn't* enter my body. Maybe he missed?

"Augh!" I heard Marco grunt and fall to the side. He was lying right beside me, rolling around from a wound to his right shoulder.

"You mothafucka—" Then she was cut short with two gunshots, and I heard a thud shortly after.

I was beaten up so badly I could barely move. I opened my eyes, but everything was a blur. All I saw was a silhouette moving toward me, maybe to kill me too? I shook my head and even thought about pleading my case, but it was over. If it was my time to die, then I would die.

"What have I told you about driving that fast, ma?" It was Braxton. His voice was like music to my ears, and his strong hands were my nurses.

"Brax," I said weakly and allowed him to put my arms around his shoulders.

"It's me," he said and helped me to my feet.

My gaze once again fell upon my aunt's dead body, and I clutched his shirt, turning my head. I couldn't believe she was gone. The woman who had saved me . . . was gone. Not too far away from her Brina lay, with half of her face missing. Her body was still twitching slightly, but she was dead. There was no getting out of that. Marco, on the other hand, was still on the ground scooting away from us. The bullet Braxton put in his shoulder must have came with enough force to make him drop his weapon because he was unarmed.

"He killed one of the best things this city had to offer. You do the honors." Braxton put his gun in my hand and kissed my forehead.

I didn't hesitate to wrap my finger around the trigger. I got my footing and limped over to where Marco was scooting in pain. He was leaving a trail of blood in the carpet, and I could see that he was trying to get to where his gun had flown to.

"Uh-uh-uhh!" I said, shaking my head. "Y-you thought that you would just come in here and kill us all off? And what, take over? After fifteen years, you have not changed a bit. But it's OK. I hope you lived a long life."

"Fuck you!" he said, not knowing that those would be his last words.

He made a face like he was trying to gather saliva to spit at me, but he never got the chance. I squeezed the trigger on Braxton's gun, close range, and emptied the clip in Marco's face. It was probably the most disgusting thing I'd ever seen in my life, all those bodies lying so close together, but when I was done, I felt no remorse. I wish I had another clip to put in him, but he was already dead.

"Come on, ma," Braxton gently grabbed the wrist of my still extended hand and pressed down so I would lower the weapon. "We need to get you out of here and to the hospital. I'ma have a cleaner team get this mess up, and I'ma have my nigga make an announcement."

"What's the announcement?" I asked as he helped me out of the room.

"That our, DBD is no more, and anyone claiming it will be murdered on sight, along with their families," he said, walking side by side with me down the stairs. "And also that we have a new queen."

"It's too early," I shook my head. "I don't even feel right leaving her body up there. I feel so empty, Brax. Why would he do that? I just got her back in my life."

Braxton didn't say anything back to me until I was secure in the passenger seat of his car. He handled me so delicately and put my seat belt on for me. When he got in the car, he started it but didn't pull off from my aunt's house. Instead, he just sat there looking forward, at nothing . . . or maybe at everything. Cars started to pull up around us, and it seemed like time was going in slow motion. I knew the people weren't EMTs, but they had stretchers and body bags to get the bodies out of the house. I had never seen the cleaners in person, but they moved quickly and deliberately.

"Some shit that happens to us is shit that we would never guess," Braxton said finally. "You not the only one hurting right now, ma. My insides are on fire. But just because I wanna murder the world doesn't mean I can. If Pat Pat taught me anything, it's to keep business moving, no matter what. That ain't the way I would have liked to see her go, but she knew the dangers of signing up for the job. Now, all we can do is learn from it and make sure the new queen has better security. This shit don't stop because one clown wants to throw a hissy fit. That nigga is dead now. We got a new deal, and that means more money. The streets respect you, JO, and I'm not going to sit here and let you pretend that this isn't what Pat Pat was preparing you for."

I didn't even know I was crying until I felt the tears running down my face. They were warm and salty, I knew, because I licked my upper lip and tasted them. I felt empty, but oddly enough, I felt whole at the same time. I watched one of the men wheel my aunt's body out on one of the stretchers, and I put a hand to my lips, kissed it, and put it on the window as they passed me.

"I know," I said and swallowed. "This war is over, but . . . but I'm ready for anything else that comes my way. I'm not going to lose anyone else I love."

"That's what I like to hear," Braxton said and finally drove out of the driveway. "And wipe them tears. We gon' be good. I promise."

"Thank you."

"For what?"

"Letting me be the one to kill him."

"That was the plan from the very beginning. It just wasn't supposed to happen like this," he said and got silent for a few moments as he drove. "So, Queen, what's the first call of business?"

I thought about the last conversation I had with my aunt. I wiped my tears away and smiled to the night sky. One of the stars was shining brighter than all the rest, and I took it as a sign. Aunt Patricia's body may have been dead, but her soul wasn't, and I was positive she was smiling down on me too.

"The first call to business is to give my auntie the best home going Houston has ever seen. She wanted a party for her birthday? Let's give her one."

The End